FEB 1 6

P9-DCD-101
3 3484 00231 6146

WITHDRAWN

Praise for Alexander McCall Smith's

44 SCOTLAND STREET SERIES

"Irresistible. . . . Packed with the charming characters, piercing perceptions, and shrewd yet generous humor that have become McCall Smith's cachet."
—*Chicago Sun-Times*

"Feel the warmth of McCall Smith's wit, deft character-ization, and overarching theme of kindness. . . . You'll be treated to an astonishing view of changes in char-acters' lives, very much like a time-lapse video in book form."   —*Booklist* (starred review)

"McCall Smith, a fine writer, paints his hometown of Edinburgh as indelibly as he captures the sunniness of Africa. We can almost feel the mists as we tread the cobblestones."   —*The Dallas Morning News*

"Just about perfect. . . . Contains a healthy helping of McCall Smith's patented charm."
—*St. Louis Post-Dispatch*

"Will make you feel as though you live in Edinburgh, if only for a short while, and it's a fine place to visit indeed. . . . Long live the folks on Scotland Street."
—*The Times-Picayune* (New Orleans)

Alexander McCall Smith

THE REVOLVING DOOR OF LIFE

Alexander McCall Smith is the author of the No. 1
Ladies' Detective Agency series, the Isabel Dalhousie
series, the Portuguese Irregular Verbs series, the 44 Scotland Street series, and the Corduroy Mansions series.
He is professor emeritus of medical law at the University of Edinburgh in Scotland and has served with many
national and international organizations concerned with
bioethics.

www.alexandermccallsmith.com

IN THE ISABEL DALHOUSIE SERIES

The Sunday Philosophy Club
Friends, Lovers, Chocolate
The Right Attitude to Rain
The Careful Use of Compliments
The Comforts of a Muddy Saturday
The Lost Art of Gratitude
The Charming Quirks of Others
The Forgotten Affairs of Youth
The Perils of Morning Coffee (eBook only)
The Uncommon Appeal of Clouds
At the Reunion Buffet
The Novel Habits of Happiness

IN THE CORDUROY MANSIONS SERIES

Corduroy Mansions
The Dog Who Came in from the Cold
A Conspiracy of Friends

IN THE PORTUGUESE IRREGULAR VERBS SERIES

Portuguese Irregular Verbs
The Finer Points of Sausage Dogs
At the Villa of Reduced Circumstances
Unusual Uses for Olive Oil

OTHER WORKS

La's Orchestra Saves the World
The Girl Who Married a Lion
and Other Tales from Africa
Trains and Lovers
The Forever Girl
Fatty O'Leary's Dinner Party (eBook only)
Emma: A Modern Retelling

THE REVOLVING
DOOR OF LIFE

A 44 Scotland Street Novel

ALEXANDER McCALL SMITH

Illustrations by Iain McIntosh

Anchor Books
A Division of Penguin Random House LLC
New York

AN ANCHOR BOOKS ORIGINAL, FEBRUARY 2016

Copyright © 2015 by Alexander McCall Smith
Illustrations copyright © 2015 by Iain McIntosh

All rights reserved. Published in the United States by
Anchor Books, a division of Penguin Random House LLC,
New York. Originally published in hardcover in Great Britain by
Polygon, an imprint of Birlinn Ltd., Edinburgh, in 2015.

Anchor Books and colophon are registered trademarks of
Penguin Random House LLC.

This is a work of fiction. Names, characters, places, and
incidents either are the product of the author's imagination or
are used fictitiously. Any resemblance to actual persons, living
or dead, events, or locales is entirely coincidental.

This book is excerpted from a series that originally appeared
in *The Scotsman* newspaper.

The Cataloging-in-Publication Data is on file at the
Library of Congress.

Anchor Books Paperback ISBN: 978-1-101-97191-8
eBook ISBN: 978-1-101-97192-5

Author illustration © Iain McIntosh

www.anchorbooks.com

Printed in the United States of America
10 9 8 7 6 5 4 3 2 1

This book is for Louise Richardson

1. Moving Can Be Good For You

Matthew had read somewhere—in one of those hoary lists with which newspapers and magazines fill their columns on quiet days—that moving house was one of the most stressful of life's experiences—even if not quite as disturbing as being the victim of an armed robbery or being elected president, nemine contradicente, of an unstable South American republic. Matthew faced no such threats, of course, but he nevertheless found the prospect of leaving India Street for the sylvan surroundings of Nine Mile Burn extremely worrying. And it made no difference that Nine Mile Burn was, as the name suggested, only nine miles from the centre of Edinburgh.

"What really worries me," he confessed to Elspeth, "is the whole business of selling India Street. What if nobody wants to buy this flat? What then?"

He looked at her with unconcealed anxiety: he could imagine what it was like not to be able to sell one's house. He had recently been at a party at which somebody had whispered pityingly of another guest: "He can't sell his flat, you know." He had looked across the room at the poor unfortunate of whom the remark was made and had seen a hodden-doon, depressed figure, visibly bent under the burden of unshiftable equity. That, he decided, was how people who couldn't sell their house looked—shadowy figures, wraiths, as dejected and without hope as the damned in Dante's *Inferno,* haunted by the absence of offers for an unmoveable property. He had shuddered at the thought and reflected on his good fortune at not being in that position himself. Yet here he was deliberately courting it . . .

Elspeth's attitude was more sanguine. She had been unruffled by their previous moves—from India Street to Moray Place, and then back again to India Street. The prospect of another flit—a Scots word that implies an attempt to evade the clutches of creditors suggests, misleadingly, that moving is an airy, inconsequential thing—did not seem to trouble her, and she had no concerns about the sale of the flat. "But of course somebody will want to buy it," she reassured him. "Why wouldn't they? It's one of the nicest flats in the street. It's got plenty of room and bags of light. Who wouldn't want to live in the middle of the Edinburgh New Town?"

Matthew frowned. "The New Town isn't for everybody," he said. "Not everybody finds the Georgian aesthetic pleasing." He paused as he tried to think of a single person he knew of whom this was true. "There are plenty of people these days who are suburban rather than urban. People who like to have . . ." He paused for thought. He knew nobody like this, but they had to exist. "Who like to have garages. *Homo suburbiensis*. Morningside man, who is a bit like Essex man but just a touch . . ."

"Superior?"

"You said it; I didn't."

Elspeth smiled. "You shouldn't worry so much, Matt, darlingest. And so what if we don't sell it? We can afford the other place anyway."

Matthew winced. "If I dip into capital," he said.

Elspeth shrugged. "But isn't money for spending? And surely there's enough there to be dipped into."

Matthew knew that she was right; at the last valuation, his portfolio of shares in the astute care of the Adam Bank had shot up and he could have bought the new house several times over if necessary. But Matthew had been imbued by his father with exactly that sense of caution that had created the fund in the first place, and the idea of selling shares in any but the direst of emergencies was anathema to him.

In general, Elspeth did not look too closely at Matthew's financial affairs. She had never been much interested in money, and very rarely spent any on anything but family essentials and the occasional outfit or pair of shoes. She was nonetheless aware of their good fortune and of the fact that thanks to the generosity of Matthew's businessman father they were spared the financial anxieties that affected most people. Her capacity for moral imagination, though, was such that she could understand the distorting effect that poverty had on any life, and she had never been, nor ever would become, indifferent to the lot of those—perhaps a majority of the population of Scotland—who were left with relatively little disposable income after the payment of monthly bills. This attitude was shared by Matthew, with the result that they were tactful about their situation—and generous too, when generosity was required.

The farmhouse near Nine Mile Burn had not been cheap. Although it was far enough from Edinburgh to avoid the high prices of the capital, it was close enough to be more expensive than houses in West Linton, a village that lay only a few miles further down the road. Their house, which they had agreed to buy from no less a person than the Duke of Johannesburg, who lived at Single Malt House not far away, had been valued at seven hundred thousand pounds. For that they got six bedrooms in the main house—along with a study, a gun room (Matthew did not have a gun, of course), and a drawing room with a good view of both the Lammermuir and Moorfoot Hills to the south and east; a tractor shed, a byre, and six acres of ground.

The Duke had been pleased that Matthew was the purchaser; they had met on several occasions before, although the Duke seemed to have only the vaguest idea of who Matthew was. Matthew's quiet demeanour, however, had been enough to endear him to the Duke.

"I must say," the Duke had remarked to a friend, "it's a great relief to have found somebody who's not in the slightest bit *shouty*. You know what I mean? Those shouty people one meets these days—all very full of themselves and brash. We used to have very few of them in Scotland, you know; now they're on the rise, it seems."

The friend knew exactly what the Duke meant. "Nouveau riche," he said. "They're flashy—they throw their money around."

The Duke nodded. "Whereas I'm *nouveau pauvre*. I've got barely a sou these days, you know—not that I ever had very much."

"And you a duke," said the friend. "Fancy that!"

"Well, a sort of duke," conceded the Duke. "I'm not in any of the stud books, you know: Debrett's and so on. Or I'm in one of them—just—but I gather it's not a very reliable one. It was rather expensive to get in; you had to buy sixty copies, as I recall, and I think quite a number of people in it are a bit on the ropey side. In fact, all of them are, I believe."

"People take you at your own evaluation, I've always thought," said the friend. "Behave like a duke and they'll swallow it."

"True," said the Duke. "But frankly, that's a bit difficult for me, old man. I'm not quite sure what the form is when it comes to being a pukka duke."

"Take a look at some of the people who are what they claim to be," advised the friend. "Watch the way they stand; the way they walk. They're very sure-footed, I'm told. And they look down at the ground a lot."

"That's because they own it," said the Duke. "Doesn't apply to me—or not very much. I've got fifty-eight acres in Midlothian and forty-one up in Lochaber, but most of it is pretty scrubby. Lots of broom and rhododendrons."

The friend looked thoughtful. "No, you're not quite the real thing, I suppose. And then there's always the risk that the Lord Lyon will catch up with you."

The mention of the Lord Lyon made the Duke blanch. This was the King of Arms, the official who supervised all matters of heraldry and succession in Scotland. He had extensive legal powers and could prosecute people for the unauthorised use of coats of arms and the like.

"Do you think Lyon would ever bother about me?" asked the Duke nervously.

His friend looked out of the window. "You never know," he said. "But I shouldn't like to be in your shoes if he did."

It was not the sort of thing a friend should say—or at least not the sort of thing that a reassuring friend should say.

2. Distressed Furniture

The Duke of Johannesburg proved to be a most considerate seller, more than prepared to include all the contents of the house in the sale without adding anything to the purchase price.

"We haven't lived in the place for years," he said. "And recently we let it out, of course. But all the stuff is ours, and some of it is actually quite good, even if it's a bit distressed, as the antique dealers say. Mind you, *distressed* is not quite strong enough for some of my furniture. My furniture has moved beyond being distressed. *Terminal* might be more accurate. I can just imagine the auction catalogues—can't you?—'a table in terminal condition' and so on. Hah!"

Matthew was keen to keep as much of the Duke's furniture as possible, but Elspeth had other ideas. "It's terrible old rubbish," she said. "Look at this." She referred to the inventory that the Duke's agent had prepared. "*A charming William IV library table with only two legs, but otherwise sound.*"

"Oh, I saw that one," said Matthew. "It had a lovely green leather top."

"That's as may be," Elspeth retorted, "but what's the use of a table with two legs? Or . . ." And here she pointed to another inventory item. "*A glass-fronted bookcase, circa 1860; no glass.*"

She looked up at Matthew. "What is the point, may I ask, of having a glass-fronted bookcase with no glass in the front? In fact, one might even go so far as to say that it's an impossibility. A glass-fronted bookcase with no glass is simply not a glass-fronted bookcase."

"Perhaps," said Matthew. "If you're intent on being pedantic."

They normally did not argue with one another, but even the most equable of couples may be expected to fall out over a move. And so Matthew decided at a very early stage that he would leave everything up to Elspeth and not dispute any of her decisions. Armed with this authority, Elspeth made all the arrangements, chose the date of departure, and did most of the packing herself. He helped, of course, mostly by taking the triplets around the Botanic Gardens in their three-seated pushchair. This inevitably brought a response from passersby—looks that ranged from amusement to sympathy and sometimes on to disapproval.

"Three!" remarked one elderly woman as Matthew and the triplets passed her on the way to the greenhouse. "My, you must have been insatiable!"

Matthew was ready to let this remark pass with a polite nod of his head, but then its implications dawned on him. Did she really think *that*? he asked himself.

"Excuse me," he said, "but I wonder what you mean by what you've just said."

The woman blushed. "Oh . . . oh, I don't really know. It's just that it must take a lot of energy to create triplets. Not every man . . . Oh dear, I'm not sure that I know what I meant."

And then there was the visiting American woman who asked the triplets' names when they were waiting together for a pedestrian light in Stockbridge. "Dear little things," she said. "They're all boys, aren't they? What are they called?"

"Tobermory, Rognvald and Fergus," answered the proud father.

"What wonderful Scottish names!" enthused the visitor. "Which is Tobermory?"

Matthew hesitated. The truth was that he did not know, as although Elspeth claimed to be able to differentiate between the three boys, he had no idea. But a father could hardly confess to being uncertain as to the identity of his own sons, and so he pointed at random to one of the boys. "Him," he said.

The woman bent forward to look more closely. "We went to Tobermory last week," she said. "We were visiting Iona and afterwards we called in at Tobermory—a lovely place . . ." Her voice trailed away. "He's wearing his brother's jumper, I see. It has Fergus knitted across the front."

Matthew waved airily. "They share their clothes," he said airily. "And of course they're far too young to dress themselves, or to care what they're wearing, for that matter."

In the last few days before the move, the boys were left in the care of Anna, their Danish au pair, while Matthew and Elspeth made final preparations. A couple of weeks before they were due to move in, the Duke agreed to meet them at the house to hand over the keys—they had already paid the purchase price—and to answer any final queries they might have.

"I shall miss the old place," he said, as he stood with them in the doorway of the large ground-floor drawing room. "We used to have such marvellous parties here back in the old days. White-tie affairs, you know. The men in Highland dress, of course, and the women in long dresses with tartan sashes. Interminable affairs, some thought, but I always enjoyed them. We used to give breakfast to anybody who was still there at six in the morning, and standing. Sometimes we even had to give them lunch. Frightful, but there we are—it's very hard to ask guests to leave, you know. Some stayed for weeks." He paused. "I never really knew how to do it until I read about what Willie Maugham said to Paddy Leigh Fermor after Paddy had for some reason been terribly rude to the old boy when he was staying as a guest at the Villa Mauresque. For some reason Paddy imitated Maugham's stutter at the dinner table—causing dreadful offence. One doesn't imitate the host's stutter in any circumstances. Anyway, Paddy did and so Maugham said to him over coffee that night, 'I shall have to say goodbye to you at this stage as when I get up tomorrow morning you will already have left.' "

The Duke laughed.

"How very tactful," said Matthew.

"I never met Maugham, of course," continued the Duke. "He was more my father's generation. In fact, Pa met him once or twice in Antibes. He said he was an ill-tempered old cove, but there we are. Leigh Fermor shouldn't have done what he did."

The Duke gazed fondly over the drawing room. "Yes, those white-tie parties were grand evenings, and people paid attention to what they wore. You can't just add a white tie to Highland Dress, you know. It all depends where you are. If you're in Perthshire, for example, you can only wear a white tie with Highland Dress if you were born in the county. In Argyll, if the invitation says white tie—and it does for occasions like the Oban gathering—you wear a jabot, as I'm sure you know."

Matthew was silent. He knew nothing about any of this and he wondered why nobody had ever taught him about these things that were so important even while being utterly unimportant.

3. *Boys Are So Physical*

After the Duke of Johannesburg left—he had an engagement with his lawyer in Edinburgh—Matthew and Elspeth made their way into their new drawing room. Elspeth flopped down on one of the Duke's faded chintz-covered sofas, now theirs, patting the cushion beside her in an invitation for Matthew to join her. As they sat there, surveying their new home about them, there was at first a silence of the sort that comes when one has done something important but not yet determined the full implications of one's actions. After a few minutes, almost in unison, they said, "So . . ." and then stopped.

"You go ahead," said Matthew.

"No you."

Matthew smiled. "I know that we haven't actually moved in yet, even if we've got the keys. But I was just going to say: *so here we are.* That's all. And you?"

"I was going to say exactly the same thing," said Elspeth.

Matthew looked thoughtful. "Do you think we've done the right thing?"

"I was just about to ask you that," said Elspeth. "My answer, though, is: yes. I can't wait to live in the country. It'll be such fun for the boys; they'll have so much room . . . Boys are so physical. They love to run around, to climb trees . . ."

". . . And bruise their knees," said Matthew.

"Exactly." She looked up at the ceiling. "What's that song about bruising both your hearts and your knees? Isn't there a song about that?"

"There is," said Matthew. "But I can't remember what it's called. It's about friendship, I seem to recall."

"Just like . . ." Elspeth tried to remember another song about friendship, but none came to mind; there were so many songs about being in love, but people did not sing quite so much about being in friendship. And yet, she thought, there was no reason that one might not "be in friendship" just as one might be in love. Could friendship intoxicate in the way in which love did? Could you feel as elated about friendship as you could about love?

"Like *John Anderson my Jo,*" suggested Matthew. "Robert Burns."

"Isn't that about being married?"

"Yes, it is. But I think it's about friendship too. You could apply those words to an old friend—to one with whom you've shared a great deal."

She looked at him. She had read an article somewhere that many men were lonely because they did not know how to handle friendship, because they did not attend to their friendships in the way in which women did. You could not simply leave friendship to look after itself. Friendship was a plant that required careful tending—and that was something that women did rather better than men.

The same article had discussed the contemporary idea of *bromances*, which were strong friendships between men. There was nothing physical about these, but they were romantic in a way in which male friendships usually were not. David and Jonathan had a famous *bromance*, the article said, and there were other examples, but male reticence and taboos meant that it was not a common thing. Those in a *bromance* could not only play golf or squash with one another, but could go out for dinner afterwards, or could simply sit and talk; in short, they could do all the things that women did so easily and so naturally with their female friends but that men were frightened to do.

Matthew was an only child, as was Elspeth. She remembered feeling lonely in her childhood and the envy she had felt for those who had brothers and sisters. Matthew, she imagined, had felt the same, although they had never talked about it, just as they had never discussed the question of friendship. What friends did he have? There was Angus Lordie, for whom Matthew had acted as best man when Angus had married Domenica, and there was Bruce Anderson, whom he occasionally met in the Cumberland Bar. Angus was older than him, though, and that must limit the friendship to some extent, and Bruce was vain and unreliable, and hardly a friend to be encouraged. Who else was there? There were various friends from his days at the Academy, and he met them at regular reunions, but none seemed to be particularly close. Big Lou? She did not count because men and women tended to be friends with one another in a totally different way— and anyway, no wife would encourage a husband to develop friendships with other women.

She wondered whether perhaps Matthew did not need male friends; perhaps he was one of these men who lived entirely through their family. Her own father had been a bit like that, she remembered. His life had revolved around his wife, his daughter, his dog, and his motorbike. That was his universe, and he seemed uninterested in engaging with anything very much outside that.

While Elspeth was thinking about this, Matthew had risen to his feet and was inspecting a bookcase at the end of the room.

"Elspeth," he said. "There's something odd about this bookcase. Come and take a look."

She got up to join him. She bent forwards to examine one of the books—part of the library that the Duke had thrown in with the sale. "I've far too many books," he had said. "And that can be so confusing."

One of the titles stood out. *Eastern Approaches* by Fitzroy Maclean. She reached for the book and opened it. Inside, on the title page, the author had written: *J: something I wrote some time ago, but I hope you enjoy it. Fitzroy.* She closed it. Her father had said something about Fitzroy Maclean, but she could not remember exactly what it was. And who was *J*? Johannesburg?

"Not the books," said Matthew. "It's just that I get the impression there's something behind this bookcase."

Elspeth laughed. "No," she said. "Don't tell me. A concealed room."

Elspeth laughed again. "There are no concealed rooms," she said. "Concealed rooms are a cliché too far: *nobody* has concealed rooms any more. Nobody." She imagined the estate agent's advertisement for a house so endowed: *four bedrooms (one concealed)* . . .

"*Au contraire*," said Matthew. "I think that's exactly what we might have."

4. *Glasgow—A Promised Land*

In Scotland Street, Bertie Pollock, now just seven, gazed out of his bedroom at the view of Edinburgh sky that his window afforded him. Bertie was reflecting on the fact that he was no longer six; he had been that age for so many years, it seemed, and he had begun to despair of ever getting any older. Other people had regular birthdays—at least one a year—and yet whatever clock determined the passage of time for him seemed to be very badly calibrated.

He had to put up with some flaunting of birthdays by those who had them. "No birthday yet, Bertie?" crowed Olive. "I've had a birthday, as you may have noticed, and Pansy has had one too. Even Tofu's had a birthday, although he didn't deserve one. What about you? Still six?"

At this rate, he thought, it would be an interminably long time before he turned eighteen—the age at which, according to the law of Scotland, he believed you could leave your mother and go to live wherever you liked. In his case, he imagined it would be Glasgow, a promised land that lay only forty miles away to the west, where there would be no psychotherapy, no yoga classes, no Italian *conversazione*, and no prohibition on owning a Swiss Army penknife. Glasgow represented freedom—a life in which you could do what you liked and do it when you liked. As a small boy who had been told what to do since as long as he could remember, he could not imagine anything headier, anything more exhilarating than that.

Yet these thoughts of freedom were tinged with guilt, for although Bertie might be forgiven for dreaming of freedom from his mother, he could not rid himself of a nagging disquiet. He had encouraged his mother to go off to the Persian Gulf, and this meant that what happened there was his fault. That, of course, is how children think: they blame themselves for the misfortunes of their parents. If something goes wrong with the world, it's my fault: I did it. That was a heavy burden of guilt for so young a set of shoulders, and the strain was telling.

The trip to the Gulf had come about after Irene had entered a competition to compose a new slogan for a desert sheikhdom, and rather to her surprise she had won. Her suggestion—*So much sand—and so close at hand!*—came to her almost without thinking, and it was this spontaneity, perhaps, along with its undoubted veracity, that made her entry stand out above others. Some of those other entries, of course, were made by those who seemed to be quite unfamiliar with the region. *From lush forests to Alpine pastures—we've got it all!* was an enthusiastic entry, but not one that disclosed much knowledge of physical geography. More truthful was the entry, *It's air-conditioned!* That had the merit, too, of being brief, but could perhaps be applied to rather too many places and did not quite capture—or so the judges thought—the particular essence of the sheikdom. And as for the entrant who suggested *Not much here!*—that was downright rude and was tossed aside without further consideration.

Irene had duly been awarded the prize, which consisted of five days on the Gulf coast with all expenses paid. Unfortunately the five days proved to be an underestimate: after having been mistaken for the new wife of a Bedouin sheikh and being consigned to a harem, Irene had now spent almost two months in a desert fastness. British diplomats had done their best to arrange for her return, but these matters can be difficult, and there had been many misunderstandings. At least a message had been allowed out, in which Irene said: *Am working on attitudes here. Don't worry about me. In fact, quite content to stay pro tem.* It was a brief and rather enigmatic message, and the British consular authorities had been doubtful as to its genuineness. Irene's husband, though, had been convinced that this was indeed Irene: *working on attitudes* had a certain ring to it that he thought could only come from his wife.

"It's the sort of thing she says," said Stuart. "It really does sound like her."

"But what can she mean?" asked a puzzled official at the other end of the telephone line.

Stuart paused. He did not wish to be disloyal. "She is very enthusiastic about changing attitudes," he volunteered.

There was a brief silence at the other end of the line. "Whose attitudes?"

Stuart thought for a moment. "I suppose everybody's," he said. "That's not to say that she doesn't recognise the validity of other points of view . . . I'm not saying that."

The official, trained in diplomacy, sensed that this was a sensitive area. "Of course," he said quickly. "And if you feel that she really wrote that, then that, at least, is a good sign. It means that relations with her . . . her host are probably quite good. And that helps, of course."

The conversation had concluded shortly after that with the advice that there was very little that anybody could do but to wait for the wheels of desert bureaucracy to grind at whatever pace they were accustomed to grinding. There was every chance, the official suggested, that Irene might return before a forthcoming round of trade talks between the United Kingdom and local states. "Nobody wants this sort of thing to be brought up at ministerial level," said the official. "It sours relations unnecessarily. She'll suddenly reappear—I'm pretty confident of that."

Stuart had passed this reassurance on to Bertie. "The people in London say that Mummy will come back," he said. "Her holiday is just taking a little bit longer than we thought."

Bertie had frowned. He was not quite sure whether he wanted his mother to come back; life without her had clear benefits, and if she was happy enough in the desert, then surely it was unkind to persuade her to come back.

"I think she might be happier over there," he said to his father. "It's much warmer than Scotland, Daddy, and you know that Mummy likes warm weather. And some of those places are really nice, you know. Look at Dubai—people love going there. Perhaps we should let her stay for . . ." He did a rapid calculation. "Eleven years?"

If Irene stayed in the desert for a further eleven years, then

when she came back to Scotland he would be eighteen, and . . .
He hardly dared hope.

5. *E Portugallia Semper Aliquid Boni*

As might be expected, Irene's absence had complicated Stuart's
life. Like most men of his generation—at least in that part of
Edinburgh, where new and reconstructed men abounded—he
believed that he shared fully in the task of bringing up a young
family. But like many men who think that of themselves, his
self-evaluation was perhaps somewhat optimistic. Day-to-day
responsibility for Bertie and his young brother, Ulysses, had
been borne almost entirely by Irene who, in spite of her views
of the tyranny of domestic drudgery, nonetheless performed
almost all the mundane tasks of running the lives of two
small boys—getting Bertie to school in the morning and then
afterwards to yoga and psychotherapy, delivering Ulysses
(in a miasma of vomit) to the East New Town pre-toddler
social awareness play sessions, laundering the endless stream
of flannelette garments in which Ulysses passed the day, and
making meals for the entire household every evening. All of
this had to be done before clearing up and preparing for the
next day in which she would do exactly the same thing.

Stuart helped, of course, but there is a major difference
between merely helping and actually shouldering the burden.
Even if he cooked the evening meal from time to time, he rarely
did the shopping required to stock the kitchen cupboard. And
even if he bundled clothes into the washing machine, very
seldom did he remove them, and even less often did he iron
them.

Like Bertie, he had encouraged Irene to take up her prize of
a five-day free holiday; like Bertie, he had imagined that these

five days would be a period of blissful freedom. And that is what they were. But at the end of the fifth day, when the news came through that Irene had gone off to a desert encampment, Stuart had begun to discover that supplies were running low in the kitchen, that the hall carpet was looking particularly dirty, and that there were very few clean flannelette rompers left in the drawer given over to Ulysses' clothing. And that was even before he had to tackle the issue of getting Bertie to school and arranging day care for Ulysses.

Stuart's solution had been to take ten days of compassionate leave from his job as a statistician with the Scottish Government. His immediate superiors had been supportive. "Of course you'll need a bit of time to get things sorted out," his departmental head reassured him. And then, with a sympathetic look, had continued, "Look, we all hope that your wife will be found—the uncertainty must be truly awful."

"Oh, they know where she is," said Stuart. "It's really a question of getting her out again."

"Of course."

Eyes were lowered. Everyone knew from the press reports that Irene was last seen entering a harem, and everyone's imagination had been working overtime to construct a picture of her there. For some, it was simply impossible, harems being so beyond the normal range of contemporary experience; surely there was some mistake, they thought, and Irene was merely the victim of some mix-up over a visa or a *permis de séjour* and everything would shortly be sorted out. Others envisaged Irene in a scene that would not have been out of place in an Orientalist painting, with blue-tiled walls, marbled pools, and great feather fans being swayed gently by sultry boys. And behind such imaginings was the awful, insistent thought: had Irene been obliged to go through some marriage ceremony with the Bedouin sheikh whose guest she had been? Stuart himself had not a single doubt in his mind but that

Irene would rapidly have taken control of the harem and engaged in the task of raising the awareness levels of the women who were quartered there. There were some indications that she had organised a book group in the harem, as Blackwell's Bookshop on South Bridge had received a bulk order for twenty copies of a novel recently reviewed positively in the *Guardian*. The delivery address for this order was in one of the Gulf states, to an office known by British consular officials to be the address of the Bedouin sheikh's coastal agent. As far as Stuart was concerned that was proof positive that Irene, although not free to travel, was not cowed.

The solution to Stuart's difficulties came from an unexpected quarter. His mother, Nicola Pollock, now in her early seventies, had lived in Portugal for the previous ten years after marrying a shipper of Douro wines. Stuart's father had died a few years before this second marriage, and Nicola had not taken well to life on her own in Melrose, where they had spent much of their married life. She had met the wine shipper on a Baltic cruise on which the women had outnumbered the men by almost three to one. Such single men as there were—and there were not more than eight of these on board—found themselves in constant demand, and indeed one or two had taken to having their meals in the seclusion of their cabins, so pursued were they if they ventured into any of the ship's public rooms.

Nicola Pollock had met Abril Tavares de Lumiares in the bridge club that took over the aft saloon every evening before dinner. Abril was a year or two older than she was and had not been married before. He had been engaged for a number of years in an arrangement that had a dynastic flavour to it—both families saw the business sense in the union—but eventually, after eleven years, he and his fiancée had drifted apart. Abril had decided that marriage, perhaps, was not for him, and had thrown himself into building up the business that sent Douro wines, fortified and table, off to markets his father had developed in the United States, Canada, and Brazil. On the cruise, though, away from the demands and pressures of the business, he had decided that he and Nicola should be for one another more than newly-discovered bridge partners.

He declared himself in the course of a bid, in what might well have been the only proposal of marriage in the history of bridge; bridge, of course, being the catalyst for many a divorce: foolish bidding, although not in itself a ground for divorce may well be a cause of divorce.

"Five hearts," he had opened.

The likely lie of the cards made this absurd, and they all laughed; it was friendly bridge.

"Are you mad?" asked Nicola.

"No," said Abril. "But perhaps I am in love. That is why I am thinking of hearts—and of the contract that might result."

This remark was greeted with silence. Then one of the other players said, "Double," greatly increasing the risk of the original bid.

"Double is better than single," said Abril.

"Beds?" asked somebody, and laughed.

6. A Mother-in-Law Reflects

"I'll drop everything," said Nicola over the telephone. "I can get a flight from Porto first thing tomorrow. I could be in Stansted by eleven and Edinburgh by lunchtime."

Stuart felt a surge of relief. He should have contacted his mother straightaway, rather than leaving it until Irene had been missing for a few days. *A boy's best friend is his mother . . .* yes, he thought, but perhaps not in every case. Perhaps that should be reworded: *A boy's most ardent champion is his mother . . .*

"I really don't want to put you out," said Stuart. "Maybe I'll be able to cope."

Nicola was brisk; she, at least, had made up her mind. "How exactly would you do that?" she asked. "You have to go back to work. Who's going to look after wee Ulysses then?"

"I'll think of something. Aren't there crèches?"

"No doubt there are. But you've got to get him there. Then you have to pick him up again, and you also have to collect Bertie from school. How do you think you're going to manage all that?" She paused. "And you have to feed them and sort out their clothes and . . ." She sighed. "You can't do it, darling—you really can't."

He knew that she was right, and he realised that it was time to concede. "It's really good of you," he said. "But what about Abril?"

"He works all the time. And anyway, he'll understand how important it is. We have a woman who helps in the house—she loves cooking. She'll hold the fort while I'm in Scotland. She'll spoil Abril rotten." A note of resentment crept into her voice. That woman would dearly love her to board a flight never to return, leaving Abril for her to feed, care for, and eventually marry. What right had a foreign woman—a Scotswoman, for the love of Maria!—to march into Portugal and snap up one of the most eligible men along the entire length of the Douro? None; that was the answer to that: none at all.

He thanked her again. He had not seen much of his mother in recent years and he would be pleased to be able to spend some time in her company. He knew that she and Irene did not get on, and it was the coolness between them that had led to Nicola's staying away. It would be far easier in Irene's absence to slip back into the comfortable relationship they had enjoyed before his marriage.

The coolness between Nicola and Irene had started at their first meeting and had continued through the years. At the bottom of the icy chasm between them was a fundamental difference of outlook: Nicola accepted things for what they were, whereas Irene engaged with the world as a potential adversary, as a place that had to be changed. Nicola was a defender of female independence but nonetheless understood that men and women might sometimes see things in a distinctively different way, and that these differences need not be an affront to either sex. Irene, by contrast, thought that men were deeply flawed and would only redeem themselves were they to renounce their maleness in favour of androgyny at the very least, but preferably femininity. "There can be no truces," she said. "Women will never be free from male oppression until men and masculinity are vanquished. That's all there is to it."

This severe view might have condemned Irene to a life devoid of male company, spent, perhaps, amongst a sisterhood united in its antipathy to masculinity. Such sisterhoods can be sustaining, and would have provided Irene with a perfectly adequate social network, but this solution was precluded by a powerful feature of Irene's makeup: at the age of fourteen, rather to her dismay, she found that she was interested in boys. There were no boys at the school she attended—Mary Erskine's—but there were plenty of boys at Daniel Stewart's, the school just round the corner, and as she waited at the bus-stop after school she found herself watching the Stewart's boys as they jostled with one another on their way to rugby practice. *She wished they would jostle her.* The Stewart's boys wore a uniform that included knee-length red socks, and Irene's eye was drawn to these socks as the eye of a female bird may be drawn to the gaudy plumage of a male bird. She felt confused and unsure of herself, but the die was in the process of being cast: the resentment of men was already there, but so was the desire to be with men, to get their attention, in short, to *possess* them.

When Stuart had told his mother that he and Irene were planning to get married, she had become very quiet. It was only for a few moments, but she needed the time to compose herself.

"But that's such exciting news, darling," she said faintly. "I'm so . . ." She stumbled. It was hard to enunciate the word "delighted" when one's heart was a cold stone of despair, but it had to be said. *Pleased* came out instead. "I'm so pleased. That's such good news." It was not; it was dreadful news. One might as well say that the eruption of Vesuvius or the sinking of the *Titanic* was good news. It was not.

"You do like her, don't you?"

"Of course, darling, I think she's . . ." She almost said *horrific* instead of *terrific*, but stopped herself in time. "She's just right for you." She was not. She would ruin his life.

Nicola was astute. Like most parents who saw their offspring making the wrong choice of partner, she understood that the options were stark: you either accepted the boyfriend or girlfriend, or you lost your son or daughter. It was that simple. She decided to make the most of the situation and went out of her way to welcome Irene to the family. Irene, though, saw through the forced bonhomie.

"I don't wish to run down your mother," she said to Stuart. "But her insincerity is staggering. I'm treated to performances that would easily win her a place at the Royal Scottish Academy of Music and Drama—a scholarship even—but I can tell she dislikes me. And she's so . . . well, sorry to have to say it, she's a major pain."

Stuart groaned at the insult. He thought it was unfortunate that Irene thought this of his mother, but it was even more unfortunate that she should have been overheard; for Nicola was outside the door at the time and heard exactly what her new daughter-in-law thought of her. From that moment on, the contours of their relationship were determined. So now, as Nicola sat back on the flight from Porto to Stansted, she was able to think: how nice it would be if Irene were never to return. She did not want anything too unpleasant to happen to her, of course; she merely wanted her exile to be permanent, or semi-permanent, perhaps; we cannot always expect permanence in our affairs and should settle for the semipermanent should it be on offer.

7. *The Transmissibility of Cowness*

"My grandmother's coming to stay," announced Bertie in the special period at school where the members of the class were invited to give their news. "She's arriving tomorrow—from Portugal."

"From Portugal!" said the teacher. "Did we all hear that, boys and girls? Bertie's grandmother is arriving from Portugal. How nice for Bertie!"

Olive looked at Bertie with interest. "To make up for your mother's running away?" she said. "As a sort of mother-substitute?"

"Olive!" exclaimed the teacher. "Bertie's mother did not run away. What a terrible thing to say!"

"Sorry," said Olive. "That slipped out. I didn't mean to say it."

"I should think not," snapped the teacher. "Poor Bertie!"

Tofu, who had been following the exchange with some interest, now joined in. "My dad says Bertie's mummy's a cow," he said. "I wonder if his granny will be a cow as well."

Olive had views on this, and expressed them before she could be stopped. "It depends on whether she's his granny on his mummy's side or on his dad's side. If it's on his mummy's side, then there's a good chance she'll be a cow too. It all depends, you see." She gave Tofu a withering look. "Mind you, you're one to talk, Tofu. My dad said that your mummy was a real tart, and my dad is always right about these things. I'm sorry to mention it now that she's dead of starvation, but there's no point hiding from the truth, is there?" She waited for an answer that did not come, and so she added, "I could have warned her about starvation, of course. That's what comes of being a vegan—I could have told her that."

"She didn't die of starvation," muttered Tofu. "She's still alive."

"Just," said Olive.

"Now, now!" said the teacher. "This is not at all nice. The important thing is that Bertie is going to have a visit from his grandmother."

"I hope she doesn't drink too much," said Olive. "Pansy's granny never stops drinking."

"Not all the time," said Pansy mildly. "Just in the evening."

Tofu sought clarification. "What time does she start?" The question was posed with a politeness that was unusual for him. Any exchanges between Tofu and Olive tended to be short, scornful, and as often as not curtailed by his spitting at her. Although Olive's principal lieutenant, Pansy, had a secret soft spot for Tofu and they usually addressed one another courteously enough, except when Olive was around, when Pansy felt that she had to follow her friend's lead.

Pansy thought for a moment. "About five," she said. "Sometimes a bit earlier, but usually at about five."

"Now listen," said the teacher. "We should not talk about other people's grannies like that, even if . . ." She hesitated. What Olive had said was probably true—children did not miss these things. And the teacher herself had seen the grandmother in question collecting Pansy from the school gate one afternoon and she had looked rather the worse for wear. It was her nose, of course, that set alarm bells ringing; that degree of red, that deep, almost purple colour seemed so unnatural. Of course, people other than drinkers could have red noses, but when you combined a red nose with a somewhat irregular gait surely there was legitimate cause for concern.

Olive took the opportunity to fill the brief silence. "Have you seen her nose, Miss Campbell? Have you seen Pansy's granny's nose close up?"

Pansy turned and gave Olive a discouraging look. She was prepared to discuss her grandmother's drinking, but to pick on her nose was a different matter.

"I've seen it," interjected Tofu. "I saw it one day last term, when she came to the school concert. When they turned the lights out in the hall for the concert, you could still see Pansy's granny's nose glowing in the dark. It was like one of those red lights that say EXIT."

It was rare for Olive to agree with Tofu, but on this occasion she did. "That's right," she said. "It was a good thing there wasn't a fire during the concert because that would have meant that everybody would have run over towards Pansy's granny's nose—by mistake of course. She could easily have been crushed."

The teacher clapped her hands together to bring this unsavoury conversation to an end. "That's quite enough," she said. "We mustn't make personal remarks. It's most unhelpful."

"Even if they're true?" asked Tofu.

"Even if they're true," repeated the teacher. "It doesn't help at all. It just makes people feel bad about themselves and it leads to arguments. The point is this, children: some people don't look the same as us, and that . . ."

"They have different noses?" interrupted Tofu.

"Yes. There are many different noses. One nose is very much the same as any other nose. It's what's *inside* the nose that counts."

It was a well-intentioned remark, but perhaps unhelpful before such an audience. Olive grimaced, and several other children tittered.

"What I meant to say, boys and girls; what I meant to say is that it's what's inside a *person* that counts. What's really important is what sort of person they are inside—not just inside their nose or indeed any other part of them, but inside *them*."

The teacher looked out over the faces of the fifteen children seated at their desks, each one, she reflected, a complex and unique personality—as her psychology tutor had drummed into them at teacher training college. "What you are going to be doing in your careers," the tutor had said, "is take that raw material, the basic personality so to speak, and enable it to develop. You should not try to make it what *you* want it to be; you should try to make it discover itself and blossom. That is what your job amounts to—that is your immense privilege."

Was it really an immense privilege to sit here and talk to these little . . . these little . . . In an awful moment of existential understanding, Miss Campbell thought: *these little savages.* And then she thought: *I must not think things like that.*

She became aware that Olive was staring at her.

"Excuse me, Miss Campbell," she said. "But I think you need to use your hanky."

Flustered, Miss Campbell took her handkerchief out of her sleeve and dabbed at her nose. *Little cow*, she thought.

8. Mitigated Beige

Angus Lordie and Domenica Macdonald had settled into the routines of married life rather more quickly—and comfortably—than either had thought possible. Both had lived a solitary existence for long enough to fear that sharing Domenica's flat in Scotland Street would involve more than a few compromises and adjustments; yet both had determined in advance that they would not allow themselves to be irritated by any aspect of the change. Angus had seen such irritation bring to an untimely end the marriage of a friend who, having married for the first time at forty-three, had found his new wife's minor idiosyncrasies to be unbearable. The straw that eventually broke the back of that marriage had been her insistence on pronouncing Gullane as it was written, rather than as *Gillane*, which was what it really was—a highly divisive issue in Scotland, even if not one that might be expected to bring a marriage to an end.

For her part, Domenica remembered the difficulty that her university friend, Janet, had encountered in persisting with the second marriage she had contracted after her first husband's parachuting accident, he having inadvertently left his parachute in the plane before the jump. The problem had revolved around physical matters—not those connected with the marital bed, but more the marital bathroom. She had confessed these to Domenica one afternoon when the two of them had been having tea together in the Portrait Gallery tearoom on Queen Street.

"He's a very generous man," Janet had said. "He's kind and considerate too."

"Everything one might want in a husband," remarked Domenica, wondering what was to follow.

Janet lowered her voice; a woman at a neighbouring table, bored with her own company, was straining to hear their conversation. "The problem is more personal."

Domenica looked away. "Oh well, that side of things can be awkward, but there are always people who can help, you know." She paused. "One should not be ashamed to talk about these matters." She said that even while reflecting on the intense embarrassment that must inevitably accompany any discussion of such things.

Her friend gasped. "Oh, it's nothing to do with *that*," she said.

Domenica was relieved. She noted that Janet used the term *that*. That was what *that* was often called, and there was rarely any difficulty in understanding exactly what *that* meant.

"So it's not *that*," said Domenica.

"Oh no," said Janet, with the sort of philosophical sigh that women often utter when discussing *that*. "*That's* not a problem. It's more . . . well, it's more to do with his *pores*. Johnny, you see, is a very greasy man. He's utterly charming—but greasy."

The eavesdropper at the next table, catching this, gave a start. Her eyes widened.

Domenica felt that this would have to be handled very delicately and was considering her response when Janet continued, "When he has a bath there is always a line of grease around the surface of the bathtub. I feel it when I use the bath myself. You know how it is? It's rather like the feeling you get when you get in and discover that the last person has used bath oil. It's slippery."

Domenica winced. She knew the feeling. But surely one might rise above such a minor thing. Or one might take steps to deal with it, asking that the bath be cleaned after use—there were abrasive powders that were designed to deal with just such issues.

"And he's ruined the furniture in the sitting room," Janet continued. "There are dark patches where his head has been."

Antimacassars, thought Domenica; they were designed specifically for that problem. Of course it would be difficult to find them these days, although they were exactly the sort of thing that might be sold by the Royal Edinburgh Repository and Self-Aid Society, one of the few remaining places to sell hand-knitted models of the Queen. As a child she had walked past the "distressed gentlewomen's" shop in Castle Street and had marvelled at the term.

"Why are they distressed?" she had asked. "What's upset them?"

Her mother had explained. "They are not distressed in the sense of being upset," she said. "Their circumstances are distressed."

"Which means?"

"Which means they have very little money. So they spend their time knitting cardigans and socks—such as you see in the window—and crocheting covers for various things. Distressed gentlewomen are very keen on covering things with crochet work—it is one of their consolations, I think."

And there had been antimacassars in the window—pieces of white embroidered linen in squares of such a size and shape as might rest neatly on the top of any chair in which a pomaded man might sit. But then they had disappeared, although there still seemed to be an abundance of doilies for other purposes—to put on tea trays or to cover jugs of milk.

She had mentioned antimacassars to Janet, along with a suggestion that her husband might find some soap or lotion that could reduce greasy exudations, but this advice, if it was ever followed, had not been enough to prevent a parting of the ways. She herself would never allow a minor matter of physical squeamishness to imperil her marriage, although no such thing ever arose, except, perhaps, in relation to Angus's wardrobe, which had to be *rationalised*, as she put it.

This process of rationalisation had involved the throwing out of most of his shirts (frayed at the collar) and trousers (frayed at the bottom of the leg). His jackets, or most of them, had been donated to a charity shop in Stockbridge, and his shoes, with the exception of a couple of newer pairs, had been consigned to the bin. This dramatic pruning had been followed by the making by Domenica of an unaccompanied trip to Stewart, Christie in Queen Street where she had engaged in a private consultation with a sympathetic assistant.

"Your husband undoubtedly has very good taste in clothes," said the assistant. "But perhaps he keeps them too long. Many men do that, you know."

Domenica agreed, and then had moved on to the choice of several tweed jackets, a waistcoat, a dozen shirts, a pair of corduroy trousers, and two pairs of chinos, one in crushed strawberry and one in mitigated beige. She then arranged for Angus to call and have these clothes fitted and, if necessary, taken in or let out according to need.

"In my experience," said the assistant, "men require slightly larger sizes after a year or two of marriage. It's undoubtedly something to do with the contentment that their new state brings, and to the effect of improved diet. This is just a general observation, please understand: there are some men who *diminish* on marriage. One person we know virtually disappeared a year or two after his wedding. Mr. Lordie, I am sure, will not fall into that category."

9. *The Ethics of Portraiture*

And Angus was indeed content. Not only was he rather pleased with his new wardrobe of clothes—particularly with the mitigated-beige chinos, which he wore rather too often, at the expense of the older, crushed strawberry pair, which remained more or less untouched in their drawer—but he was also delighted with the encouragement Domenica gave him in his artistic life.

Over the years, Angus had acquired a reputation as one of the most sympathetic portrait painters in Scotland. This sympathy was for his sitters, with whom he usually developed a strong rapport even in the earliest minutes of the first sitting. Having a portrait painted is a potentially stressful experience for anybody: how will I look? Will *both* my chins be painted? Will I appear older than I am? Will I look ridiculous? These are the questions that even the most selfless, least egotistical sitters will ask themselves, for, after all, who does not hope to be remembered in the best possible light? Who, if given the choice, would not opt to be portrayed at sixteen rather than at sixty? Who does not have at least some feature, some minor imperfection perhaps, that he or she would not want at least softened, if not totally obscured, by a more forgiving rather than a harsher light?

The fact that Angus was so gentle in his treatment of his sitters meant that they relaxed and, in the ensuing state of trust, allowed their true personality to emerge. In most cases he judged this true personality to be benevolent, but even where the qualities that emerged were unattractive, Angus was still inclined to play these down and to look for something positive in an otherwise unpromising personality.

This could give rise to a challenge, as it did when he was asked by a Glasgow industrialist to paint his fourteen-year-old son, a boy whose dismaying appearance would be difficult to disguise. The diplomatic problem was exacerbated by the fact that the father looked very much the same as the son—both were of simian appearance, with heavy, beetle brows, wide mouths, and the flared nostrils usually found on chimpanzees. They had come to see Angus in Edinburgh, father and son, visiting him in his studio.

"They say my boy is very much a chip off the old block," said the father, smiling with pride. "And I suppose when I look at the photographs of me as a youngster I can see it too."

Angus made a noncommittal response.

"He's a keen tennis player," went on the father. "Maybe you could paint him on the tennis court, about to serve."

Angus stared at the boy, who was sitting awkwardly in his studio chair. The similarity to a monkey was quite striking, he thought. Perhaps he could be painted sitting in a tree, or foraging for berries, as chimps do . . .

"What's that stink?" the boy suddenly asked. "There's a real stink here."

Rather than reproaching his son, the father sniffed at the air, his already copious nostrils widening even further.

"I can't smell anything," said the father.

"Turpentine," said Angus, glaring at the boy. "I use it to clean my brushes. The oil paint, you see, would dry on them if I didn't and then the bristles would be ruined."

"See," said the father. "You see, Billy, that's something you've learned already. You come through to Edinburgh and you learn something." He laughed. "And the other way round, of course."

"Hah!" said Angus. And it was then that a possibility occurred. "Tennis," he continued. "You know, that's a rather intriguing idea. A portrait of Billy playing tennis would be rather interesting—rather like Raeburn's picture of the *Skating Minister.*"

"You hear that?" said the father. "That picture we saw in

the National Gallery of the minister on his skates—remember it?"

The boy nodded vaguely.

"And I think," said Angus, coming to the point of his idea, "that it would be best to paint Billy from behind, just as he's tossing the ball up into the air for his serve. It could be a powerful portrayal of the . . . of the sheer physicality of the game—the power of the serve. Beyond us, so to speak, would be the trajectory of the ball, the open court stretching out before him—symbolic of life's challenges, perhaps. Billy, though, would fill the foreground with his shoulders and with his racquet up in the air ready to be brought down upon the ball."

The father looked thoughtful. "That sounds very interesting, Mr. Lordie. But would Billy be recognisable? You see, I assume that we would just see the back of his head, not his actual face."

"You don't need to see my face," said Billy. "You and Mom know what I look like."

Angus smiled. "Billy has a point," he said. "Art does not need to be too representational. We've gone beyond that now." *The Devil may quote scripture for his own devices*, thought Angus, reproaching himself. Perhaps he should just grasp the nettle and paint this unfortunate boy with full frontal physiognomy; the notion of painting just the back of his head was no real solution to the delicate issue of truthfulness in portraiture.

"I suppose we'll know it's him," said the father.

"That will be very clear," said Angus. "Posture is very revealing. And the cranium itself, viewed from whatever angle, is quite distinctive."

The father's mind was made up. "Very well," he said. "You've persuaded me."

But then Angus changed his mind. He had been sorely tempted, but this option, he saw, was meretricious to the core, and he resisted it. "No," he said. "I don't think that will work. I shall paint Billy more or less as we see him here—seated in my studio. I shall capture him far better that way."

There had been three sittings, and eventually the painting was complete. Angus had not flinched from presenting his subject as he saw him, but even with that truthfulness he had somehow painted the boy in such a way that in spite of his unprepossessing face he looked appealing, caught at that odd stage of transition between childhood and youth, to all intents and purposes like a Norman Rockwell portrait for the cover of *Life* magazine of some freckled, optimistic boy.

The boy's mother had cried when she saw it, and had planted a kiss on Angus's surprised cheek.

"Dear Mr. Lordie," she whispered. "I know my son's no oil painting but . . ." She sighed. "But now he is."

Angus reflected on the truth of this statement as both metaphor and fact, and smiled in modest acknowledgement of the compliment.

10. Lions, Sociobiology, and Maleness

Domenica appreciated Angus's ability to get the best out of his sitters. That, she thought, was one of his better qualities—a social ease that she felt she herself lacked. It was not that she was in any way awkward in her dealings with people—none of her many friends would have described her as being difficult to get on with—the difference between her and Angus was more subtle than that, residing somewhere in the tricky territory of male-female distinctions. The trickiness lay in the fact that in a society with an official commitment to removing salience, such matters as the differences between men and women were rarely talked about openly.

Both Domenica and Angus were in their late forties. Both were old enough, then, to have witnessed the dismantling of patriarchal society. Both had welcomed this change—Angus because he had never seen the justification for male assumptions of entitlement, and in Domenica's case because, like any woman of her age, she had encountered male condescension—or, as she put it, male pushiness—and had resented it. She had never struck an overtly feminist pose, but had understood why there were those who felt they had to do just that. The walls of bastions had to be pulled down if a new, just architecture were to be established—she knew that had to happen—but she had never liked the anger with which that process was sometimes tainted. In claiming a right, Domenica felt, you did not necessarily have to humiliate whole swathes of humanity. So she had never felt comfortable with the distaste that some of the more aggressive warriors in the struggle for women's rights expressed for men in general.

"Men may be misguided and, indeed, at times arrogant," she said to a friend. "But try as I might, I can't dislike them with quite the intensity that some feminists manage."

. The friend had smiled. "Nor I. In fact, I rather like men.

I know that's a very unfashionable view, but there we are. I suppose the issue is maleness, isn't it?"

"Well, yes, but . . ."

The friend had expanded on the theme. "Maleness exists as a phenomenon in nature, doesn't it? You can observe it in . . . well, I suppose, in any animals you care to examine. Lions. Cats. Elephants. Everything, come to think of it. The male is usually larger, stronger, and more assertive."

Domenica looked thoughtful. "Perhaps."

"No, not perhaps. Definitely. Male creatures tend to dominate. Look at lions. You have your head lion, or whatever he's called . . ."

"Leader of the pride, I suppose."

"Yes, him. And he's the one who calls the shots. He's the boss."

Domenica shook her head. "I'm not sure that these sociobiological arguments are going to get us very far. Human society is far more complex than that. Yes we have biology in the background, but social organisation is something that isn't determined solely by biological impulses."

Her friend sighed, as if faced with some nit-picking scholastic objection. "But these impulses drive it. They do! Men are the ones who do the hunting and fighting. Women do the nurturing."

Domenica was cautious. "Possibly. But lionesses, you know, make the kill much of the time. Then the male comes along and eats what she's caught." She paused. "I don't know where this is taking us. The trouble with sociobiological arguments is that they end up justifying a very bleak vision of what humanity can be or do. They're a dead end because they see human society as being red in tooth and claw and that's it."

"But perhaps we are. Perhaps life—all life—is just a matter of competition for control of space and resources. Ultimately, most arguments are about who gets what." She looked at Domenica with the expression of one who had uncovered some fundamental truth. "That's what wars are, don't you think? One group wants something—land, water, food, whatever—and another group wants it too. Result? Conflict."

"Yes, but . . ." Domenica was struggling. The grim, reductionist logic of her friend's position did not appeal to her, and yet was difficult to refute. Yet there was an answer, and that, she felt lay in reason. Reason was the straw at which we might grasp.

But her friend had lost interest, and was returning to the subject that had launched their debate: maleness.

"Maleness exists, don't you think?"

Domenica nodded. "Yes. Yes, it does."

"But what exactly is it?"

Domenica thought it was an approach to the world. "It's an attitude. It's an attitude of engagement."

"Engagement?"

Domenica was pleased with the term, and warmed to the subject. "Yes. Look at the way in which a little boy plays. He prods. He investigates things all around him. He moves them. He tries to push them over. Then look at girls. They touch things gently. They watch them. They don't try to push them about. They . . ." She searched for the right word. "They *cherish* them."

The friend agreed. "Yes," she said. "It's exactly that."

"So," continued Domenica. "If we're agreed that maleness is something to do with engagement, then why do we find it attractive? Assuming, of course, that we do find it attractive."

The friend smiled. "Yes, we do. As women, we do. We like it. We like men, or at least, those of us who like men like it."

Domenica raised an objection. "And we don't like men who don't have that maleness about them?"

This was problematic. "No, we do like them. Women like sensitive men—men who aren't interested in pushing or shoving things about."

Domenica thought of the sensitive men she knew. She had several friends in that category. "But we don't like them for their maleness, do we?"

"No, we like them because they're easy company. Because we can talk to them. It has nothing to do with maleness."

They looked at one another, and smiled. Their discussion had come back to that central mystery of the way in which men and women saw one another and why, because of that, the ancient dance of fascination took place.

"So, why do we do it?" asked Domenica.

"Get involved with men? Fall for maleness?"

"Yes."

The friend hesitated. "Because we want to possess it," she said. "Because we want to possess men, to tame them, to own them." She paused. "Remember D.H. Lawrence's essay, 'Flowery Tuscany'?"

"Of course," said Domenica, perhaps a little bit too quickly.

"Because he points out," the friend continued, "that when women see flowers they feel the need to pick them—to possess them—whereas men don't."

Domenica said nothing. She could not abide Lawrence. And anyway, if men didn't pick flowers it was probably because they didn't see them in the first place.

11. A Selfish Climber

There was an overlap of just over two weeks between the getting of the keys to the house at Nine Mile Burn and the handing over of the flat in India Street to its purchasers. During that period, Matthew and Elspeth found themselves owners of two properties—a situation that for most people is made distinctly uncomfortable by the need to have a bridging loan between mortgages. For a brief spell interest is paid not only on the old mortgage but on the new loan too—a potentially crippling burden. People on bridging loans can be seen in restaurants eating only one course or, indeed, nothing at all, so pressing is the enforced parsimony a bridging loan entails.

In Matthew's case, such exigencies were unnecessary, as he had found the purchase price of the new house from capital—an unusual position for one in his late twenties to be in. But even so, being insulated from harsh economic reality does not mean that one is unaware of the stringencies under which most people live.

"How does anybody do it?" he remarked to Elspeth as they sat in their kitchen in India Street, amidst the half-packed crates of pots and pans, cutlery and crockery.

"It helps to have packers," said Elspeth. "Those guys move in—bang, bang—and everything's wrapped up in crumpled newspaper and stacked away."

"Not that," said Matthew. "I meant financially, but since you mentioned it, what if you can't afford movers? What do you do?"

Elspeth looked at him. There was the odd occasion—such as now—when the difference in their backgrounds showed. Had Matthew never done a flat move as a student? Had he been able to afford removal men even then?

"You pack everything yourself," she said. "But it depends on how much stuff you have. Lots of people don't have all that much stuff, you know."

"Oh, I know that," said Matthew. He was sensitive to any suggestion of privilege.

"Then you hire a van," Elspeth went on. "And you get your friends to help."

"Of course."

Elspeth continued. "There's a certain stage in your life, though, when you realise that you're not going to help anybody else to move. You say to yourself: that's it—no more helping friends with their move."

Matthew smiled. He had done that; only a few months ago he had declined an invitation to have a drink with a friend when the friend had casually added to the invitation that there was a wardrobe that needed shifting afterwards.

"It comes at about twenty-eight," Elspeth continued. "You turn twenty-eight and you decide that you've helped enough friends to move flats. And that's the point at which you say . . ."

"My back," interjected Matthew.

"Exactly. You say: 'Sorry, I've got this back, you see.' It always works."

Matthew looked thoughtful. "There's a limit to what one can do for friends—whether or not you have a tendency to put your back out."

Elspeth agreed. "Of course, some people are so selfish they'll do nothing for others—even for their friends."

Matthew thought about this. He had several very generous friends—their names came to him quite readily, even if they were all from his pre-Elspeth days—but it was difficult to call to mind entirely selfish ones. But then he remembered. "Yes," he said. "I knew somebody like that. I remember driving with her up to Fort William once—we both belonged to a climbing club at university. We were going somewhere up there—I forget exactly which mountain we were going to climb—it wasn't Ben Nevis."

"I'm not sure I would want to climb with a selfish person,"

mused Elspeth. "She'd let go of the rope rather than try to save you—if you fell, that is."

"It's unusual to find a selfish climber," said Matthew. "Generally speaking climbers help one another. But this woman, well . . ."

He related to Elspeth how they stopped at Tyndrum, before the road began its ascent to Rannoch Moor and to Glencoe beyond. He told her how in the car park of the Green Welly they had sat down to an improvised picnic lunch. Matthew had gone into the shop to buy some food, and had returned with ready-made sandwiches and two apples. He had offered his companion a sandwich and he had seen her glance discreetly at the sell-by date on the packaging. One sandwich was fresher than the other—and it was this one she chose. Then she had turned to the apples and again he had seen a quick appraisal of desirability before she left him with the smaller and less inviting of the two.

"In those two quick glances she gave herself away," he said. "She said everything about her personality that needed to be said, and I realised that I was in the company of a consummately selfish person."

Elspeth agreed. "Imagine giving somebody else the older sandwich," she said. "A good person would not have done that, would she?"

"No," said Matthew. "She would not."

"Where does generosity come from?" Elspeth asked.

It was a strange question, and Matthew wondered whether the same question might be asked of any of the virtues. "I suspect that generosity is determined at a very early age," he said. "Probably in one's very earliest years, and then it becomes cemented through the habits of the heart."

"Like everything else," said Elspeth. "Like kindness; like sympathy; like the ability to think yourself into the shoes of another."

"Yes," said Matthew. "Like all of that."

"Mind you," said Elspeth. "Our characters are partly a matter of genes, aren't they?"

"Could be."

"I think they are. You know, when I was doing my teaching qualification we were advised to read a book on twins. It was fascinating. It was all about those studies in which twins who are separated at birth and who have had totally different upbringings are later assessed by psychologists. And you know what? They are often remarkably similar in their behaviour and their preferences."

"Really?"

"Yes. In one case two men turned up who had not seen one another since birth. They were twins who had been adopted by different families. And when the researchers saw them in their thirties or whatever age they were, they wore similar clothes, voted for the same party, watched the same movies, had the same hobbies, and drove the same make of car."

"No!"

"Yes. And there was something else—they had each married a woman with the same first name."

"Well!" exclaimed Matthew.

"Yes," said Elspeth. "So much for the idea that nurture beats nature."

"Oh," said Matthew, vaguely depressed at the thought that our fate was so much a question of deoxyribonucleic acid.

12. Alpha Males and Sociopathy

Matthew and Elspeth may have had packers to help them in their move, but there was still a daunting amount of sorting out that Elspeth, in particular, felt they would have to do themselves.

"We acquire so much," she sighed, looking about the disarray in the kitchen. "Just by existing, we seem to acquire so much."

Matthew glanced at the shelf behind his chair. Elspeth was right: a tin soldier in the uniform of a Highland regiment stood beside a broken wally dug; beside the china dog was a small stack of recipe books, an assortment of unlikely shelf-fellows—the ubiquitous *Delia, The Scots Kitchen, The River Café Cookbook*—and alongside that was a fankle of string, mixed with old bills and receipts.

He thought of his study: the movers had been told to pack the books, of which there were at least five hundred, but he had asked them to leave the papers to him. These were stacked in piles at the bottom of the bookshelves, or crammed into the drawers of the two low filing cabinets on either side of his desk. *If I am like this at this stage in my life*, he thought, *then what will I be like at fifty? Or sixty?*

Elspeth hardly helped his anxiety. She had been reading an article in a Sunday newspaper and had passed it over with the suggestion that he read it.

"I'm not saying that this is you," she said, pointing to the page in question. "All I'm saying is that you have to be careful. OCD." She uttered the acronym OCD as if it were QED.

"OCD? Me?"

"Hoarding," she said. "Read it. It's caused by OCD."

Matthew took the newspaper but did not begin to read. "Do you think I've got OCD?" he asked. "Do you really think . . ."

Elspeth shook her head. "No . . . or maybe just a touch. Apparently lots of people have mild OCD, or at least a tendency to it. It's nothing to be ashamed of."

She saw the look of dismay on Matthew's face and sought to reassure him. "No, seriously, if you read that, you'll see you're nowhere near as bad as the real McCoy. It talks about these two brothers in New York, you see—they were called the Collyers."

Matthew glanced at a photograph above the article. He read the names below it. "Homer and Langley Collyer?"

"Yes, that's them. They lived in a mansion in New York, apparently, and they filled it up with so much stuff that they had to get from room to room by tunnel through all the junk. Their tunnels collapsed and they died."

"Oh." Matthew thought: *I'm nowhere near needing a tunnel . . .*

Elspeth continued with the story. "It took the police ages to work their way through all the things stacked in the rooms before they could find their bodies. They had been dead for weeks—entombed in all the rubbish."

"Poor guys . . ."

"Yes," said Elspeth. "And it tells you there some of the things they found in the house. It wasn't just old newspapers and so on: they had fourteen pianos, an X-ray machine, a number of violins, a car chassis, countless telephone directories, the pickled body of a baby in a jar . . . and so on. There were 140 tons of rubbish in the house."

Matthew looked about the kitchen. There were the old receipts, of course, and the cookery books, but no car chassis nor X-ray machine.

"I'm going to tidy up," he said. He was filled with resolve, but he still looked at her reproachfully. "Do you really think I'm obsessive-compulsive? I only wash my hands once or twice a day, you know, and I never come back upstairs to check I've turned off the iron. Or hardly ever . . ."

"No," she said. "I don't. I just think that you . . . or rather we—that is, all of us—need to watch ourselves for signs of some of these common conditions. We might just be very slightly . . . just a teensie-weensie bit on the spectrum . . ."

Matthew looked up in alarm. "On the spectrum? Of what? Asperger's? Do you think I've got Asperger's?"

She did not. "Of course I don't think that. Lots of other people are just a little bit on the spectrum, but you aren't. And you're not a psychopath either. Or a sociopath, as they call them now."

"Can one be just a touch sociopathic?" asked Matthew.

"Oh, I think so. I know plenty of people who are a touch sociopathic. I think psychiatrists say that it's perfectly possible to have a mild degree of a personality disorder, don't they? Lots of alpha males are like that—politicians and so on."

"Really?"

Elspeth nodded. "Yes. Sociopaths are attracted to politics because they see it as a sphere in which you can be ruthless and step all over people. That fact that some politicians can tell such awful lies is another example of sociopathy. Sociopaths lie—they see nothing wrong with it."

Matthew remembered a line of poetry he had learned a long time ago. "Matilda," he began . . .

"*Told such dreadful lies,*" supplied Elspeth. "*It made one gasp and stretch one's eyes.*" She laughed. "Belloc. I read it to the children when I was teaching. I used to look at Bertie's little friend, Tofu, as I read it to them, because he was a terrific liar. But he just looked back at me as if butter wouldn't melt in his mouth."

"So Matilda was a psychopath—I mean, a sociopath?"

Elspeth nodded. "Probably. Of course she was burned to a cinder. Nobody heeded her calls for help when her house actually did go up in flames. *For every time she shouted 'Fire!' They simply answered 'Little Liar!'*"

"Poor girl."

"But that's what happens in morality tales. People come to a sticky end, or, in her case, a fiery one." Elspeth paused. "Talking of OCD, do you know who really had it? Full-blown?"

Matthew waited.

"Lady Macbeth," said Elspeth. "Remember? *All the perfumes of Araby . . .*"

"Ah," said Matthew. "Of course. I thought that was guilt."

"It can be the same thing," said Elspeth. "Or so I've read."

Matthew sighed. "I'm going to have to start throwing things out."

Then he remembered something. "The people who bought the flat," he said, looking at his watch. "They were going to come round to see us. I'd forgotten."

Elspeth had forgotten too. But what she remembered was what their lawyer, who had already met them, had said. "Apparently they're well-known," he had remarked. "He's . . . well, I forget what he does, but I gather he's some sort of celebrity. B-list, or possibly even C, but beggars can't be choosers, so to speak. Scotland has only a handful of A-list celebrities, and most of those live abroad. All the rest are distinctly B-list . . . and below."

"Really?" said Elspeth.

"Yes," said the lawyer. "Everybody knows that—except for the B-listers, of course. They don't know they're B-list."

"The whole notion of celebrity is absurd, anyway," said Elspeth.

The lawyer was inclined to agree. "Everybody knows that," he said. "Except the celebs themselves, perhaps."

13. Enter Nairn MacTaggart

It was Matthew who opened the door to the new purchasers of the India Street flat. Standing before him on the landing were a man and a woman, the man in his early forties, the woman a good ten years or so his junior, or so it seemed to Matthew. The man was well-built, but with a slightly drawn face; the woman, who was considerably shorter than him, had an interesting and intelligent face but also had that look, indefinable but quite recognisable, of somebody who lived in the shadow of another.

The man extended a hand to Matthew. "I'm Nairn," he said. "Nairn MacTaggart."

The accent was more West of Scotland than East, with the upward swirl, like the movement of a wave, that marked the speech patterns of Glasgow or its satellites. It was in a friendly register, though, unlike the sometimes disapproving tones of Edinburgh that could inhibit a conversation even as it started.

The woman also proffered her hand. "And I'm Chrissie."

Matthew invited them in. "Welcome to your new home," he said, ushering them into the hall.

"Not quite," said Nairn, smiling.

For a brief moment, Matthew wondered whether the sale had fallen through. He laughed nervously. "Well, it will be in . . . what? Ten days, I think."

"Yes," said Nairn. "Ten days."

"And we're looking forward to that," said Chrissie. "We're staying with friends at the moment—we've been there for three weeks, ever since we sold our old place at . . ."

Nairn interrupted her. "Staying with friends can be a very rewarding experience," he said, "but not necessarily for the friends."

"Hah!" said Matthew.

Chrissie looked at Nairn appreciatively. "That's very clever, Nairn," she said.

Reasonably clever, thought Matthew. I wouldn't say *very* clever.

"You begin to notice their faults," said Nairn. "Living with somebody brings you up against the reality of other people, doesn't it?"

Chrissie nodded her agreement. "That's absolutely true," she said.

"Oh well," said Matthew. "At least you have some friends."

Nairn gave him a sideways glance.

"Of course I imagine you have plenty of friends," Matthew said hastily. "But at least you have . . . you have some you can stay with."

Nairn looked up at the ceiling. "Friends are a mirror," he said. "If we want to see ourselves, then we only have to look at our friends."

"Totally," said Chrissie, and then, as if to forestall any contradiction, repeated, "It's there staring us in the face. Self-knowledge."

Matthew felt that he should introduce the couple to Elspeth, who had remained in the kitchen.

"We tend to live in the kitchen," he said, as he led his guests through. "It gets the afternoon sunlight."

"The gentlest of lights," said Nairn. "Ready to forgive; preparing us for night."

"Possibly," said Matthew.

Nairn stared at Matthew, as if challenged. "Definitely," said Nairn, pronouncing it the Glasgow way—*defin-ately.*

They entered the kitchen, where Matthew introduced the MacTaggarts to Elspeth. Tea was offered, and accepted.

"So," said Matthew as they sat down at the table, "so, you're going to enjoy living in India Street. We have great neighbours, and you're just a toddle away from Stockbridge. There are plenty of great shops down there."

"We lived in Stockbridge years ago," said Nairn. "In St. Bernard's Crescent. It was our first flat after we married."

"Only for a year or so," said Chrissie. "Before we went away."

"Where?" asked Matthew. "Where did you go away?"

"America," said Nairn. "Then Italy. We were in Bologna for a couple of years. Then Milan. Then home."

"You got around," said Matthew. "You went to quite a few places."

"Most places are much the same," said Nairn. "At least that's what I've found. You get what you get, don't you? You get some of this, and then you get some of that."

Chrissie seemed to brighten at this comment. "Very true," she said.

Matthew glanced at Elspeth, who was frowning slightly. He was not sure that he understood Nairn's comment, and he could see that Elspeth was also puzzled.

"What did you do in Bologna?" he asked.

Nairn made a slightly dismissive gesture, as if Bologna meant very little. Or perhaps, thought Matthew, it was to demonstrate that Bologna came to him, rather than the other way round.

Matthew waited for an answer, but none came.

"You must have been busy," he said, rather lamely. "Bologna and then Milan. Were you busy in Milan?"

Chrissie answered for Nairn. "Frantic," she said.

"Milan was very heavy," said Nairn.

Matthew glanced at Elspeth again. He decided to try another tack. "And America? Did you work there?"

"America is all about work," said Nairn. "New York in particular."

Matthew seized at the scrap of information. "You were in New York?"

Nairn nodded. "On and off," he said.

"Mostly on," said Chrissie.

Nairn shrugged. "Or off."

"And Chicago," added Chrissie. "We were in Chicago. Do you know Chicago?"

Matthew had been there once some time ago; Elspeth had not.

"Everybody likes Chicago," Chrissie said.

"Except those who don't," interjected Matthew, a note of disagreement in his tone.

Chrissie accepted the rebuke. "If you don't like Chicago, then it's not for you," she said.

Elspeth joined in. "It's the same as anywhere," she said. "If you don't like it, then you don't like it. There's not much more to be said, I suppose." She paused. "But what did you do in Chicago?"

"Work," said Nairn. "Not too strenuously, but it was work nonetheless."

"You worked very hard, Nairn," said Chrissie. "You did, you know." She turned to Elspeth. "He was worn out after a few months. We had to go to San Diego to recover."

"But that's far away," said Matthew. "Isn't that in Southern California?"

"It was when we were last there," said Nairn.

There was a silence. Matthew, who now felt irritation growing with him, made a last attempt. "What exactly did you do in Chicago? It was obviously stressful work."

"Whose work isn't stressful?" asked Nairn.

"Let's not talk about work," said Chrissie. "Let's talk about the flat. Is there anything you think we should know?"

Matthew thought: *but I want to talk about work; I want to find out what you do.* But he did not say that, and instead he said, "We've made you a list of what's where—you know, the controls for the central heating and so on."

"That's great," said Nairn. "I always find those things rather hard."

"So you're not an engineer," said Matthew quickly. That, at least, excluded one possibility.

Nairn laughed. "Me? An engineer? Certainly not."

"Nairn can do many things," said Chrissie. "But he can't change a lightbulb."

Matthew smiled. "What's that joke? How many psychiatrists does it take to change a lightbulb? You aren't a psychiatrist, are you?"

"Nairn would have been a great psychiatrist," ventured Chrissie.

"But he isn't?" asked Matthew.

"Not in a narrow, formalistic sense," said Nairn. "But we can all be the things we aren't, don't you think? So we can all be engineers, if that's what we want to be—engineers of the human self."

Matthew bit his lip at the pretentiousness. But he was piqued by the mystery. Who was this Nairn character and what exactly did he do? Matthew suspected that the answer to these questions was as follows: nobody, and nothing. But he could not be sure, and he was determined to find out.

14. *Above Edinburgh Airport, She Wept*

Nicola Pollock was the grandmother of Bertie Pollock, the mother of Stuart Pollock, and the widow of the late

Henderson MacDougall Pollock, barley broker and distillery director. Henderson had been her first love—she had met him at a dance in Kelso when they had both been seventeen, and they had married at twenty-four. He was the man by whom she judged all other men, and found, more often than not, them lacking. If a politician, for example, wanted her vote, the question she asked herself was this: *Would Henderson have voted for him?* If he would, then the matter was settled; if he would not, then no amount of argument would obtain her support. And the same went for books—*Would Henderson have read it?*—for holiday destinations—*Would Henderson have gone there?*—and indeed for her own choice of outfits—*Would Henderson have liked this particular outfit?*

To lead one's life in the shadow of another is hardly anybody's idea of self-fulfilment. For a feminist, it is, understandably, abhorrent; so many women's lives have been stunted by the infliction of male decisions and preferences—blighted lives that made up a vast historical hinterland of oppression, unhappiness, and sheer waste. In Nicola's case, though, marriage had not been that. Henderson Pollock had been anything but an overbearing husband and never sought to impose his views on his wife. On the contrary, he had encouraged her to develop her own interests and tastes, and if she tended to follow his lead, it was no doing of his. No, this was sheer admiration at work—admiration inspired and fueled by love. And when Henderson had died at the age of forty-nine, Nicola had settled into a life of quiet reflection on how fortunate she had been in the marriage that had molded every aspect of her life.

Her widowhood was a sociable one, and she met the occasional man who was available and who might have been interested in this vivacious and unusually attractive widow, but these men were few and far between and anyway routinely failed comparison with Henderson's memory. They were few in number because of the brute facts of demography: for every single woman aged over forty there is only 0.3 of a man— which is another way of saying that there are three times as many single women looking for a husband than there are single men looking for a wife.

This paucity of suitable males is something that first dawns on women in their late teens. Prior to that, the composition of school classes conveys an impression of rough equality of numbers. But this impression of equality is misleading, and males are favoured—in the reproductive sense—by the fact that their rate of mortality is higher—men are greater risk-takers and risk goes hand-in-hand with earlier demise.

And so it is that young women begin to find out in their twenties that there are not quite as many eligible young men as they had earlier imagined. But other factors come into play: the liberation of both men and women from pressure to conform sexually further diminished the number of those men looking for a female partner. The personal fulfillment that many men now found in being able to acknowledge and engage with an alternative sexuality made many much happier, but was not always greeted with the same whole-hearted enthusiasm by women. Whatever their publicly professed views, many women discreetly regretted the loss of precisely those men who were the most sympathetic, the most amusing company, the most prepared to help in the kitchen; of course these men should be allowed to be themselves, but what a pity—many women thought—that quite so many intelligent and artistic men should be lost to them.

Nicola had never imagined that she would meet another man with whom she would be prepared to share her life, but rather to her astonishment she did. With Abril, she found both a partner and a whole new identity within a culture very far removed from the douce world of bourgeois Melrose.

Over the years, that Borders world seemed to become more distant; the clothes she wore changed—no more tweeds; her palate became accustomed to a whole different range of tastes; her very soul, she felt, broadened and acquired a Portuguese sensibility. Scotland now seemed almost alien, at that distance—a world of muted colours and hushed voices, a world in which so much was unspoken, a world in which cold somehow seemed at the heart of things.

But it was still home. However she redefined herself, that part of one that made for the core of the self, that part that we think of as the ultimate, inner being—that was ineradicably Scottish. That part spoke with a Scottish voice; that part looked out through Scottish eyes; and it was that part that now welled within her as she gazed out through the window of the descending plane and saw below her the rolling Borders hills . . . and there, in their midst, a loch, and a large one at that. St. Mary's Loch? She strained to see, but the plane banked slightly to the right and the sun shone in her eyes. She raised a shading hand to her brow; a few minutes later, a road snaked through a glen and then climbed a broad hill—Soutra, perhaps, still there, still commanding, although marred now by a forest of great wind turbines, a monument to our indifference to our environment. The sight saddened her, and she wondered how long it would be before Scotland disappeared under these Quixote-provoking structures and we had only a memory of our beautiful hills remaining, a memory of Eden before we wrecked it with machines.

She gripped the armrest of her seat. She felt her eyes begin to fill with tears. She fought the welling up within her, but unsuccessfully. She began to cry—silently, as she was surrounded by people and she did not want to make an exhibition of herself. But she could not suppress her tears.

"Are you all right?" the man beside her whispered.

She nodded. "I'm sorry," she said. "It's just that . . ." Words failed her and she gestured through the window at the scene below.

"Scotland," muttered the man.

"Yes," she said. "Home."

The man placed his hand gently on her forearm, and left it there. It is such an easy thing to do—to touch another in sympathy—but it is such a hard thing too.

15. *The Sad Fate of the Danish Car Industry*

Stuart Pollock, together with Bertie and Ulysses, left in good time for the airport—or would have done so had he remembered where he had parked the car. This was a recurring issue in the Pollock household, and had led to a number of fairly sharp domestic disagreements.

The problem sprang from the fact that Scotland Street, a short street by the standards of the New Town, did not have enough parking for its residents, who were obliged to find a space—if they could—in one of the neighbouring streets. This was easy enough when the residents of those streets were using their cars, but was considerably more difficult when they chose to be at home and to be parked. At such times, it could become necessary for Stuart or Irene to drive to the far end of Cumberland Street, or even up into Heriot Row to find a vacant spot. That was no great hardship, of course, but if one regularly put the car in a different place it could become difficult to remember where that place was, especially if the car was not used for a week or two, as sometimes happened.

Thus it was that the Pollock family's aged Volvo had been forgotten about in Northumberland Street, Great King Street, North West Circus Place, and Dublin Street. Then, when the car was suddenly needed, there would be a moment of panic that nobody knew where it was. This led to accusations and recriminations, often of an unseemly sort.

"You'd think that with something as significant as a car," said Irene sarcastically, "one might remember where one put it. We're not talking about a small item here, you know, Stuart: we are talking about a large chunk of Danish engineering."

"Swedish," corrected Stuart.

"Don't change the subject, Stuart. It matters not a jot whether the Danes or the Swedes make these things—the point is . . ."

"But it does matter," protested Stuart. "The Danes don't make cars."

Bertie had been listening. "Excuse me, Daddy," he interjected. "I think they did make some cars. Not many, but they did make some. I read about them."

Both Irene and Stuart looked down at Bertie with astonishment. Although barely seven, Bertie was a voracious reader and had soaked up information on a range of topics that constantly surprised them.

"They made electric cars," said Bertie. "They were very nice, but they didn't work." He paused; he had remembered something else. "And then they made a sort of sports car and they sent it over to the BBC to film on one of those programme about cars that Tofu likes so much. The one with . . ."

"Ridiculous programme!" snapped Irene.

"And then the Danish sports car caught fire," Bertie continued.

Irene brushed this diversion aside. "Danish or Swedish—the point is this, Stuart: you need to *concentrate* when you park the car. Say to yourself *I have parked the car in Drummond Place*—commit it to memory. Then this sort of situation wouldn't arise."

Stuart took a deep breath. "Unless *you* used it last," he said between clenched teeth. "Who went to her Melanie Klein Reading Group in Barnton—of all places—by car, may I ask? Oh yes! Anybody around here *drive* to Melanie Klein Reading Group by any chance? Anybody round here then leave their Volvo right down by Canonmills—and forget where she had parked it until her husband just happened to be walking that way and noticed a whole stack of Melanie Klein books on the back seat of a Volvo that looked slightly familiar? Ring any bells?"

And so the arguments continued. Neither Stuart nor Irene was blameless, but, on balance Stuart mislaid the car more often than Irene did. And the occasions on which he did, it had more dramatic consequences—as when he went through to Glasgow by car for a meeting and then returned by train. This was easily done, of course: everyone else at the meeting was returning by train and it was the most natural thing in the world to accompany them back to Queen Street, continuing the discussion on the train. That oversight, though, had unexpected consequences, in that it had resulted in Stuart and Bertie having to return to Glasgow—by train—and discovering that their car, that had been parked, coincidentally, outside the house of the well-known Glasgow gangster, Lard O'Connor (RIP), had been stolen.

Lard had proved to be helpful in recovering the car—although the one he had delivered to them was not quite the same car, being a similar model but with one more gear than their own. He had also befriended Bertie, and had helpfully taken him and his father to see the Burrell Collection before they returned, by car, to Edinburgh.

Bertie was proud of his car. It seemed to him, as it seems to most children, that other families led a more normal life than his own. Other people's mothers did not insist on psychotherapy and yoga lessons; other people's mothers did not breast-feed their babies on the 23 bus, as Irene did: *Nihil humanum mihi alienum est,* she said to Bertie as he squirmed with embarrassment—*Nothing human is strange to me,* but even the most reconstructed boy of seven would be mortified by his mother breast-feeding on the bus, no matter how socially accepted such things were. At least when it came to their car, he had no reason to feel ashamed, as there were several members of his class at the Steiner School who had very odd vehicles in the family. Tofu's father, for instance, had converted his car to run on olive oil, which made its exhaust fumes smell like ciabatta bread—Bertie did not have to contend with anything like that; nor did he have to endure being picked up in an old Dormobile covered with *Nuclear Power? No thanks!* stickers, as did Olive's friend, Pansy. At least an old red Volvo would hardly be noticed, which is what most children want; and it would be missed, too, when, through some awful confusion it was mistaken for a part of an avant-garde artist's installation and sent down to London, where it in due course won the Turner Prize.

With their car subsumed into the world of conceptual art, they had to find another one, and it was this car, an anodyne grey station wagon, that they eventually located just in time to arrive at Edinburgh Airport as the flight carrying Nicola Pollock touched down on the runway, bounced back into the air, but only briefly, and for no more than a few feet, and then settled down again onto terra firma with a smouldering of expensive rubber and a transitory puff of smoke.

16. Hen Parties and the Scottish Enlightenment

Bertie, his father, and Ulysses arrived in the hall where liveried drivers, some bearing small boards on which names were displayed, were waiting to whisk their charges off to their destination. A driver from Gleneagles Hotel patiently waited for the Yamimoto party—golf was their goal—while Stuart imagined a more prosaic day awaited a couple of accountants from London being met by a driver holding up a placard announcing *Deloittes*.

"Should we not have a placard with Granny's name on it?" asked Bertie. "Just so that she knows."

Stuart laughed. "I think she just might recognise us, Bertie, whereas Mr. Yamimoto and his friends won't know the driver who's taking them up to Gleneagles. That's why he needs a sign."

"But we haven't seen her for ages," persisted Bertie. "And she's never even met Ulysses. She doesn't know how ugly he is."

"Poor wee Ulysses," said Stuart, and then reprovingly to Bertie, "Your brother's not ugly!"

Bertie looked down at his brother, strapped into his pushchair. He was fond of Ulysses, but he felt nothing could disguise the fact that he was a girning little boy who was prone to regurgitation. "I'm not saying it's his fault," Bertie protested. "It's just that his face looks so funny. Olive said that she thought he was upside down when she saw him for the first time. She thought that his face was actually his bottom."

Stuart made a dismissive gesture. "Olive is badly informed," he muttered.

"I told her he was the right way up," Bertie continued.

"Good," said Stuart. "Now perhaps we should concentrate. Passengers are beginning to come through and any moment we'll see Granny. Pay attention, Bertie."

They had only a couple of minutes to wait before Nicola emerged through the arrivals door. She was pushing a wheeled cabin-bag, and she left this to one side as she opened her arms in delight. Bertie, feeling himself being gently pushed forward by his father, hesitantly took the few steps that separated him from his grandmother.

"Bertie," said Nicola, embracing the small boy. "Darlingest, dearest Bertie!"

Small boys are undemonstrative; small boys may freeze when enveloped by the arms of relatives; but on this occasion Bertie did not. He closed his eyes and took a deep breath. His grandmother smelled of perfume and aniseed.

She reached into a pocket of her jumper and extracted a small bar of Toblerone that she thrust into his hands. "I love this stuff, Bertie," she said. "It's got honey in it. Chocolate and honey is such a delicious combination."

Bertie fumbled with the yellow cardboard and the silver wrapping paper beneath it. He sank his teeth into the hard, delicious confection; she was right—he could taste the honey.

Nicola stood up again and embraced her son, planting a kiss on each cheek. "Stuart, my dear," she muttered, and for a moment the tears that had welled up when she first saw Scotland from above reappeared. "So this is dear little Ulysses," she said, bending down to kiss the infant. "Oh dear, has he been sick?" She dabbed at his front with a muslin cloth that had been lying on his lap. "Poor wee fellow."

"He's always sick," volunteered Bertie, mumbling somewhat as his mouth was full of Swiss chocolate. "Mostly he's sick when he sees Mummy, but he's still a bit sick even when she's away." He paused. "Mummy's in the desert, you know."

Nicola glanced at Stuart. "Oh well, there we are; that's cleaned him up a bit."

"We should pick up your cases," said Stuart. "Carousel five."

They moved across to the baggage carousel, where a number of Nicola's fellow passengers were milling about, waiting for their suitcases to appear from behind an opaque flap of thick plastic.

"Look out for a large red suitcase," said Nicola to Bertie, "and a medium-sized black one with a striped strap round it. You see if you can recognise them, Bertie. A fifty pence prize if you can."

Bertie, whose pocket money had long been pegged by his mother at twenty pence a week, was immediately excited by the prospect of such riches. "Can I hold Ulysses?" he asked. "We don't want him to be sick over everybody's luggage, and he's never sick if I pick him up."

"Yes, you may," said Stuart. "But be careful with him—he's getting a bit heavier. Don't let him drop."

"You dropped him once, Daddy," said Bertie. "Remember? He landed on his head. It was in the kitchen."

Nicola laughed. "They bounce, thank heavens. I dropped you, Stuart, when you were about two. It was at Kelso Races, and you landed on the grass and seemed perfectly happy."

A warning light was suddenly switched on and a discordant siren sounded. "Stand well back, Bertie," said Stuart. "The luggage belt is about to move."

Holding Ulysses was an effort for Bertie, and his arms were beginning to ache. But Ulysses himself, for whom nothing was nicer than to be held by his much-admired older brother, was

emitting satisfied cooing sounds, and this made Bertie determined to persist.

Suitcases started to emerge. There were many more people
around Bertie now, including the members of a rowdy hen
party who had travelled up from Stansted to spend a weekend
in Edinburgh; a weekend of binge drinking, of screeching
in the streets, of tottering along the pavements from club
to club on unsteady high heels and clad in absurdly short
skirts. Stuart tried to control his visceral distaste; Essex girls,
he thought, and then silently reproached himself; Edinburgh
had people every bit as awful as these and they were just
here to enjoy some harmless fun. "I'm going to get seriously
wrecked," shrieked one of the girls, addressing her friends,
but also all those standing round the carousel. "First bar
we get to!" This brought cheers from others of her party.
"Wicked!" shouted another. "And I'm going to find a . . ."
The end of this statement of intent was drowned out by the
delighted screeching that greeted it. Stuart heard a whining
sound outside; a jet engine revving up, he thought, or the
sound of Enlightenment philosophers, not to say John Knox
himself, birling in their graves.

A large red suitcase hove into sight and Bertie, in the
excitement of recognition, and in eager anticipation of his
reward, put Ulysses down. On the carousel.

17. *Suitcases as Hostages to Fortune*

As his grandmother's suitcase drew level with him, Bertie
struggled to manoeuvre it off the carousel. A preliminary
pull succeeded in getting it to the edge and then a further tug,
administered as he ran alongside it, brought it tumbling to the
ground. From where he had been standing with Nicola, Stuart

suddenly realised what Bertie was up to, and rushed forward
to help him.

"You should have called me, old fellow," he said, laying a
hand on his son's shoulder. "That looks a bit heavy."

Stuart leaned forward to check the label. "Well, at least it's
the right one. You have to be careful that you don't take . . ."
He stopped, straightened up, and looked about him. "Where's
Ulysses?"

Bertie who had followed his father's lead and had been
examining the label, gave a start. "He's over there," he said,
pointing to the suitcase-laden carousel. "I had to . . ."

He became aware of his father's look of alarm. "I'm sure
he's all right, Daddy. Maybe he's . . ." Unable to think of
anything to say, he became quiet.

Stuart lunged forward and pressed a large red button
prominently placed on a nearby pillar. As he pressed it, the
carousel lurched to a stop.

"What did you do that for?" complained a young man
standing by. "That's for emergencies."

"This is an emergency," hissed Stuart. "My son!" He began
to run round the side of the carousel, pushing people out of
his way, desperately scanning the luggage piled on the belt.
In a few seconds he had reached the point where the luggage
disappeared once again through a hatch before reappearing a
minute or so later on the other side of the hall.

Bertie had followed him. "Maybe somebody picked him
up," he panted. "Maybe they've taken him to the lost property.
Do you think that might have happened, Daddy?"

Stuart did not answer his question. "You wait here, Bertie,"
he shouted. "I'm going to climb through there." He pointed
to the hatch and began to clear the now static suitcases that
were blocking it.

"Be careful, Daddy!" shouted Bertie. "There's a notice that
says you shouldn't . . ."

His words were drowned in the sound of the carousel starting up again. Stuart, on his hands and knees, felt the belt jerk into motion, and was then carried ignominiously through the hatch, the plastic curtain brushing roughly against him as he made the transition into the behind-the-scenes region of the airport; so might it feel descending to Hades; so might one be greeted by Charon; so might one first see the waters of Lethe.

Instead of which he saw a small group of astonished men dressed in blue work outfits standing around a small tractor and its attendant cart. One of the men detached himself from the group and strode over towards Stuart, apparently ready to admonish him. But then Stuart saw that one of the other men was holding Ulysses, while another spoke urgently into a mobile phone.

Stuart brushed past the man coming towards him and ran over towards Ulysses.

"This yours, Jim?" one of the men asked.

Stuart was relieved to hear the traditional Scottish honorific—Jim. The world of officials and busybodies would never use the term. *Jim* was friendly; *Jim* was understanding, implicitly recognising that anybody might leave his baby on a luggage carousel—it could happen to the best of us just as easily as to the worst.

"Yes," he said. "My other son put him on the belt. Sorry about that."

The man who had been holding Ulysses passed him over to Stuart. "Aye, well, he's none the worse for wear," he said. "Mind you—it could have ended differently."

One of the other men nodded. "That's right," he said. "Somebody put their baby on the luggage belt at check-in the other day. It was a mistake, of course, but the baby was checked through to Antigua via Gatwick. Fortunately they noticed in time."

Stuart blanched. "Well, thanks to you that's not happening."

He looked at the men. "I'll leave you to finish loading the luggage. Thanks very much for . . . for taking care of him. Sorry to keep you from your work."

"Oh, there's no hurry," said one of the men, looking at his watch. "It's almost time for our coffee break. We'll start that a bit early."

Stuart frowned. "But you've still got all that luggage to load on the carousel," he said.

"There'll be plenty of time for that after our coffee break," said the man who had been holding Ulysses.

Stuart raised an eyebrow. These men had done him a favour, and he did not wish to press them, but he could not help but wonder about the people awaiting their luggage in the other side.

Picking up his concern, one of the men gave an explanation. "Those folk will be all right," he said. "They've got their mobile phones and their Blackberries. They can read their e-mail for a while. They'll get their suitcases all in good time."

"Instant gratification can be bad for you," said one of the others. They all laughed—except Stuart.

"You disapprove?" asked one of the men. "You think it takes too long for your luggage to come out?"

"Well," began Stuart, tentatively. "I would have thought . . ."

The tallest of the men approached him menacingly. "Listen, Jim," he said. "You do your job and we'll do ours. Ken what I mean?"

"I understand perfectly," said Stuart.

"Technically that baby should have been handed into lost property," said the baggage handler. "We could still do that, you know." He paused. "And hand you in as well."

Stuart edged away. "Thank you very much," he said hurriedly. "I'll be making my way now."

"One final thing," called out one of the men. "You keep what you've seen back here to yourself. Understand?"

Stuart said that he did understand—perfectly.

"Because every so often people come through that hatch and see things they shouldn't see," continued the handler. "They see suitcases being dropped . . ."

"Never our fault," chipped in one of the other men. "Weak handles."

There was general laughter at this.

"Of course," said Stuart.

"And people who talk about what happens to their suitcases in the airport," the man continued. "Well, they find out—or rather their suitcases find out just how unwise that is. Suitcases can be made to encounter problems, you know. To come adrift, for instance, and spill all their contents on the floor. You wouldn't believe what we see."

Stuart gasped. And then, as if one man, the baggage handlers burst out laughing. "Don't believe a word of what we say," one said. "We're just having our little joke. You see, we get a bit bored here behind the scenes. Anything to liven things up a bit."

"Yes," said another. "Although we do have a very good game we play. It's called *Test the Strength of the Suitcase*."

"Sshh," said one of the other handlers. "Not for publication."

"Tell it not in Gath," said another. "Publish it not in the streets of Ashkelon."

"Or indeed of Edinburgh," said yet another, to general laughter.

18. *Tartan Light*

For Big Lou, owner of the newly renamed *Big Lou's Coffee and Conversation Bar*, the summer, which had started late, damp and miserable, was at last starting to pick up. And not before time, she felt: winter, with its dreich days and snell winds, had kept a longer grip on Scotland than was usual. Arctic air, trapped by the jet stream, had settled over the land for weeks, whitening the hills in both highlands and lowlands with a democratic sternness. The mercury fell, and stayed low; waterfalls froze in mid-leap, delighting hardy practitioners of curling. Some of the older curlers remembered regular competitions on open ice. The severe winter made such things possible, although caution was still advisable: two curlers, tempting thin ice on Duddingston Loch, paid the price: ignominious rescue by their fellows and frozen extremities. All those years ago the Reverend Robert Walker, of course, had had no such fears when he went out on the ice in that exact spot and was noticed by Raeburn, who happened to pass by and witness the sharp-nosed minister skate by. The Reverend Walker had less fickle climate patterns to rely on, otherwise he would not have been looking so confidently ahead, as he is in the painting, but down, prepared for the tell-tale cracks that precede the breaking of ice.

The animal world was so much more vulnerable: in the north, deer became more and more bedraggled and increasingly miserable; at Tomintoul, birds fell from the air, their tiny wings heavy with rime, the sun—their only deicer—too far away to help. Sheep on hill farms huddled together for warmth, their breath hanging in tiny clouds above them; cattle sought the shelter of trees and dykes; a stray cat was found frozen to the Playfair Steps, a small death in the scale of things, but the end of a fellow creature's life, thought the man who found it, and regretted it for that.

Big Lou was made of stern stuff, of course; you don't grow up on a farm in Angus without being able to withstand a blast of cold. Throughout her childhood there had been no central heating in the farmhouse, the kitchen being warmed by the range, the living room by a log fire, and the bedrooms by the body heat of those sleeping within. That was entirely natural—and bearable. Nobody sat around very much, and therefore nobody complained of the cold. When you went outside you wrapped up; when you came inside you took off the outer wrapping but not the inner: two sweaters, in Big Lou's case, knitted for her by her Shetland aunt, Mrs. Spence of Unst, whose intricate handed-down patterns identified each sweater as being by her and by nobody else. These served Big Lou well, and were replaced every other year at Christmas, which was in January, as Mrs. Spence, who was originally from Foula, observed the old Norse Christmas and could not be doing, she said, with the modern Christmas nonsense from more southerly latitudes. If they miscalculated the date of Christmas, she was fond of saying, then who should be surprised that they got so much else wrong? She supplied the answer to that: nobody.

Mrs. Spence had other distinctions in life apart from that of being Big Lou's aunt. She was a well-known teller of traditional tales, mostly concerning seals, kelpies, and various other unidentifiable creatures, and mostly taking place in or around peat cuttings, cliffs, and remote crofts. She was interviewed several times by folklorists from the School of

Scottish Studies, and even entertained Professor Sandy Fenton, regaling him with accounts of her grandfather's herring fishing and his stories of his time as a flenser on a Salvesen whaler in the South Atlantic. She prepared Professor Fenton oatcakes on her griddle and showed him her cupboard of natural wool dyes. And all the time she knitted with prodigious energy.

In her flat in Canonmills, in the depth of one particularly severe winter, Big Lou remembered her Shetland sweaters. Mrs. Spence was no more, and with her had died a whole world of knowledge of wool and its possibilities. Even if the Borders mills continued heroically, so many sweaters now came from other places, the products of soulless machines and relentless globalisation; people seemed to want them in spite of their inadequacy for the Scottish climate, and in spite of the fact that no human eye had conceived them and no human fingers had brought them into existence stitch by stitch, row by row.

Big Lou, of course, now had central heating, but she used this frugally and still believed in dressing warmly for indoors. That winter, though, had made her realise something that she had not previously understood: she had a vitamin D deficiency. And having read about serotonin levels, she concluded, too, that hers were low—a common winter complaint in northern countries.

It was Angus Lordie who suggested the remedy. "A light box, Lou," he said. "Put it on a table and sit beside it for forty minutes a day. It makes your brain believe you live in Italy or somewhere like that. It gives you a blast of light—something we can be a bit short of in the Scottish winter."

Big Lou had heeded his advice and ordered a catalogue from a firm in England. She had been intrigued by some of the lamps on offer: one acted as an alarm clock, gradually filling the bedroom with the equivalent of morning sunlight; another, a Scottish offering, had the bulbs behind a panel of tartan glass—this bathed the user in tartan light, said to be of particular benefit to those in whose heart a dark winter might diminish positive feelings of Scottishness, or might indeed encourage a feeling of the wrong sort of Scottishness. It was impossible, the catalogue claimed, to feel at all dour if you sat in this light each day, even in places, of which there were admittedly one or two in Scotland, where one might be inclined to feel slightly on the dour side.

19. *Big Lou Makes a Change*

As Big Lou's light box gradually had its effect, she found herself looking forward to spring rather than dwelling on the reality of prolonged winter. And when spring eventually arrived—in May that year—she was ready for the transition. It was a brief spring, modulating within weeks to full-blown summer, but in that short period she made a number of important decisions.

The first of these was that she would change the name of her coffee bar. She had never been entirely happy with *The Morning After Coffee Bar* as a name. It was suggestive, first and foremost, of a hangover—something that, for most people, had entirely negative associations. Then there was a slight whiff of guilt to it: the morning after, even if one had not been drinking, could be a time of regret for what had been done the night before—for an unfortunate encounter or a tactless word. What was needed, she felt, was something that played to the particular appeal of her coffee bar. The result was *Big Lou's Coffee and Conversation Bar*, a name that was welcoming on several counts. The inclusion of a reference to the owner in a business name made everything more personal. If we go to *Harry's Bar*, for instance, we know that a friendly host awaits us; if we enter a restaurant called *Marco's*, we know that Marco will be there to ensure that all goes well.

Less reassuring are those establishments where the noun is not a proper one. It is unwise to eat in a restaurant called *Mama's*, or, even more so, *Doc's*. In each case the claim is probably suspect: there will be no *mama* in *Mama's* and anyone called *Doc* is surely apocryphal.

The new name told you what you might expect if you descended those somewhat hazardous steps that led down from Dundas Street: Big Lou, coffee, and conversation. Those steps, of course, had a history, particularly when the coffee bar was still a bookshop: it was on the fourth step from the top that Christopher Murray Grieve, the poet Hugh MacDiarmid, tripped. He did not fall far, and was unharmed; other literary figures had been less fortunate, although none as unfortunate as the late Lard O'Connor, who succumbed to a heart attack halfway down and could not be resuscitated even when an ambulance arrived within minutes. The heart attack had nothing to do with the steps, of course, since Lard was descending rather than ascending when it struck him; it had everything to do with the Glasgow diet, with year after year of overindulgence in fried foods, sugar, and a complete lack of exposure to anything green. In fact, Lard had been heard to say that green things were generally poisonous, and that those who ate vegetables were asking for trouble, although he exempted onions from this category as they could be made palatable if covered in batter, fried, and served as onion rings.

If you reached the bottom of the steps unharmed, you would then find Big Lou and the promised conversation. Big Lou would not have been described as unduly chatty—where she came from there was a general reluctance to use words unnecessarily—*nae time fur Marcel Proust*, as the common Angus saying has it—but she was always prepared to engage with any customer who wanted to pass the time of day or even to move on to meaty issues. When Big Lou had bought the premises, she had acquired the stock of secondhand books still on the shelves, and had transferred them to her flat in Canonmills. There she had started to work through them, title by title, with all the determination of the autodidact. So it was that she could discuss the philosophical theories of David Hume, Adam Smith, and, with great enthusiasm, Thomas Reid; so it was that she had read the first four volumes of the Scott Moncrieff translation of Proust; and so it was that she was familiar with George Davie's *The Democratic Intellect* and Professor Youngson's *The Making of Classical Edinburgh*. Occasionally—very occasionally—a customer might share her interest in these matters and an exchange of ideas might result, but more often people simply looked blank if Big Lou mentioned any of these saliences in Scottish intellectual history.

She wondered about this. "Do folk know *anything* any more?" she once asked Angus Lordie.

And Angus replied, "Depends on how old they are, Lou."

"What's that got to do with it?"

Angus shrugged. "It all depends on what schools teach. I'm not sure how much that is, these days." He paused. "Are we producing people who are more literate and better-informed than they used to be? I don't know, Lou, but somehow I hae ma doots."

For Lou, it was a question of facts. "Geography, Angus? Capitals of the world? Major rivers? Contour lines?"

Angus shook his head. "I'm not sure any of that is taught any more, Lou."

"Robert Burns?" she said.

Angus shook his head again. "They don't learn poetry. Not off by heart."

"Why?"

"Could it be . . ." Angus hesitated. "Could it be that the teachers . . ."

"Dinnae ken any themselves?" prompted Big Lou.

Angus scratched his head. "I don't know, I'm afraid."

Big Lou sighed. "Are we facing a new Dark Age, Angus?"

"Possibly, Lou. A dark age in which our concentration spell is this long." He held up his little finger. "And there's another thing, Lou—I heard the other day that in some schools in America they were no longer teaching children handwriting. Kids can't write any more."

"What do they do?"

"They print. Or they type on their iPads. But no actual cursive script."

Big Lou thought for a moment. "And their signatures? How will they sign things?"

"They'll make a mark," said Angus. "Just like the old days. Or I suppose they could print their names."

"And is it true that teachers don't bother about correcting spelling mistakes any more?"

"People say that. But then, a lot of people sound off about these things without knowing what they're talking about."

Angus finished his coffee and wiped the milk from his lips with his handkerchief. "Oh well, Lou, *O tempora, O mores . . .*" He paused. "Not that one would say that to the teachers."

20. The Sodium Chloride of the Earth

The change in name of the coffee bar was one of Big Lou's major decisions that late spring; the other was the employment of an assistant. For Lou that was a very significant milestone: she had always been the one to be employed as a handmaid to the efforts of others—to have an assistant herself seemed all wrong to her; seemed to be a reversal of the natural order.

It was Matthew who had persuaded her to consider the possibility. "Look Lou," he had said one morning. "All sorts of people have assistants these days. I have one in the gallery. Remember that girl, Pat MacGregor? She's working for me again."

"Well you're you and I'm me," said Big Lou.

Matthew laughed. "That's no answer, Lou. If somebody gives you advice, you can't just rebuff him by saying *You're you and I'm me*. What sort of answer is that?"

"Mine," said Big Lou. "It's my answer."

Matthew sighed. "What did Burns say, Lou?"

"An awfie lot," said Lou, wiping the counter of her coffee bar with a cloth. She kept the bar scrupulously clean, but sometimes the top had to be wiped for emphasis.

"He said *A wad some Pow'r the giftie gie us to see oursels as ithers see us*."

"Well?" said Big Lou. "I'm well aware of myself, Matthew."

Matthew was undeterred. "You see, Lou, I see you as somebody who just works and works. You've been working all your life, haven't you? On the farm, up at Montrose . . ."

"Arbroath," corrected Lou.

"Well, up there. I know how hard people work in that part of the world. Aberdeen's the same."

"Well, if there's work to be done, Matthew . . ."

It was hard going, thought Matthew. Big Lou was the *sodium chloride* of the earth, but sometimes convincing the salt of the earth about something—about anything—could be difficult. But he continued. "Then you went off to that place, didn't you? To the Granite Nursing Home, or whatever it was called. That place in Aberdeen."

"Aye, that was it."

"And what did you do there, Lou? You worked all the time to look after other people. I can just imagine it. Cleaning, scrubbing. All that stuff they get up to in Aberdeen. Then you came here and you worked really hard to get this place going. I saw you, Lou. You never stopped. Six days a week, from . . . what time do you get in here in the mornings, Lou? Seven? Eight?"

Big Lou paused in her polishing of the counter. "It's eight these days, because of wee Findlay."

"Of course. And that's another thing, Lou. You've taken on that wee boy and all the work that goes with bringing up a child. But that's more work, isn't it? All for other people."

She said nothing, but she asked herself: what does he expect? If there was work to be done, then it had to be done. That was the way the world was. It was the way it was in Arbroath, Aberdeen, and Edinburgh. Work had to be done, and if you were around, then you had to do it. You couldn't sit about and expect others to do it.

She met Matthew's gaze. "I'm all right, Matthew."

"No, you aren't, Lou. I've seen how busy you get when there are a lot of people in here. You need somebody to help you." He paused. "And how about offering food as well? People come in here and it would be nice if they could get a scone, maybe, with their coffee. Or one of those rolls you have up in Aberdeen. Those butteries. How about that, Lou?"

"Butteries," she said, and closed her eyes for a moment.

He pressed his point. "Well, why not? Grow the business a bit—that's what they say you should do, isn't it? They're always going on about how a business that doesn't grow is going to get smaller. Well, you could grow yours by offering a bit more."

Matthew had thought it was one of those inconclusive conversations that he sometimes had with Big Lou—conversations that raised issues that were never resolved—and had not thought much more of it. But he had planted a seed in Big Lou's mind, and only a week or so later Big Lou received a visit that was to bring the idea to the fore.

The visit was from a younger cousin, Hettie. Wee Hettie, as Big Lou called her, was not as small as the sobriquet suggested. In Arbroath the honorifics *big,* or sometimes its Scots variant *muckle*, and *wee* were used in a relative sense, and indeed sometimes ironically. Thus Big Jimmy could be so called because he was actually small, and Wee Eck, possibly named after the small character in a popular newspaper cartoon strip, could, in fact, be considerably bigger than Big Jimmy, or indeed more generously built than Fat Bob, another very popular name for a thin boy who happened to be called Robert. That was the ironical usage; the relative usage involved calling somebody *big* to differentiate him or her from some other person in the same circle. That other person may not be big in the objective sense, and indeed could be quite small, but was, at least, clearly not the same person as the one who was called *wee*.

Big Lou's cousin, Wee Hettie, was not quite as large as Lou, who was tall and well-built, but she was by no means small. She and Lou had seen a lot of one another as children, as Hettie came from the next farm but one, an arable farm called Snell Mains. She had three brothers, two of whom were, for some inexplicable reason, called Graeme. This led to confusion, of course—a confusion that was resolved by one being called Big Graeme and the other being known as Wee Graeme. Unfortunately Big Graeme, who was physically larger than Wee Graeme, was also younger, which led to considerable difficulty amongst those who thought that he, being called Big Graeme, would naturally be older than Wee Graeme.

It was Wee Hettie who telephoned Big Lou and said, "Big Lou, is that you?"

"Aye."

"It's Wee Hettie."

That was how it started.

21. Wee Hettie

Big Lou had not seen Wee Hettie for almost five years. Their last meeting had been at the family wedding at which their cousin Maggie had married an irascible farmer from Kelso, a man whom nobody liked. Lou and Hettie had sat together in the church, neither expressing the foreboding that each felt—at least not expressing it in words, body language being another matter. As Maggie and her new husband made their way back down the aisle, the expression on the faces of the congregation ranged from mute resignation to outright despair. At the reception that followed, though, the atmosphere of gloom lifted, and Lou and Hettie were able to catch up on their own news and that of other relatives.

Wee Hettie had just completed a degree in chemistry at the University of Aberdeen. She had hoped to get a job, but had been called back to Snell Mains, the family farm, to help her father, who was crippled with arthritis. Her brothers, both called Graeme, were younger than she was, and neither would be in a position to take over the running of the farm for several years. One of them, Big Graeme, had shown great promise as a rugby player and had already been selected to play for Scotland in an international Under-21 match against Wales. It would be wrong, thought Hettie's father, to nip a

distinguished rugby career in the bud, and it was tacitly agreed
that he would be brought under no pressure to return to the
farm.

That left Wee Graeme, who had also enrolled at Aberdeen
University, though several years behind his sister. His course
in agricultural science would take four years to complete,
which meant that the spotlight of responsibility fell solely on
Hettie. She did not protest, although her heart sank at the
thought of being trapped at Snell Mains for an indeterminate
and probably lengthy period.

Hettie's real ambition—confessed to Big Lou during their
conversation at that family wedding—was to become a dieti-
cian. She had decided this during her chemistry course and
had enquired about doing a course in Edinburgh, but her
hopes had been dashed by the plaintive message from the
farm that if she were unable to come home, then Snell Mains
would have to be sold. And that meant that not only would
her father have to leave the house in which he had spent his
entire life, but that Wee Graeme would have no farm to take
over. She could not let either of these things happen, and so
Hettie went home to do her duty, as uncomplainingly as she,
and her mother before her, had tackled all the tasks that went
with being the daughter or the wife of an Angus farmer.

That was five years ago, and now here was Hettie contacting
Lou in Edinburgh and arranging to come to see her at eleven
the following morning. It was a good time for their meeting:
Lou would have finished with the going-to-work rush and
would not yet be dealing with the first of the lunch customers.
She found herself anticipating the visit with some excitement:
five years was a long gap and there would be much ground to
cover.

Each commented positively on the appearance of the other.
"You're no worse," said Hettie—a common compliment in
their part of rural Angus.

"Aye, and your heid's still there," replied Big Lou—high praise in the same circles, negative versions of the same remark being, "Your heid's awa, I see," or "Your heid's mince."

That established, Big Lou made Wee Hettie a cup of coffee and they began their conversation. At length Big Lou asked the question that had been in her mind since Hettie had telephoned the day before. Why was she in Edinburgh?

"It's a long story," said Hettie, "but the short version is this: I'm here because I no longer have to be there."

Big Lou knew exactly what she meant. Wee Hettie was talking about freedom: freedom from getting up at four to do the milking; freedom from mucking out the byre; freedom from struggling with fencing and tractor tyres and ewes in the distress of difficult lambings; freedom from listening to long sermons in the kirk on Sunday and from hearing the same lengthy stories from visiting aunts time after time; freedom from baking scones every day, and freedom from eating them with the aunts as they told their long-winded tales of local events.

And what was Hettie planning to do? Big Lou listened as her cousin explained the part-time course in dietetics she would be starting a couple of months later. Her degree in chemistry had stood her application in good stead, and she had been given credits that would allow her to complete the course in two years rather than three.

Hettie, seated on one of the coffee bar's high stools, looked at her cousin across the polished surface of Lou's counter. "It's what I have to do, Lou," she said. "I've found my . . . my . . ."

"Vocation?" offered Big Lou.

Hettie nodded enthusiastically. "I want to make a difference, Lou. I want to do whatever I can to change what Scotland eats. This is not about me, Lou—it's about our diet—the diet of all of us—everyone."

"Even Glasgow?" asked Lou.

Hettie's expression showed no sign of reservation. "Even Glasgow, Lou. Yes, even Glasgow."

Lou took a sip of her coffee. "That's a pretty big job, Hettie. You know what they're like over there. You know what they like to eat."

"Of course I do, Lou," said Hettie.

Lou looked down at the ground. It was never pleasant to throw cold water on enthusiasm, but she wondered whether Wee Hettie, this woman of . . . what age was Hettie now? . . . twenty-seven . . . could seriously entertain thoughts of changing the Scottish diet through what? Advice? Moral suasion? Political engagement?

She looked back at Hettie, at the familiar face, a face that represented so naturally and unself-consciously the world of those quiet farms, that uneventful landscape, that unchanging hinterland. It was the face of one who had very little experience of the cynical world of cities, the face of one who simply had no idea how large things were, how immutable—and how bad.

"Tell me about it, Hettie," she said.

Hettie frowned. "It's a sad story, Lou," she said. "In fact, it makes me want to cry, you know. It makes me want to cry buckets."

22. Scotland's Shameful Diet

So Hettie told her sad story—and Big Lou listened.

"You see," she began, "you see the Scots diet, Lou?"

Big Lou nodded. "Aye, Hettie, I think I know which way this is going."

Hettie looked out of the window as she spoke. There was not much to see, as the steps that descended sharply from the street—those steps down which the poet Hugh MacDiarmid had once fallen—blocked out everything but a view of the lower legs of passersby. And at that moment, as if a visual aid ordered to illustrate the point that Hettie intended to make, a pair of generously proportioned legs, threatening to burst the seams of the cloth that contained them, walked past.

Both Lou and Hettie sensed the synchronicity, but made no comment. "I never judge those legs," Big Lou had once said to Angus. "I see every sort of leg in Scotland walk past during the day, Angus, but I draw no conclusions."

Hettie continued. "You see, Lou, we used to have a pretty good diet in Scotland. Used to have. And I'm not talking here about a few years ago—even fifty years ago—I'm talking about way back. I'm talking about the days when people still lived in the country and Glasgow and Edinburgh were tiny wee places. Those days."

"Before the Industrial Revolution?" prompted Lou.

"Yes," said Hettie. "Before that."

"But times were hard, weren't they? If you were a High-lander, for instance, scratching away at your wee bittie of land, trying to grow something with all that rain and hum-mocks and whatnot—it wasn't easy."

Hettie accepted this. "Yes, there were bad times, but the diet that most people had in the country was reasonably good. There were oats—so you had your porridge—and there was a bit of kale and so on. And you could catch fish if there was a river or loch nearby, or the sea, of course. There were plenty of mackerel in the sea."

"I suppose so."

"Folk went hungry, of course," Hettie conceded, "but by and large what they had was healthy. There was no rubbish, Lou. And very little sugar, although they loved making preserves out of the fruit they grew. They were all right."

"Oatmeal was the thing," mused Lou. "Oatmeal, oatmeal, oatmeal."

A great deal of Big Lou's extensive, if unstructured, reading stuck. Now she remembered Carlyle's remark about Macaulay. "An honest, good sort of fellow, made out of oatmeal." She looked at Hettie, and smiled; she thought the same thing might be said of Hettie's brothers—and of so many people she had been brought up with in Angus. They were made out of oatmeal. And Scotland was still populated by oatmeal people, she thought. Fondly. They were still there.

Hettie agreed about oatmeal. "It made us," she said, a note of sadness in her voice.

But Lou's thoughts had moved on to the injustices of diet. In the story of food, she reflected, all the wrongs of Scotland's past were displayed. You needed land to grow food—even to support your tiny domestic kailyard—but there had always been avaricious eyes on land. "Some folk," she said, "ate very well, didn't they? The gentry. Prosperous farmers."

Big Lou remembered Marian McNeil's book on Scottish breakfasts and the surprising information it contained about the breakfast table in more prosperous houses. Claret was a popular item on that table—and quaffed with enthusiasm, as was whisky and Jamaica rum. For breakfast. And to accompany these unlikely breakfast drinks—how different from today's orange juice, thought Lou—there was mutton and sheep's heid, haggis, ham, cheeses of various descriptions, bannocks, venison pie, pastries . . . the list seemed endless.

"But the ordinary folk didn't do too badly," said Hettie. "As long as they were prepared to grow their vegetables—which some of them didn't seem all that interested in. And as long as they could take a wee bit of fish and game. Meat was available."

"But not always very much," observed Lou. "You've heard of a *tattie and a pass*? That was when there was only enough meat for the faither. So the bairns had to content themselves with passing the tattie over the top of the stew to get a bit of a whiff of it."

They sat in silence for a moment. Talking about how life had been in the country made Lou sad; that had been her world, and its echoes were still there, no matter how things appeared to have changed.

"And then," said Hettie after a while. "And then, when folk went off to live in the towns, they lost all that. All that good food that had been there for the taking was no longer available. They had to content themselves with potatoes and a bit of this and that: watered-down milk, bread made from adulterated flour. A poor, poor diet."

"It's a miracle they survived," said Lou.

"Yes, a major miracle. Of course, many of them didn't. People didn't last very long because there were all sorts of illnesses that went with living in a tenement in Glasgow or Edinburgh. You had a good range of infections to choose from and you also had rickets. Think of what rickets did."

Lou had recently seen an old photograph of children playing in a Glasgow street in the early years of the twentieth century. The children all seemed so small for their ages—stunted by poverty—and not a few had the characteristic bandy legs that rickets brought to those it affected.

She mentioned this to Hettie, who nodded sadly. "Vitamin D deficiency," she said. "They never saw the sun because it was blotted out by the smoke. So their bodies couldn't . . ." She did not finish. She shrugged.

"Well, at least they got rid of rickets," said Lou. "At least that happened."

"Yes, but what happened when we had more money to spend on food? What did we do? We spent it on the wrong stuff. On sugary things. On fried things. And so now obesity has replaced rickets."

"You'd think we'd learn," said Lou.

"No," said Hettie. "I'm not sure if I think that, Lou. You know that our Glasgow diet is the worst in the developed world, Lou. You know that?"

"Aye, I've heard that."

"And yet," said Hettie with a smile, "we still say *Here's tae us, wha's like us?*"

Lou did not complete the well-known toast: it was inappropriate in the circumstances, she thought.

"So what are you going to do, Hettie?" she asked.

Hettie misunderstood her question. "Well," she said. "I thought I'd come and stay with you, if you don't mind, Lou."

23. A Tram Goes Past

Bertie felt a considerable civic pride as he spoke to his grandmother on the way in from the airport.

"We have trams now, Granny," he said. "Nobody goes in them, but it's nice to have them, I think."

"Nobody goes in them, Bertie?" asked Nicola. "Surely *somebody* does . . ."

From behind the wheel of the aged Volvo-substitute, Stuart confirmed what Bertie had said. "Bertie's right," he said. "Trams were a wonderful idea, but the whole project went wrong somewhere along the line—or all along the line, perhaps."

"The lines don't go where anybody wants to go," said Bertie. "They go from a place where nobody lives to another place where nobody lives. And they only go in one direction— and back, of course." He paused. "Look, there's one over there."

Nicola watched the comfortable-looking white tram pass by.

"You see," said Bertie. 'There was only the driver. That's all."

"How very strange," said Nicola. "That would never have happened in the old days."

"Ah," said Stuart. "The old days. What a blissful time it must have been."

"You may mock if you must, Stuart," snapped Nicola. "But I can assure you in the old days Edinburgh would never have done anything quite as stupid as that. Our City Fathers may have been a crusty old bunch but they knew how to control the purse strings."

"Mummy says we should call them *City Parents*," said Bertie.

Nicola rolled her eyes, but only very slightly, and in such a way as not to be seen by Bertie.

"Your Mummy is so . . . so attentive to what people say," she muttered.

"She says you're very old-fashioned," Bertie continued brightly. "She says that you're probably a fascist." He paused. "A crypto-fascist. Is that true, Granny? Are you really a crypto-fascist, like Mummy says?"

Stuart gasped, and the car swerved slightly. "Bertie, I don't think Mummy ever said *that* . . ."

"Oh yes she did," protested Bertie. "She said that Granny probably wore black underwear, like all fascists wear. That was what she said, Daddy. She said it over the phone to one of her Melanie Klein Reading Group people. I heard her; I promise you."

Nicola laughed. "Oh, I'm sure it's all a misunderstanding, Stuart. Don't worry about it. Probably a joke. Just as I was joking when I called her a self-righteous cow once. Nothing serious—and least said, soonest mended."

But now there were other things to think about. They had taken a circuitous route onto Lothian Road and would shortly be in Charlotte Square. Towering above them, caught in the sunlight, was the towering shape of the Castle, its ramparts incised against a cloudless sky. "Such a sight," muttered Nicola. "Such a heart-stopping sight."

"I went to the Castle once," said Bertie. "I could take you there, Granny. We could go and see the Stone of Scone. It's up there, you know. The English pinched it from us and sat on it for years and years. Somebody pinched it back once, but they found it and took it away again. But they gave it back eventually."

"As well they should," said Nicola. "Nothing is to be gained by hanging on to stolen property. The English should know that."

"But a Scotsman pinched those Marbles from the Greeks, didn't he?" asked Bertie.

"Oh well," said Nicola. "The Turks would have destroyed them if Lord Elgin hadn't come to the rescue, Bertie. They were grinding them up to sell as mortar. He *rescued* them—and that's quite different from pinching. We can all feel very grateful towards Lord Elgin. He was a very distinguished Bruce, moreover, and when Bruce blood flows in your veins you are well placed to do heroic things."

"I don't think the Greeks think that," said Bertie. "Tofu says the Greeks want them back."

Nicola laughed. "Just as the Germans want their money back from the Greeks," she said lightly. "It's such a complicated world, Bertie!"

They were now in Charlotte Square. "That's where the First Minister lives," said Bertie, pointing to an impressive Georgian house. "They have lots of parties there. Just for important people, but everybody else is allowed to stand outside and watch the important people go in."

Again Nicola laughed. (Nicola, the Granny, that is . . .)

Ulysses now made his presence known, chuckling contentedly from his car seat.

"Ulysses can't really talk yet," said Bertie. "He can think, though. You can tell when he's thinking—his face goes all red."

"He's a bonnie wee boy," said Nicola.

"He's quite smelly, most of the time," said Bertie. "And he vomits a lot, especially when he sees Mummy. And makes really rude noises when Mummy tries to talk to him." He paused, and looked admiringly at his father. "Daddy said he was so looking forward to your coming from Portugal, as he won't have to change Ulysses anymore."

"I did not," spluttered Stuart. "Bertie, you mustn't say things . . ."

"It's quite all right," said Nicola, reassuringly. "I understand you, and I understand men in general. Even entirely reconstructed men have issues with changing babies. I quite understand. And if the younger generation can't keep us alive to change babies, then what can they keep us alive for?"

Bertie now saw a familiar building on Queen Street and pointed it out to his grandmother. "That's where I go for psychotherapy," he said. "I go every Saturday morning. Ulysses hasn't started yet, but Mummy says he will—once he learns how to talk. It's difficult to do Free Association if you can't talk."

Nicola glanced at Stuart. "I see," she said. "I shouldn't have thought you needed psychotherapy, Bertie."

Bertie was electrified by this remark. "Did you hear that, Daddy? Granny says I don't need psychotherapy. She said it herself. Can you phone them up and cancel?"

"Your mother," began Stuart . . .

Nicola did not let him finish. "Stuart, how can you possibly go along with that claptrap? Bertie is an entirely well-adjusted little boy. If ever anybody didn't need psychotherapy, it's him."

"Irene made it clear," began Stuart. "She said that . . ."

Again he did not finish "Oh, phooey!" exclaimed Nicola.

It was a moment of shattering discovery for Bertie. Here was somebody—his grandmother no less—who dared to say phooey about his mother. It was astonishing; it was liberating; it was as if the heavens had opened and Themis herself, guarantor of justice and good order, had made some divine pronouncement from a throne set on high. *Phooey* announced Themis; and all the hills and lochs, all the glens and moors and high places of Scotland echoed her judgement so that none could claim not to have heard it. *Phooey!*

24. Drummond Place Issues

Into Drummond Place swept the anodyne grey station wagon in which the Pollock family (*sans* Irene) travelled with Stuart's mother, Nicola Tavares de Lumiares (*née* McCullough) freshly arrived from Portugal and ready to assume day-to-day responsibility for her grandsons Bertie and Ulysses.

"Drummond Place!" she exclaimed. "Oh Edinburgh, dearest Edinburgh! Slow down, Stuart, so that I can luxuriate in all of this. Drummond Place and there, if I'm not mistaken, is Dundonald Street. That flat on the corner was lived in by Nigel McIsaac and his wife, Mary. He was a very accomplished artist, you know, and I used to visit them when we came in from the Borders. We had lunch there and we talked about every subject under the sun. We did, you know. They had a great talent for friendship."

"I can imagine," said Stuart, complying with the request to slow down.

"And round the corner," went on Nicola, "just round there is the flat that Sydney Goodsir Smith lived in. And Compton Mackenzie was further along that side of the square. He was a remarkable man—my father knew him, you know. They used to play chess together sometimes. And he was the President of the Siamese Cat Club: he was a very major figure in Siamese cat circles, word has it. He married his housekeeper, Chrissie

McSween, and then, after she died, he married her sister, which was so considerate of him."

Bertie joined in. "He wrote a book about whisky, Granny," he said.

Nicola turned to smile at Bertie. "Of course he did, Bertie. It was called *Whisky Galore*, wasn't it?"

"I think so," said Bertie. "I haven't read it myself, but Mr. Lordie likes it. He says it's far better than the rubbish people write these days."

"Hah!" said Nicola. "It was a very good story. Those people on that island were very pleased to find all that whisky, I imagine."

"There are a lot of people over there waiting for things to wash up on their shores," said Stuart. "Government grants, mainly."

Nicola laughed, and changed the subject. "Civil servants shouldn't make jokes like that," she said, smiling. She looked appreciatively out of the car window at the Drummond Place gardens. "I do love all that greenery. Those great towering trees."

"A source of great contention at present," said Stuart. "There's an issue about access. Some people are allowed to take their dogs in there, and others not. I think it's something to do with the positioning of your windows. And some dogs are not allowed in at all because they're the wrong breed."

Nicola gave a whoop of delight. "Oh, how priceless! So Edinburgh hasn't changed all that much has it? Such delicious pettiness."

They had now reached Scotland Street itself, and Stuart was keeping an eye out for a parking place. Fortunately one materialised, and he was able to nose the Volvo-substitute into it before another driver, who had also spotted it, was able to stake his claim. Once parked, Bertie helped his grandmother with her suitcases while Stuart extracted Ulysses from his car seat and wiped the small trail of vomit from the front of his jersey.

They made slow progress upstairs. Bertie insisted on managing one of the suitcases himself, and bumped it up step by step, pausing every so often to regain his strength.

"You're doing so well, Bertie," said Nicola. "You must be a very strong boy."

Bertie beamed with pleasure. Nobody had called him strong before, and his liking for his grandmother was increasing by the minute. Not only had she derided his mother's view that he needed psychotherapy, but now she was calling him strong. His mother had never commented on his strength; modern boys, she had once said to him, are indifferent to strength.

Bertie had listened patiently, but in his heart he knew that his mother was wrong. Boys did worry about strength, for the simple reason that if you were not concerned about strength you would be certain to be hit by somebody far stronger than you—somebody like Larch, a boy in Bertie's class who had already been referred for anger management classes. He had gone to these classes and returned to give them a glowing recommendation. "You don't have to do what they tell you," he said triumphantly. "You just have to think *not* whenever they say anything. That way you learn how to be really angry."

Tofu was much the same. Although he was less violent than Larch, Tofu still had a mature understanding of the advantages conferred by strength. "You don't have to hit people, Larch," he had said scornfully. "You can just *threaten* to hit them. That's much more effective. That way you save your energy, see."

They reached their floor on the common stair.

"This is our place," said Bertie proudly. "My Dad owns this whole flat."

"Does he now?" said Nicola. "Well, that's very satisfactory."

"With the help of a mortgage," Stuart muttered. "Quite an expensive one, actually."

He could not resist that reference. His mother, he knew, was quite well-off; not only did she have the money she had inherited from her late husband, Henderson, but her second husband, Abril, was rumoured to have a considerable fortune. He, too, could afford to pay off their mortgage, if only he would loosen the purse strings.

"Mortgages are such a burden," remarked Nicola.

"They certainly are," said Stuart.

"But they are character-forming, aren't they?" Nicola continued brightly. "If one receives everything in this life on a plate, Stuart, I think one misses out on certain experiences that we all need to go through."

Stuart groaned inwardly. Perhaps once she had had a few of those sherries she liked, he might be able to wheedle out of her some agreement to do something about the mortgage, but he did not hold out much hope for that. They would have to wait until she died, he thought guiltily. There would be plenty of money then. He stopped himself: one should not think that about one's mother—one simply shouldn't. A lot of people, though, he told himself, did exactly that. There were countless grown-up children watching the health of their aged parents with what could only be described as vulturine interest; watching for every telltale sign of weakness, for every symptom of a weakening heart or of a faltering step. He looked at his mother. She seemed so hale and hearty, but that, he remembered, was no guarantee of anything.

25. He Never Thought of Love

The Pollock flat in Scotland Street had three generously proportioned bedrooms and one cramped box-bedroom. Irene and Stuart occupied the largest of these rooms: Irene, in particular, appreciated the view it afforded out over the former marshalling yards of the old Newhaven railway. These yards were still largely an empty expanse of ground, one of those urban spaces that somehow seem to survive the avaricious eyes of developers. "Spaces are important," she said to Bertie. "There are things, you see, and then there is the space that lies next to things. The space defines the thing every bit as much as the thing defines itself. You understand that, don't you Bertie?" Bertie had nodded. The idea could be put more simply, he thought, but he understood.

The second bedroom was Bertie's. He was inordinately proud of this room, which was his sanctuary, his retreat—his boy-cave. The room had been much-painted: Irene had decorated it in pink to begin with, as a gesture against stereotyping, but shortly afterwards Stuart, egged on by Bertie, had painted it white, to the considerable annoyance of Irene. Unfortunately for Bertie, who had been thoroughly embarrassed about living in a pink room, the coat of white paint had been insufficiently thick to prevent pink from somehow seeping through, with the result that his room was now of a shade in between the two colours but still recognisably pink in the eyes of any of Bertie's friends who came to the house.

"How nice that you live in a pink room," pronounced Olive when she was brought to play—without invitation from Bertie, but at the insistence of Irene. "I thoroughly approve of *new boys*, Bertie—I really do. You'd never get somebody like Tofu living in a pink bedroom. He doesn't have the courage."

"It's not really pink," muttered Bertie. "It's . . . it's crushed strawberry."

"Oh no, Bertie," said Olive. "It's not crushed strawberry. I know what crushed strawberry looks like, and this isn't it. This is dusty pink. I saw this exact colour in a magazine and it said it was pink. There was a picture of a girl in a dusty pink bedroom. They said it was the ideal feminine colour."

"It's not," muttered Bertie. "It's nothing to do with that."

"Of course these days things like that don't matter," continued Olive. "Girls are very happy that boys want to be like them. We are going into the Age of the Girl, you know. I read that too. This is the Age of the Girl. Boys are finished—did you know that, Bertie? Boys are finished."

Contiguous with Bertie's bedroom was the third bedroom, the smallest of the three, but larger, of course, than the windowless boxroom next door. This bedroom was now the nursery, and was occupied by Ulysses and the extraordinarily large quantity of impedimenta that constitute the support system for any baby: changing mats, stacked cartons of wet wipes, plastic devices for serving, catching, and disposing of food, piles of muslin cloth, bins for detritus of every category, and so on. Hanging from the ceiling were various mobiles, devices with strings that played repetitive tunes, and small silver stars intended somehow to induce a feeling of sleepiness at bedtime.

This bedroom had been cleared by Stuart in preparation for his mother's visit. The cot in which Ulysses slept had been shifted into the boxroom, and the various support systems had been dispersed about the house. With the infantile objects now elsewhere, the room had shrugged off its nursery feel. A small writing desk from the main bedroom had been moved in, along with an easy chair from the living room. With flowers on the desk and a fresh potpourri on the windowsill, the feel of the room was welcoming, even if a slight smell, inadequately masked by the potpourri, still lingered in the air.

"My Dad says your room won't smell too much of Ulysses after a couple of days," said Bertie as he showed his grandmother into her room.

"I'm sure it'll be just fine," said Nicola, moving across the room to open the window. "I hope poor little Ulysses won't mind having been moved out of his room."

Bertie shook his head. "He doesn't know what's going on," he said. "He's got no idea of anything, really."

"Oh Bertie, I'm sure Ulysses is drinking it all in," said Nicola brightly. "Babies know more than we give them credit for."

"You can use his chest of drawers over there," said Bertie. "We chucked all his stuff out."

Nicola opened her suitcase and began to unpack. It was a strange feeling, she decided, this going back in time. How long was it since she had looked after a child? She did not like to count the years. Decades, rather. So long ago. And now these two little souls, this lovely little boy, Bertie, with his serious expression and his odd way of putting things; and that funny little scrap of humanity that was his brother . . . My flesh and blood, she thought. Mine.

And in the kitchen, where he was making a cup of tea to welcome Nicola, Stuart thought: I still have a mother. A mother. There is still somebody who can say *That is my son.* Me. He watched the water in the glass-side kettle begin to move—tiny currents of heated water mixing with layers of colder water, a miniature watery turmoil. It all started there, he thought. It all started with the movement of water. It's very easy to go back. It's very easy to go back to being the child in the relationship, the dependent one; no matter how many years have intervened, it is easy to revert to how it was before, to the time when you knew instinctively that your mother loved you and that her love was always there like the sun, constant, always available, never for a moment critical or conditional.

Love. He never thought of love. Did other people? Did other people go about their daily business thinking about love; about the people they loved and the people who loved them? Did people wake up in the morning and say to themselves *Perhaps this will be the day I find love?* Did they really do that?

Did he love anybody at all? Did he love his mother, as he knew she loved him? He loved her, of course, but he was not sure exactly *how* he loved her. Did he love his boys? Yes, he did. He loved them—even Ulysses, sometimes. But did he love Irene, his wife? Did he love her? Why had he never cried, not once, since she went away? Was that the test—the real test—whether we could cry for somebody?

26. *Because It's Small and It's Ours . . .*

"It's extraordinary what a difference moving in has made," said Matthew. "When we were here last—before all our stuff came—this place seemed . . ."

"Unlived in?" prompted Elspeth.

"Yes, unlived in. But it's more than that. It somehow seemed cold."

Elspeth smiled. "I've turned on the heating. I know it's summer, but I felt there was a bit of dampness."

"The Duke hadn't used this place for ages," said Matthew. "A house somehow loses its spirit if there's nobody living in it."

"*Lares* and *penates*," said Elspeth. "The Romans' household spirits. And then they became gods. They put statues of them on the dining table."

"Whereas we put pepper and salt."

"Yes: we being devoid of any sense of things beyond us."

Matthew raised an eyebrow. "My, we are getting philosophical. But I do like the idea of household gods—shall we get some? A set of little statues and bring the boys up to believe in them?"

"I hope they believe in something," said Elspeth. "Imagine believing in nothing at all—not even in love, or justice, or any of the things that can make people passionate."

"Such as a country?"

Elspeth thought about this. "I suppose there are lots of people who believe in Scotland. Or the European Union, for that matter. Their belief enables them to . . . well, to talk about the future with enthusiasm. They don't like things as they are and they are convinced that things will be much improved once they are otherwise."

"Well, why not?" asked Matthew.

"I didn't say there was any reason why not. I'm just commenting on that sort of belief. The trouble is that it might make discussion difficult. If somebody believes so strongly in one particular solution to the world's problems, then it may obscure the nuances. That's all I was saying." Elspeth paused. "They may not see that there are others who have a different view. You can love things in a whole lot of different ways, can't you?"

Matthew did not answer her question. "I believe in Scotland," he said, "because I love it. I love it because this is where I come from and where I intend to stay. I love it because it's . . ." He shrugged. "Because it's small and it's ours."

"Both are good reasons," said Elspeth. "Just like our boys—they're small, and they're ours."

They had been seated during this conversation; now Matthew stood up. "You know, there's something that's still niggling away. I measured up the outside walls of the house yesterday. I noted down the measurements."

"Why?"

"Because I wanted to calculate the floor area—at least of the ground floor."

"And?"

"Well, it was quite simple measuring the outside walls, because they were fairly regular. There's that bit that sticks out at the back, but I was able to factor that in. Anyway, I measured it all and then took into account the thickness of the walls. I deducted that from the total."

Elspeth was unsure where this was leading. "Why did you do all this? I thought that the solicitors' particulars gave the floor area."

"They did," said Matthew. "But I wanted to check up on something. So I then measured the rooms inside—everything. I worked out the size of each room, including the hallway and corridors. I added it all up."

Elspeth frowned. Matthew had a slight tendency to what she termed—quite fondly—*geekiness*, and she wondered whether he was going to turn into one of those men who became obsessed with facts and figures. They were terribly tedious—they knew much of the *Guinness Book of Records* off by heart and could recite batting averages for the Australian cricket team back to 1954. They were only one rung above the train-spotters, those lost characters who stand on platforms in anoraks and note down the numbers of passing trains. Presumably measuring floor areas was exactly the sort of thing that the off-duty train-spotter might do.

"I added it all up," repeated Matthew. "And then I compared the two figures. And you know what? There are just over sixteen square metres unaccounted for."

"Surely not."

"No, there are. Remember I said right at the beginning that I thought there might be a concealed room? Remember what I said?"

"Vaguely," said Elspeth. She remembered rejecting the possibility and thinking no more of it.

"Well there must be one," said Matthew. "Because I've done the maths and there's only one conclusion."

"Just like Professor Higgs," said Elspeth lightly. "He did the maths all those years ago and concluded that the Higgs Boson must exist."

"Elspeth, I'm not joking!"

She put on a serious expression. "No, I can see that. Well, what are we going to do?"

"I want to take that bookcase off the drawing room wall," said Matthew. "The bookcase on the left. I'm pretty sure it's in there."

Elspeth sighed. She knew that when Matthew got hold of an idea, it could be difficult to persuade him to drop it. "All right," she said. "I'll help you."

"Good," said Matthew. "I'll fetch something from the garage."

He returned a few minutes later with a crowbar and they went into the drawing room together. Matthew began by taking the books out of the bookcase and stacking them on a library table that stood against the opposite wall. Then, when the bookcase was bare, he tapped loudly on the inner layer of wood that separated it from the wall.

"That doesn't sound at all hollow," said Elspeth. "That sounds as if it's just wall."

Matthew, though, was still convinced, and he now moved round to the side of the bookcase and inserted the tip of the crowbar between it and the wall. He began to prise.

It was slow work, but after a while he had prised the bookcase from its setting. It had been held in place with just a few screws, and these had eventually wrenched themselves free of plaster and lathe.

Elspeth peered into the new space created. There was an opening—a door-sized opening—and it gave into a dark area beyond.

"You see," said Matthew. "I knew I was right."

Elspeth fetched a torch and played the beam into the darkness that lay beyond the newly exposed doorway.

"It's not empty," she said, her voice faltering with the significance of the moment.

"So I see," said Matthew.

"I have a strong sense of implausibility."

"But we all do," said Matthew. "Anybody who thinks about the human condition must feel that." He paused; he had more to say on that subject, but this, he thought, was not the time; not with a concealed room freshly unconcealed before him. "But shall we inspect what we see beyond?" he went on. "Please, after you . . ."

Elspeth thought: *I am so fortunate. I am married to a man who says "Please, after you." How fortunate is that?* And she thought of a friend who did not even have a husband, although she dearly would have loved one, and how her life would be transformed, would be made perfect, if she had one who said, "Please, after you" or indeed by one who did not even say that, who said nothing, in fact. *Bless you, my darling,* she thought. *And thank you for this: for this house, for our marriage, for our three boys, for bothering to say "Please, after you."*

27. *Hand Sanitiser Issues*

They stood at the entrance of the concealed room, both slightly awed by what they were doing—how often in this life do we enter concealed rooms? Matthew, at least, remembered something he had read many years ago, as a boy at the Edinburgh Academy, when George Harris, his inspiring history teacher, had happened to mention the story of the archaeologists who had opened the sealed tombs of Egyptian pharaohs and who had all died within a few short years. That was just the sort of thing to engage the attention of a fourteen-year-old boy with a budding interest in science—of course it was asking for trouble to open something that had been sealed for so many years. What could one expect? It was not a question of curses or anything of that sort; it was more an issue of bacteria and viruses. Microorganisms could lie dormant indefinitely until somebody came along and kicked up the dust, metaphorical and real, under which they had been concealed.

He half-turned to Elspeth. "Do you remember those stories of the Egyptian tombs? Lord Carnarvon and his team? How they all died after they'd opened the tombs? Probably pathogens inside. Rare moulds and so on."

"Oh nonsense!" said Elspeth. "They were probably much safer inside the tomb than outside, given sanitary conditions in Egypt at the time. And even these days you have to be careful. Everybody who goes for a cruise on the Nile gets the most awful tummy upsets. They just do. It's the water. Morag McAndrew was really ill after she went on that boat on the Nile. She said the boat itself was very clean but she saw the galley staff washing the plates in the actual Nile. They had a big basket and they put all the plates in it apparently and then lowered it into the Nile and shoogled it around for a while."

Matthew bit his lip. "Have you got any hand sanitiser?"

"Hand sanitiser!" exclaimed Elspeth. "Really, Matthew, you mustn't get caught up in all that. Those people who carry those little bottles of gel and keep rubbing it on their hands . . . Really!"

Matthew bit his lip again. He had developed the habit of taking hand sanitiser with him to work, and he used it several times a day; certainly after handling the door in the small staff washroom that led off his office at the gallery. Recently he had also resorted to opening and closing that door with a handkerchief—a precaution that he also used when he went for coffee at Big Lou's café, where the handle of the main door must be, he thought, a major vector of transmission of every sore throat and chest infection in the New Town.

And what was wrong with being careful? It was all very well for Elspeth to imply that hand sanitiser was a step too far, but why subject oneself to more germs than necessary? It was not as if he had taken to wearing those face masks that you see people in Japan wearing as a matter of course. Indeed, he had seen a group of young Japanese tourists in Edinburgh recently and several of them had been wearing white face masks. Not only was that absurd, it was, he thought, insulting.

And where would it end: would people start walking about in those clumsy white suits with portable piped air supplies? Would we go to dinner at friends' houses wearing protective clothing, and say, *Nothing personal, of course?* No, all that was a good mile away from the sensible precaution of using hand sanitiser when opening certain doors or when entering concealed rooms . . .

It was unfair of Elspeth to criticise him for carrying hand sanitiser. He had seen her use it herself, and he also remembered how careful she had been in the days when she had still been teaching. He remembered her exact words. "Children," she said, "are walking reservoirs of infection. They get everything and they pass it on really efficiently. And you should smell their hands! They look very cute but smell their hands! Disgusting!" She had gone on to tell him how she had always carried a packet of wet wipes with which she would discreetly wipe the hands and faces of the smellier children and then give them a quick spray from a small bottle of personal freshener that she kept with the wet wipes. She did all that—quite sensibly—and yet she laughed at his carrying his hand sanitiser.

"So you haven't got any?"

Elspeth sounded short. "Of course I haven't. And look, we're going into a concealed room and you're going on about hand sanitiser!"

"Sorry," said Matthew. "It's just that I suddenly remembered those archaeologists and I thought . . ."

"Matthew!"

"All right, all right."

They went into the room, the beam of the torch moving quickly round its confines.

"It's a storeroom," said Elspeth. "That's all it is."

Matthew sounded disappointed. "I'd rather hoped . . ." He was not sure what he had hoped. Certainly he would have preferred something different and not these stacks of ordinary household articles, exactly the sort of thing that one would expect to find in a typical attic.

There was a child's toy pram. There was a rolled-up rug, tied with white string. There were several dining-room chairs, stacked one upon another. There was an old leather suitcase on which the labels of shipping companies had been stuck and then inexpertly peeled off. There was a typewriter—one of those old uprights that weighed so much they were almost impossible to lift. There was a canvas stretcher bed, half-folded, its crisscross legs an example of the intricate over-engineering of the time.

And then Matthew saw the pictures. "May I have the torch?"

Elspeth passed it to him. "That typewriter . . ."

"No, it's not that. It's the pictures. Look, over there."

They were stacked against the far wall, four of them, a cloth of some sort draped over their top, as if to conceal them. But their shape revealed what lay beneath.

Matthew negotiated his way between the stretcher bed and the suitcase and stood before the pictures. Slowly and somewhat gingerly he took off the dusty cloth and laid it to one side. Then he bent down to look at the first of the pictures. Elspeth joined him.

"What are they?" she asked. "The glass on that one looks broken."

"Just cracked," said Matthew.

He handed the torch back to Elspeth while he lifted up the painting. "Just shine it on the middle bit there. That's it."

He drew in his breath.

"What?" asked Elspeth.

He did not answer, and so she said, "What?" again.

But he did not answer. He was rapt.

28. *French* Intimisme

"I'm pretty sure this is James Cowie," muttered Matthew.

Elspeth leaned over his shoulder to get a better view of the painting. As she did so, the beam of the torch moved, to fall on the painting behind the one they were examining. Only a small part of it was visible, but it was enough to elicit a gasp from Matthew.

"Fergusson," he said.

"Let's take them into the drawing room," said Elspeth. "We can't really see them in here."

Matthew picked up the first of the paintings and carried it gingerly back past the now detached bookcase. He returned for the other three, coughing from the dust that had settled on the frames in spite of the covering cloth.

"These must have been here for ages," he said, as he laid the final painting against a sofa. "Years and years."

Elspeth joined him, brushing the dust off her hands. "I'll fetch the vacuum cleaner," she said. "I don't want the boys to be exposed to all this dust." Tobermory, she suspected, had a slight tendency to asthma and she did not want him to start one of his sneezing attacks.

While Elspeth was out of the room, Matthew bent down to examine the Cowie. It was a finely worked watercolour, the subject being what appeared to be an artist's studio. Two girls and a boy, young enough still to be in their teens, were perched on high stools while before them was an easel holding a drawing block. One of the girls was staring directly out of the picture, her face passive but somehow expectant. The other girl and the boy were gazing out of the window, their attention held by something beyond the scope of the painting.

Elspeth returned with the vacuum cleaner.

"Their clothes," said Matthew. "Look at their clothes."

"Nineteen thirties? Forties?"

"Yes," said Matthew. "The children in Cowie's paintings all wear the same things—the girls wear a sort of tunic—you see it there—the boys have these long shorts. Schoolchildren of the time were dressed like that."

"And the faces," mused Elspeth.

Matthew nodded. "Yes. Innocent, weren't they?"

"Unlike modern teenagers?"

Matthew smiled. "Modern teenagers look more knowing."

"And jaded?"

"Much more. They've seen it all, haven't they? On the web."

He took out a handkerchief and rubbed it across the face of the glass. "Cowie taught up at Hospitalfield," he said. "You know, that place up in Angus. We went there for a jazz evening with Alan Steadman."

"Yes, I remember."

"This was probably painted up in Aberdeen, though. These are schoolchildren."

"And the other paintings?"

Matthew took a deep breath. He had already looked at the Fergusson, and he was sure of that. But there were two more, both glazed and shrouded in dust. "We should use the vacuum on those two," he said. "The dust's really thick. I'll do it."

He plugged in the cleaner and placed the head up against the glass of one of the paintings. As the machine whined into life, the dust flew off the surface; there was a glint of silver from where the glass now reflected the light. Pushing the vacuum head backwards and forwards, he had soon removed the dust. He turned to the other.

Elspeth watched him with anticipation. "And?" she said.

Matthew switched off the vacuum cleaner and crouched down in front of the two paintings. "Both are oil on canvas," he said. "I'm glad that whoever had these had the good sense to put them behind the glass. Otherwise all that dust would have been on the surface itself."

"And?" prompted Elspeth again.

"I have no idea what this one is," he said, pointing to the larger of the two. He put on his art-dealer's voice. "An unremarkable nineteenth-century genre painting, probably. Highland cattle? Yes, there they are. A stag? Yes, in the background."

He moved to the next. She watched him. It fascinated her to see Matthew reacting to a painting; she had seen him doing this before. You could almost *see* the thought process, the elimination of possibilities, the reaction to some deep, inbuilt feeling for what was before him.

She did not want to rush him, but she was excited. If the others were a Cowie and a Fergusson, then this was not just a collection of odd bits and pieces. Fergusson was one of the most highly prized of the Scottish Colourists, and Cowie, although less widely appreciated, was interesting.

"Anything?" she asked.

Matthew said nothing. Now he reached forward and lifted up the painting, holding it at such an angle that the light fell more directly on it.

"This isn't Scottish," he said.

She saw that the picture was of a kitchen scene. A woman stood at a cooking range with her back to the artist; above the range, a line of copper saucepans was hanging; a rabbit, trussed for the larder, had been tossed onto a pine table to the woman's right, its fate the pot. The painting had a richness to it; reds predominated, with orange and copper in support. There was a visible warmth to the painting that emanated from the range with its glowing heart and its steaming pan.

"That's a French kitchen," said Elspeth. She was not sure why she said this; she simply knew.

Matthew agreed. "You know what this is," he said quietly. "Not only is it French, but it's . . ." He turned to face Elspeth. "Edouard Vuillard."

Elspeth's knowledge of art history was sketchy, but she had picked up the outlines.

"Bonnard and Vuillard. That Vuillard?"

Matthew's face broke into a smile. "Yes, that Vuillard. One of the French *intimistes*."

She reached out to touch the painting. It was as if she wanted to satisfy herself that it was real.

"Obviously I'll have to ask Belinda," said Matthew.

"Belinda?"

"Belinda Thomson. She's the Vuillard expert and she lives in Edinburgh. She's the person who authenticated that Vuillard café scene last year."

"And if it is?" asked Elspeth.

"If Belinda says it's a Vuillard," said Matthew. "Then it's a Vuillard. It looks like it to me."

Elspeth sat down on the sofa. "Matthew," she said. "If that's a Vuillard and the other two are a Fergusson and a Cowie, then we've . . ."

"Discovered rather an important haul," said Matthew.

Elspeth opened her hands in a gesture of puzzlement. "But who owns them?"

Matthew frowned. "I hadn't thought about that."

"But you'll have to think of it," said Elspeth. "These paintings are valuable, aren't they?"

"Very."

"Just how much is very?"

"The Vuillard is the most valuable, I'd say. One hundred and twenty thousand. One hundred and fifty. Something like that. The Fergusson would be a bit less. The Cowie, about twenty. Even the other one might fetch a thousand."

"So all in all, something like a quarter of a million?"

Matthew nodded.

"A quarter of a million in our concealed room," said Elspeth.

"How many concealed rooms have something quite as valuable as that in them?"

Matthew seemed puzzled. "But you think it might not be ours?" he asked. "How come?"

29. *We See More of the Scottish Nudists*

The Association of Scottish Nudists, with its headquarters in Moray Place, perhaps Edinburgh's most fashionable address, had not inconsiderable assets. The Association owned its main office outright, and free from any standard security or other encumbrance ("My clients, The Association of Scottish Nudists, have more than *naked title*," quipped their lawyer, continuing, "although one should always be aware of the possibility that they have unadvisedly entered into a *nudum pactum*, a *bare promise* being a somewhat tricky matter in Scots Law!" These subtle allusions, of course, would not be generally appreciated, but for their audience, a small group of lawyers meeting for a Friday evening drink in Whighams Wine Bar on Hope Street, they were wildly funny, provoking peals of appreciative laughter sufficient to drown out the normal hubbub of the bar, and to occasion envious looks from the fund managers and land agents in the bar whose own wordplay, they knew, would never match that of the lawyers).

In addition to the valuable premises in Moray Place, recently valued at nine hundred and fifty thousand pounds—they included a substantial garden running down to Lord Moray's Pleasure Gardens on the north side of the square—the Association owned a flat in Ainslie Place nearby. This was let out at a rent that was more than enough to cover the cost of employing the full-time secretary who ran the office in Moray

Place, answering the phone and dealing with the Association's day-to-day correspondence. Other tasks, including the organisation of meetings and outings, were handled by members of the Association's Committee, all of whom were volunteers and who therefore required no payment.

Yet even if payment had been required, there would have been more than sufficient funds to cover it: over the years the Association had received generous legacies from a number of late members, and these formed the core of an endowment fund that would see the Association through any conceivable difficulties. It was this fund that supported the annual travel awards that sent Scottish representatives to naturist conventions all over the world—to the annual meeting of the International Naturist Association in San Diego and to the prestigious Nudist International, known unofficially as the Nuditern, that was the governing body of the international nudist movement and that had recently been given United Nations recognition as a significant body in international civic society. *International No-Clothes Day* had been a result of that recognition, although the inclusion of this date in the calendar had been the subject of opposition and even derision.

The Scottish Government had recognised it, on the grounds that they recognised all official UN special days, and felt that it might be considered noninclusive to discriminate against those who wished to take off their clothes. "This does not imply that the Scottish Government considers the taking off of clothes as mandatory," it was announced at a press conference. "The Scottish Government believes that those who wish to take off their clothes should be entitled to do so except in such circumstances where no such entitlement is deemed to exist. For this reason, we shall be calling the day *International No-Clothes Day Where Appropriate*. This in no way suggests that we disapprove of those who . . ." The statement had not been finished, being drowned out by roars of laughter from the attending journalists.

The Association
of
Scottish Nudists

MORAY PLACE

But even if the Association was healthy in the financial sense, the same could not be said of its constitutional status; that had been the subject of bitter internal feuds, culminating in the recent removal of the Association's long-serving committee and its replacement with an entirely new governing body. The background to this development was complex, revolving around the peculiar terms of the Association's original constitution. This had been drafted by an Edinburgh solicitor in such a way as to ensure that Edinburgh members could control the committee indefinitely, having, as they did, three votes each while all other members had only one. The attempt by the Edinburgh-dominated committee to justify this failed, and the result was a reconstituted committee on which nudists from Glasgow, Hawick, Aberdeen and Perth now outnumbered the Edinburgh nudists by two to one.

The new committee took office shortly after that Extraordinary General Meeting at which the constitution had been amended. The chairman was now from Glasgow, the vice-chairman from Paisley, and the secretary and treasurer from Hawick and Aberdeen respectively. At the first meeting of the new committee, the controversial decision was taken to reverse several resolutions that the Edinburgh-dominated committee had passed shortly before demitting office. These resolutions were of no real importance, but their recall underlined the profound change that had taken place in the balance of nudist power.

"It reflects what has happened in the country," wrote one of the new committee members in a letter to a friend. "People think that we nudists are merely a special interest group much like any other—bridge players, curlers, ornithologists and so on—but we are emphatically not! We are far more representative: we are people without clothes, with the emphasis on 'people' rather than on 'clothes.' There's a big difference.

"What happens in our circles merely reflects what's happening in the wider society," the letter went on. "So if there is a swing to the left, for instance, in the wider society, then there is a swing to the left in the nudist movement. We are a mirror.

"For a very long time Edinburgh has been telling the rest of Scotland what to do. Power in Scotland was unaccountable for a very long time—exercised remotely by an establishment that controlled the few domestic Scottish institutions that survived the Act of Union. That arrangement suited Edinburgh down to the ground—it was a very comfortable setup indeed, with a Secretary of State for Scotland acting as a sort of colonial governor. (Not a single Secretary of State, be it noted, was a nudist—which speaks volumes in my view.) And then it all changed. Suddenly we had a Parliament again and the levers of power were in plain view. There was a new spirit abroad, and nowhere more so than in our nudist movement. The clothes we took off now were *our* clothes. The nakedness we celebrated was *our* nakedness. We now had control over our problems—over *our* midges, *our* weather. We acted authentically again, and showed that out-of-date, unrepresentative, smug, collaborationist Edinburgh establishment that the real Scotland, the authentic Scotland, the Scotland of local, community nudists was in control of its destiny again, after a long period of being swaddled in the clothing of oppression."

30. *Nudist Disharmony*

But it was not that simple. The changes in the constitution of the Association of Scottish Nudists were admittedly long overdue: nobody could mount a defence of a constitution of a society that discriminated against its members on the grounds of their postal address—nobody, that is, with any political sense. But that, unfortunately, is just what the Edinburgh clique controlling the Association lacked; their attempts to justify a permanent Edinburgh weighting on the committee on the grounds of stability and good governance were nothing but a provocation to those members of the Association who came from other places.

"Are you suggesting," asked one outraged Glasgow member, "that we in Glasgow—we Weegies, as you so condescendingly call us—are more confrontational and excitable than you people in Edinburgh, because if you are, Jimmy, I've got news for you. Jeez I'm gonna . . ."

There were many such exchanges and it became apparent to the Edinburgh committee that, as one of their number drily observed, "The game's up, chaps—the Weegies have finally rumbled us." The constitution of the Association was changed so as to allow for equal voting rights to be given to all parts of the country, and the new committee elected under these provisions became much more representative of Scotland as a whole. The defeated Edinburgh clique, although bemoaning its changed circumstances, nonetheless felt that vague sense of relief that any toppled undemocratic group must feel when it abandons the power to which it was not entitled.

"I keep thinking of Cavafy," said the former secretary. "You know, his poem about the people waiting for the invaders. You know that one? I feel a bit like that."

"Entirely understandable," said the former chairman. "I imagine Napoleon must have felt like that when he finally realised that his ambitions were unachievable. You dread the moment but then you feel that a great weight has been taken off your shoulders."

They mused on this for some moments.

"Like dressing for dinner," said the secretary. "People used to do that. Remember? And then they stopped."

"Of course, we used to undress for dinner, didn't we?" said the chairman. "But the idea was much the same."

The secretary looked thoughtful. "I think that this takes us right to the heart of the problem of civilisation. Nobody likes to talk about civilisation these days, do they? It's regarded as *passé*, as reactionary—as if talk of civilisation implies that one's values are superior to the values of others—which is pretty much anathema to most people these days—most people having been cowed into accepting moral relativism. And yet . . ."

"And yet," supplied the chairman, "if we don't have a concept of civilisation, what is the alternative? A free-for-all? A Hobbesian society in which liberal individualism rules the roost and people can pretty much do what they want provided they don't overstep some rather minimal boundaries?"

The secretary nodded. "Mind you, I'm not sure that I'd call such a society Hobbesian. That suggests that Hobbes would have approved of such a society, whereas that's exactly what he was warning us against."

The chairman did not respond to this. He had always felt that the secretary had a slight tendency to pedantry, but that, of course, was a desirable quality in a secretary: pedants kept good minutes, by and large.

"Manners," said the chairman, returning to the theme of their discussion. "Manners are the basic building block of any civilisation. Manners spring from a shared sense of membership—or create it, rather. And membership is right at the heart of any concept of civilisation. You participate in something. You are part of it. It gives you something to which you can aspire. And on those tiny little personal aspirations are constructed the great glories—great art, great architecture, great poetry, great . . . great acts of humanity and generosity. We must not forget those."

The secretary thought about this. It was all very well, he felt, to talk about manners, but what justified manners in any particular instance? Could they not be mere meaningless custom? You raised your hat (or you used to raise your hat) because it was considered polite, but raising your hat was meaningless when you came to examine the act itself. Or did you raise your hat to signal an inner attitude—an attitude of respect for the other—for the person to whom you raised your hat (if you had one)? That was obviously it.

A thought occurred to him. "Raising one's hat?" he said.

The chairman looked puzzled. "Raising your hat? Well, that's important—yes it is. It shows that you value the other person—that you acknowledge their presence and give it weight."

"You'd always raise your hat?" asked the secretary.

"Of course. Call me old-fashioned if you will, but of course I would."

The secretary shook his head. He saw difficulties. "But we nudists don't wear hats," he said.

The chairman frowned. "Yes we do. We can wear hats if it's

sunny. Look at the Australian members of the movement—
they wear hats."

"But we should only wear hats for protection," said the
secretary. "Is that right? We shouldn't wear them for adornment."

The chairman agreed that this was so. But even as he
pronounced on the subject, he felt a sudden weariness. "I don't
know if I have the heart for all this," he said. "It used to be so
nice before we had to start thinking about all these issues. We
just ran the Association from Edinburgh as we wanted to and
everything worked out well enough. And now . . ."

"And now it's all changed," said the secretary. He paused.
"Have you heard, by the way?"

The chairman sighed. "What now?"

"The new committee wants to change the name to Nudism
Scotland. It's all the rage. Police Scotland, for example;
Transport Scotland. And so on."

The chairman sighed even more deeply. "It's really most
vexing. People think that it's clever to put two nouns together
like that. Look at the BBC. They've abandoned adjectives
altogether. So we get things like 'Italy Prime Minister' for
'Italian Prime Minister.' Where do they get that from?"

"Education Scotland has a major task ahead," said the
secretary, with feeling.

And it was at this point that the former chairman had an
idea—an idea so seditious and unsettling as to cause, once
revealed, a sharp intake of breath in the former secretary.

"No!" said the secretary when the chairman finished. But
then he said, "Do you think it possible? Do you really think
we might get away with it?"

The chairman nodded. "Indubitably," he said, adding,
"*Audaces fortuna iuvat.*"

The secretary smirked. "Would the Weegies get that?" he
asked.

But the chairman rose above such crude taunts. "We must

be charitable to our dear friends from Glasgow," he said. "The least we can do is furnish them with a translation."

"Hah!" said the secretary.

"What fun we're having," concluded the chairman.

31. Ankles and Temptation

When he had lived in India Street, Matthew's journey to work was rarely more than ten minutes. That is how long it took him to walk up to Heriot Row, turn left, stroll to the junction with Dundas Street, cross the road, and then take the few steps down the eastern side of Dundas Street to his gallery. If that simple journey took more than ten minutes it was always for social reasons, usually one involving a chance encounter with Angus Lordie and his dog Cyril, a word with the postman, or a brief chat with an India Street neighbour, perhaps James Holloway, who lived several doors away and who could sometimes be seen, sleeves rolled up, polishing his Ducati motorbike in the street.

Any meeting with Angus and Cyril was always welcome, and could result in a substantial delay as they considered the news of the day. Of course they would have a subsequent opportunity to do exactly this, as they normally met at midmorning coffee time in Big Lou's coffee bar, but bumping into one another on the street provided an opportunity for an informal setting of the agenda for their subsequent conversation.

Unknown to Matthew, these meetings in the street were an occasion of almost unbearable temptation for Cyril. Although Cyril's inclination was to wag his tail and smile at any human he met, he had an inner life that was less straightforward. Cyril subscribed, of course, to the prevailing worldview that virtually all dogs accept: a canine *Weltanschauung* constructed on the simple notion that an immutable order of things existed, and this order was based on packs. You were allocated to a pack by a process that was not for you to question: it was simply there, in the same way as the weather, or trees, or rabbit holes were there. Man may have tried a whole raft of cosmologies to explain how it is that we—and the world—came to be; dogs are spared that dilemma by virtue of their limited intellect (which, of course, is not to be disparaging about *your* dog, who is undoubtedly of immense intelligence and has an uncanny ability to empathise with the feelings of humans; but no matter how much we admire their intelligence, we have to remember that dogs have never made anything, and have no literature or art to speak of).

For dogs, the world is there, and it is owned by packs. It is the canine destiny to belong to a particular pack and to find an appropriate position in it. For most dogs this will entail subservience to a more dominant dog—if there is one—and thereafter to a human who outranks that more dominant dog. That is just the way it is. There are few dogs to whom it occurs to contest this: one may as well argue with the sun. But if a dog does take it into his head to challenge the natural order of human dominance, he will soon find out that such questioning is not tolerated for long: the fate of radical dogs is celebrated in no ballads of freedom; it tends to be ignominious and final.

Cyril was certainly not a radical dog. He accepted that Angus was divinely ordained to determine the shape of his days. He fully appreciated that food came at Angus's whim, and that the highlights of the day, the walks along Northumberland Street, the moments of blissful freedom in Drummond Place Gardens, the occasional outing to the Pentlands or the beach at Gullane, were all within Angus's gift and the subject of his sole discretion.

Cyril also understood the rules, of which the most important was that you did not, in any circumstances, nip ankles. This was a cruelly restrictive rule, but it admitted of no exception, even in those cases where the ankles were flaunted before one's nose in such a way as to suggest that being nipped was exactly what the owner of the ankles wanted. That was so obvious, but Cyril knew that this made no difference to the severity of the legislation under which he lived.

In general, he had abided by this natural law. But every so often, the temptation was just too great, and he had been unable to resist. That had happened once in Big Lou's café, when he had succumbed and had given Matthew a quick bite on the right ankle—just a momentary one, and of insufficient force to break the skin, but a nip nonetheless. And he had been forgiven: to his utter astonishment, the punishment he had expected had not been meted out. This had strengthened the knowledge, harboured somewhere deep inside him, that the human heart was one of infinite compassion, that it loved dogs even in their moments of weakness, and that this is how the world would be forever. It was, in short, a theology as complete as any devised by any theologian in Geneva, Rome, or any holy place on the Ganges.

But it was still tempting, particularly because there was something about Matthew's ankles that drove dogs to distraction. It was not smell—although that must have come into it somewhere—it had more to do with canine ley lines. These were the dogs' version of those invisible currents of energy that crisscross our world and make special those places where they converge, or surface, or do whatever it is that believers in ley lines think they do.

So when Matthew stopped on his way in to work to talk to Angus, Cyril, although civil, would deliberately look away, so as not to be confronted with the sight of those ankles. And there was usually enough to engage him: a squirrel might be spotted scampering up a tree trunk in Queen Street Gardens; a cat might be seen glowering in an upstairs window in Heriot Row, with all the arrogance and contempt that only cats can muster; another dog might pass on a lead—there was usually enough to keep the mind off ankles.

But now those moments of temptation would be far fewer—at least in Heriot Row—as Matthew no longer went that way to work. Instead, his new routine was to leave Nine Mile Burn shortly after nine, to drive down the Biggar Road to Hillend, and then make his way to the small mews behind Nelson Street on the other side of town. There Matthew was the owner of a lockup garage with a small flat above it.

He parked the car that day and took out a neatly wrapped parcel. In the back of the car were three other similarly wrapped parcels. He would leave those there and fetch them later with the help of Pat MacGregor, his assistant, to whom he was burning to show the result of his breaking into the concealed room. He knew that Pat loved Vuillard—and Cowie and Fergusson too. She would be so excited . . .

But then he thought: what if she says, "Excuse me, Matthew: who actually owns these paintings?"

32. Stepmother Days

Rather to Matthew's surprise, Pat showed no interest in his parcel. She had arrived in the gallery ten minutes before he had that morning, and was already seated at her desk when he came in. He laid the wrapped painting beside his chair without opening it and looked at her. Normally, her innate curiosity would have prompted her to ask what was behind the bland packaging, but that did not happen now.

It was the start of another week, and so Matthew began, "Well here we are," and then added with a weary smile, "Again."

This was not an unreasonable thing to say. It may have been a somewhat trite remark, but there was no reason why it should have provoked tears—which is what it now appeared to do.

Matthew stared at Pat in incomprehension. Was the prospect of another week *that* depressing?

"Did I say something?" he muttered after a few moments. "I know it's Monday, but . . ."

This seemed only to make matters worse. As the volume of her sobs increased, Pat reached into a drawer for a tissue. She dabbed at her eyes and then blew her nose. "I'm sorry," she stuttered. "It's got nothing to do with Monday . . . or with you."

Matthew left his desk and crossed the gallery floor. Putting an arm about Pat's shoulder, he gave her a hug.

"Has something happened?"

She sighed; her sobbing now abating. "Everything," she managed to say. "Absolutely everything."

He hugged her again. It was a strange sensation—one about which he felt a certain caution. He and Pat had been emotionally involved some time ago —indeed, he had once even proposed to her—but things had changed since then: he now had a wife and three small sons . . . and yet, and yet . . .

the heart could still be stirred by proximity to one with whom an intimacy had been shared. He reduced the pressure of his embrace, and moved away just enough so that only his arm touched her. They could be seen from the street outside, and if anybody were to peer through the large expanse of the glass display window they would see him with an arm around his young assistant. Any explanation of such a situation would sound so hollow: *She was crying and I was comforting her . . .*

That, he realised, was impermissible: we could no longer put our arms around others to comfort them. The most natural of human reactions—to embrace, to touch in sympathy— had now been forbidden by lecturing moralists who had interdicted ordinary tactile reactions and put in their place a cold rectitude. Latin cultures, of course, had ignored this, but in northern latitudes this coldness had settled on the human landscape like a thick layer of frost.

He drew up a chair and sat down. "Tell me," he said. "Is somebody ill?"

Pat shook her head. "No, it's nothing like that. It's just that . . ." She broke off, staring morosely at the floor.

"You don't have to," said Matthew. "Only if you want to . . ." He thought: it's that boy. Of course it's that boy. What was his name? Michael, that was it. He was a woodworker, wasn't he? He made the table that Pat had pointed out so proudly in the Scottish Gallery over the road when they had called in to see Guy Peploe.

"It's my father," Pat said suddenly "It's him . . . and other things."

Then the other things must involve that boy, thought Matthew; but first things first.

"Is your dad in some sort of trouble?"

Pat sniffed. Her tears had stopped now and her voice had returned to normal. "I think he is. I'm not sure if he realises it—in fact, I suspect that he doesn't."

Matthew frowned. Pat had said something about her father the other day, but he had not taken it in. He did not know Dr. MacGregor all that well, but he liked him. He seemed so grounded, so reasonable in his views—which he had to be, Matthew decided, given the nature of his work. If one spent the entire day dealing with disturbed people, then one's own world would have to be fairly firmly anchored.

"You know that he's been seeing this woman?" said Pat.

Matthew tried to remember whether she had mentioned a woman. "Not really," he said. "Have they split up?"

"No, that's the problem. They haven't split up. They're . . ." She paused, and looked at Matthew as if she were expecting his help. "They're now engaged and he's going to marry her."

"Ah," said Matthew. "And you don't think that's a very good idea?"

"No," said Pat. "It's a very bad idea."

"You don't like her?" It was such a trite question, and the answer was perhaps obvious, but there did not seem much else that he could say.

"I hate her," said Pat. "I hate her."

"Ah."

"With good reason."

"Oh?"

He waited. He was trying to remember something somebody had said to him about the Wicked Stepmother Syndrome. He himself had had a stepmother and knew that the relationship was a potentially difficult one, but what had surprised him was to hear that the concept of the wicked stepmother had such profound roots. In classical times, a good day was called a "mother day" while a bad day was called a "stepmother day." And in a hundred other traditions and practices was this relationship cast as entirely negative. And here was Pat expressing it in its very essence . . .

"Are you sure you hate her?" he asked.

His question was mildly put, but it triggered a passionate answer. "Of course I'm sure! And let me tell you just why I'm so sure . . ."

He recoiled at the intensity of her response. "Shall I make you a cup of tea?" he asked.

It was the classic response to crisis practised throughout these islands—in England, Scotland, and elsewhere. Emotional turmoil, danger, even disaster could be faced with far greater equanimity if the kettle was switched on. *War has been declared! There's been a major earthquake! The stock market has collapsed! Oh really? Let me put the kettle on . . .*

Pat nodded. "Thanks," she said.

He went into the small kitchen at the back of the gallery, filled the kettle and plugged it into the wall. Immediately he felt calmer.

33. *The Czechess*

Pat looked at Matthew over the top of her mug of tea. "I feel so disloyal," she said.

"Talking about your father? Is that what makes you feel disloyal?"

She nodded. "We don't like to criticise our parents to others; somehow it seems so wrong."

Matthew thought about this. He knew a number of people who found fault in their parents—on occasion, serious fault. There were others, of course, who would never do this— who elevated their parents to some sort of pedestal and who would never face up even to the most obvious defects in character. Presumably, as in all human affairs there would be a *via media*—an attitude of charity that was not blind to parental shortcomings but that was discreet about them, and understanding too.

"I don't think you should reproach yourself," Matthew reassured her. "And if you can't talk about your parents reasonably objectively, then you may not be able to help them."

Pat seemed to take comfort from this. "I do want to help him," she said. "It's probably too late, but I really would like to help him."

"Why not tell me?" said Matthew.

Pat was silent for a few moments. Then she said, "That woman is after his money. It's glaringly obvious and the only person who can't see it is my father."

Matthew frowned. "Are you sure? Just because she may be younger than he is doesn't mean that she's a gold digger. There are plenty of people who fall in love with older people who . . ."

". . . Who have more money than they have."

"Not just that," said Matthew. "Some of them may not be interested in money at all."

Pat made a face. "Highly unlikely."

Matthew shrugged. "You're being very cynical."

"I'm being realistic," said Pat. "Look at those ads you see in the lonely hearts columns."

"Which ones?"

"The ones that make it crystal clear," answered Pat. "Inadvertently, of course. *Young woman (27) seeks male friend. Age not an issue.* Well, you know what responses that'll get: late middle-aged men who don't see the trap they're walking into." She paused. "I saw one the other day placed by a young man of twenty-two looking for a male friend over sixty, preferably with a house abroad and a yacht. How transparent can you get? And if I were that guy with the yacht I'd be careful about falling into the sea. And careful about signing a new will."

Matthew looked incredulous. "Surely not."

"Well, why else would he put in an ad like that?"

Matthew shrugged again. "People are looking for different things. Emotional security. A substitute parent. All sorts of things."

"Including money," said Pat.

"Maybe." He paused. "Have you got any evidence that this women . . ."

"She's called Anichka," said Pat. "Although I can hardly bring myself to utter the name."

"Have you got any evidence that Anichka's interested in your father's money? The fact that she's Eastern European doesn't automatically mean that she's out to improve her financial situation. A lot of these marriages to foreign women work very well because people love one another. It happens, you know."

Pat was dismissive. "I know what she's like because that's all she talks about. Money. What things cost. All the time."

She gave Matthew some examples. "She reads *The Scotsman* property supplement every Thursday. I've seen her. And I've picked the paper up afterwards and she will have circled the ads for any houses that are at all like my father's. And she underlines the price. That's so that she knows what ours will be worth—she's watching the price."

"Perhaps she's thinking of moving."

"No, they aren't thinking of that. My father told me that she loves his place and is looking forward to living there. And here's another example. She had his pictures valued, and some of the furniture too. I came across the valuation report."

"Perhaps it was for insurance. People do that, you know. You have to make sure you're not underinsured."

She brushed this off. "No, it wasn't for insurance. And there's another thing. My father goes to a bank where you still have a bank manager who looks after you. I happen to know his manager, because he's also my godfather. And he came to see me. He was very embarrassed, and a bit furtive too. He said that he really shouldn't talk to me about it, but he felt that he had to. He said my father had given Anichka signing rights on his deposit account and money was being transferred out of it and sent to the Czech Republic and to some account in Toronto. He said that quite a bit of money had gone."

Matthew winced. "Oh," he said. "That doesn't sound very good."

"No," said Pat.

"Have you talked to him?"

This seemed to trigger a painful memory. "Yes, I did. And he said that he was very disappointed in me for being so suspicious. He said that Anichka was not at all materialistic. I said then why did she take such an interest in the price of everything. And he said that he thought this was because she was trying to get used to this country and it was important to know what things cost if you were to understand a place."

"Oh really!"

"Exactly."

Matthew sighed. "I don't think there's much you can do. Unless . . ."

"Yes?"

"Unless you set some sort of trap."

The possibility appealed to Pat. "A financial trap?"

Matthew shook his head. "No, a honey trap."

Pat was hesitant. "A honey trap?"

Matthew looked a bit sheepish. "I feel a bit embarrassed to suggest this," he said. "But it has to be considered. What if he were to find that she had a thing for another man. Would the scales fall from his eyes?"

Pat considered this. "I suppose it would show that she wasn't really interested in him."

"Yes."

"But how do you arrange a honey trap?"

"You bait it with the most irresistible man you can find. The man tries to tempt her. She falls for him and you make sure you get the evidence. Bingo!"

Matthew could hardly believe that he was actually suggesting this, and neither could Pat—at first. It was reckless; it was absurd; it was dangerous. But as they thought about it, they realised that it was exactly what they needed to do. And they both realised, almost at the same time, who was the obvious bait.

"Bruce?" said Matthew tentatively.

"I was just thinking of him," said Pat.

"Synchronicity," said Matthew. "It happens all the time." He paused. "Of course, it's neutral. Bad ideas no doubt occur together in much the same way as good."

"Have you changed your mind?"

"No. Bruce is ideal. He'll love it. It's just the assignment for somebody like him."

Pat looked doubtful. "I don't think we should do it."

"No, we probably shouldn't," said Matthew. "But shouldn't doesn't mean shan't. And . . ." He was looking at her intently. "And come on, Pat, this is a . . . this is a rescue."

34. Verbalisation Precedes Resolution

Verbalisation precedes resolution, said Dr. Parry in his *Principles of Psychotherapy*—and he was right. Now that Pat had expressed her fears over her father's engagement to the mercenary Czechess, Anichka, her agitation seemed to abate. Matthew thought too that her mind had been taken off her troubles by their hatching of the plan to use Bruce Anderson as bait in a honey trap. Bruce was Matthew's occasional drinking companion in the Cumberland Bar, a surveyor, *echt* narcissist, proponent of clove-scented hair gel, and former pupil of Morrison's Academy in Crieff. He was not to everybody's taste, but there was little doubt as to his attractiveness to women, who flocked to him as moths to light, fascinated by his aura of seething sexuality, his chin, his *en brosse* hairstyle, and his smooth, moisturised skin. Pat, like everybody else, had fallen for all that, although she had woken from the trance in time to avoid the eventual distress felt by most of Bruce's conquests once he moved on—"Actually they're not really conquests," Bruce said suavely. "They surrender without firing a shot. Unconditional surrender. Odd, but there it is."

But with their plan conceived in principle, Matthew did not wish to dwell on Bruce or on the other problem barely adumbrated by Pat. He suspected what that other problem was, but, rather than get tied up in her emotional affairs, he was keen to show her his new pictures, the first of which was leaning against his desk, still wrapped in brown paper with a protective layer of bubble-wrap within.

"I've got hold of a few new pictures," he said, taking a sip of his tea. "Some rather nice things, actually."

"The Bonhams' auction?" asked Pat. There had been an auction in Queen Street at the end of the previous week and Matthew had left a few successful bids with the auction house.

"No, Miranda Grant's holding on to those for me," he said. "These ones I . . ."

Pat looked at him expectantly.

I can't say *I found them*, thought Matthew. You didn't *find* pictures like that, unless of course you used *find* in a metaphorical sense.

"Yes?" said Pat. "A private sale?" People were always coming into the gallery keen to negotiate the private sale of pictures they did not wish to sell publicly. In some cases they had the pictures copied before they consigned the originals for sale, thus allowing their friends to think they still possessed them. These newly minted copies were hung in the originals' exact position and in most cases nobody was any the wiser—except sometimes. Matthew remembered going to dinner at a house in Heriot Row and inadvertently touching the surface of a small Cadell only to find that the paint was still slightly wet. He had gasped, and the host had caught his eye, guilt and embarrassment writ large on his face.

Matthew almost said, "Obviously a very *late* Cadell," but stopped himself in time, thus allowing the host the opportunity to say, "We had a leak. It's attended to now, but one or two of the pictures got a bit wet."

"Cadell's the sort of artist who can take a spot of rain," said Matthew charitably.

A friend had later told him the full story. "The poor chap invested a lot in expensive clarets just before the market collapsed. People stopped using them for bribes in China, and nobody wanted Chateau *N'importe Quoi* at however many thousand pounds a case. He had to sell his Cadell to recoup. So he very understandably had a copy made by one of those firms that will reproduce anything for a couple of hundred quid and pop it in the post from Shanghai. Amazing. He put the copy on the wall and sold the original rather well."

"Such a sad tale," said Matthew.

"Edinburgh is full of such stories," said his friend. "Hidden suffering . . ."

Pat repeated her question. "You bought them?"

Matthew shook his head. "Not quite. I'll come to that later . . . Let me show you first."

He unwrapped the painting and held it up so that the light from the large window fell squarely upon it. Pat leaned forward to examine it.

"But it's lovely," she said. "Absolutely charming."

Matthew beamed. "Yes, isn't it?"

Pat leaned further forward to scrutinise a corner of the picture. "Those lovely reds," she said. "They're . . ."

"So rich?" supplied Matthew.

"Yes. Exactly that."

"Let me guess who it is," said Pat. "Don't tell me—let me guess."

"Of course."

Pat sat back in her chair. "It's not Moira what's her name? . . ."

"Moira Beaty? No, it's not her."

"Could it be Sarah Longley? Remember those rather nice paintings of hers we showed a little while ago? She did something quite like that."

"It's not Sarah Longley," said Matthew.

"Adam Bruce Thomson? He painted the occasional kitchen."

Matthew shook his head. "*Nyet*. Don't think Scottish. Think . . . well, maybe think French."

Pat's eyes widened. "French? Well, it can't be Vuillard, although it definitely looks like him. Follower of Vuillard, shall we say?"

Matthew lowered the painting, his arms beginning to ache from holding it up. He smiled widely. "Vuillard," he said. "It *is* Vuillard."

Pat let out a shriek of delight. "But Matthew," she exclaimed. "How do you know?"

"I looked it up in the *catalogue raisonné*," he said. "It's there. There's a picture of it. It gives the date he painted it and there's a note on the subject. Then it says: *current whereabouts unknown.*"

Pat frowned. "It could be a copy."

Matthew hesitated. "Yes . . ." he began tentatively. "It could be, but no, I think it's the real thing. It's got that . . . that *feel*."

Pat knew what he meant. There were people who could sense the genuine, and she had always thought that Matthew was one. It was a sixth sense that enabled those who had it to raise the alarm well before anybody else had started to doubt.

"Can you get confirmation?"

"Yes," said Matthew. "I've already spoken to Belinda Thomson. She's agreed to look at it."

Pat seemed satisfied with that. She had been a student of Belinda's at the University and she knew of her interest in Vuillard. But then she said, "But tell me how you got hold of it. Do you actually own it or are you going to sell it on commission?"

"It's mine," said Matthew.

He spoke so quickly, and so firmly, that Pat immediately doubted him.

"You're hiding something," she said. "I can tell."

Matthew sighed. "I *think* it's mine," he said.

Pat groaned. "That means it's not. If you only *think* you own something, then you probably don't." She paused. "I think you need to tell me about it."

It was a moment or two before Matthew began. "You see," he said, "our new house has a concealed room . . ."

It was not a good beginning. "Oh come on, Matthew. Spare me the Famous Five stuff."

"I always liked the Famous Five," said Matthew.

"They were very middle class," said Pat.

"So are you," snapped Matthew. "And so are most of the people who sneer at others for being middle class."

35. The Conversation of Men

"Now, Angus," said Matthew as he sat down in Big Lou's coffee bar with Angus Lordie and, rather exceptionally, Domenica Macdonald.

Angus waited for more to be said, but that, it seemed, was the extent of Matthew's greeting. Not that its brevity made it insignificant: a whole and satisfying conversation, Angus thought, could consist of very few words, provided the words were well chosen and had behind them sufficient richness of association. In this respect he recalled a conversation he had once overheard on the Black Isle, in which one man, coming upon another in the street, said, in long drawn-out tones, "Aye," to be answered with "Aye" from the other—a slightly different *aye*, of course, and one accompanied by a slight movement of the head. This was followed by "Aye, well" from the instigator of the exchange, to which the reply was a further "Aye." The conversation was brought to a meaningful end with "Aye, then" from one, followed by a conclusive "Aye, aye" from the other.

Dr. Johnson might have been scathing about such dialogue, but to view it as meaningless or banal is to misread it. That exchange, monosyllabic though it was, said a great deal about the burdens of this life, about the Sisyphean nature of our existence; it said something about resilience and stoicism; it said something about the state of Scotland, about local issues of which an outsider could be quite ignorant; it said something about Scottish history, about Bannockburn, Flodden and Culloden; it said something about the whole pageant of life—its glory, its sadness, its ineffable mystery. No lengthy exchange in the grandest of literary salons or in the halls of the most prolix philosophers could have said more than those few words.

Few words are needed—that, thought Angus, is the insight that a loquacious culture of television windbags persistently fails to grasp. A reference to the *chattering classes* may be an unduly dismissive put-down of a certain sector of society— but underneath that pejorative expression lies an important truth: most ideas can be expressed succinctly and in a fraction of the words usually devoted to them.

Domenica, who rarely joined Angus and Matthew for coffee, was concerned that her presence might have inhibited the conversation, resulting in this apparently taciturn beginning. "I hope you don't mind my being here," she said.

Matthew looked surprised. "Why should we?"

Domenica shrugged. "It's just that men like to talk among themselves, so that we women have no idea what you talk about."

"Nonsense," said Angus. "You know perfectly well what we talk about."

Domenica looked doubtful. "Do I? I've always thought

that women don't really know what men talk about among themselves because they're inevitably excluded from all-male conversations—by definition, so to speak." She paused. "And vice versa, of course. Men don't really know what women say when only other women are present. They can't know, can they?"

Matthew frowned. "Unless women and men talk about the same thing. Then it doesn't matter whether it's just men or just women. The conversation will be the same—in both groups."

Domenica's expression made her disagreement plain. "No," she said, firmly. "There is female conversation and there is male conversation. I'm convinced of that."

"Aren't you in danger of stereotyping?" asked Matthew.

"No," said Domenica. "To suggest otherwise is merely to impose a new stereotype—the androgyne."

Matthew looked unconvinced. "Really? I thought that was exactly what society was becoming—more androgynous."

He looked to Angus for support, but Angus was struggling with the concept of androgyny.

"It doesn't matter anymore whether we are male or female," Matthew continued, wondering, as he spoke, whether he really believed what he was saying. *We new men*, he thought, *have been taught what to say.* "We've escaped the constraints of imposed gender roles. We can just be . . . people, I suppose. People rather than male people or female people." *If they could hear me at the rugby club*, thought Matthew.

"Except we aren't," said Domenica. "Oh, we may be getting rid of irrelevant distinctions—and entirely unjust and indefensible distinctions—such as the idea that a woman can't be a firefighter or a man can't be a nurse, but that doesn't change certain instincts. Those are a matter of genes—of chromosomes. And it's not something we can wish out of existence just because we believe—quite rightly—in equality."

"You're at risk of sounding old-fashioned," said Angus.

Domenica defended herself. "Is it old-fashioned to observe differences in the way people behave?"

"Possibly," said Matthew.

"Well then, I don't care," said Domenica. "I happen to believe there is a difference between male conversation and female conversation."

"In what respect?" asked Matthew.

Domenica thought for a moment. "Women's conversation is more subjective. Women talk about feelings and reactions. Men *may* talk about these things, but they tend not to—at least when talking to other men. They may talk to women friends about their feelings, but they don't to other men. That's why so many men are lonely. That's why so many men suffer to such a degree: they can't talk to anybody about how they feel."

Matthew suggested that this was exactly what was changing. "Men can do that now," he said. "Men are now allowed to talk about their feelings—because they don't have to conform to the straitjacket of masculine identity. Men can just be people, in the same way that women can be people." He paused. "Men can cry now. They used not to be able to cry—now they can."

"Perhaps," said Domenica. "But I was just thinking: can you tell whether something is written by a man or a woman? If you read it and don't know the name of the author: can you tell?"

"Always," said Angus.

"Never," said Matthew.

Domenica looked from one to the other. "An interesting difference of opinion," she said.

"Well, can you?" asked Matthew.

"Invariably," replied Domenica. "Look at Jane Austen. How could that voice be a man's?"

"That's a compromised example," said Matthew. "We

know that it's Austen because it sounds like her. And we know she was a woman."

"And Hemingway?" asked Angus. "Could anybody ever mistake a passage of Hemingway for something written by a woman?"

"Hemingway is another dubious case," said Matthew. "Hemingway was a writer who wanted to sound like a particular sort of man. Most men don't think—or speak—like Hemingway. Being Hemingway must have been tremendously exhausting."

Angus was reminded of something. "Have you seen that photograph of Hemingway when he was a small boy? The one where he's dressed in a skirt?"

Matthew raised an eyebrow. "Hemingway in a skirt?"

"Yes," said Angus, smiling. "Little boys used to be dressed in skirts until they reached a certain age. Look at Dutch seventeenth-century portraits of little boys. They all wear skirts."

"I'm sure he didn't like it," mused Matthew.

"I bet he didn't," said Angus. "That probably explains everything. The hunting. The big game fishing. The whisky. It was probably all an attempt to get over the knowledge that he once wore a skirt."

"How sad," said Matthew. "Whereas all the time he was interested in interior decoration?"

Domenica laughed. "And you accuse *me* of stereotyping," she said.

36. Clothing Speaks

"I'm not convinced," said Matthew.

"Not convinced of what?" asked Angus.

"Of the ability of people to judge whether something is written by a man or a woman. I just don't see how you do it. The language is the same, surely."

Domenica had views on that. "I seem to recollect reading something somewhere," she said. "Yes, it was an essay by Ved Mehta. He said that it was more difficult to tell now whether a writer was male or female because language itself has become so bland. Style has gone out of the window; all that matters now is that meaning is conveyed in as uncluttered a way as possible."

"Interesting," said Matthew. "But I'm not sure whether I would look at style. I'd look at content—if I were going to find any difference, I imagine I'd find it there."

"Clothing?" said Angus. "I've found that male authors don't mention what their characters are wearing. Female authors always describe clothing."

"Are you sure about that?" asked Matthew. "Or is that just another of these stereotypes?"

Angus smiled. "I'm trying to think whether Hemingway describes people's clothing—since we seem to be taking him as the quintessentially male author."

"I can't recall," said Matthew. "I've read a little Hemingway, but not very much. I can't take the intensity of it. He's like D. H. Lawrence in that sense—too intense."

"Well, I do remember something," said Angus. "I remember his description of Francis Macomber. He is described as wearing new safari clothing—and the clothing has a great deal of work to do, as I recall."

Matthew raised an eyebrow. "How can clothing have work to do?"

"It says something about character. Put a character in fancy clothing and you have a popinjay personality. Vain. Selfish, perhaps. Put him in modest, simple clothing and you have a modest, simple personality. It's that straightforward."

"So this new safari clothing was symbolic?"

Angus nodded. "The new safari clothing says: *no substance. What do the Texans say? All hat, no cattle.*"

"I love that," said Domenica. "The converse, I imagine, must be *all cattle, no hat.* When would one use that, I wonder?"

"When you were talking about somebody who's a bit too unrefined," suggested Matthew. "You might say *all cattle, no hat* of somebody who has the substance all right, but is pretty unsophisticated."

"This man with the new safari clothing," said Domenica. "What sort of character was he?"

"He ran away from a lion," said Angus. "That gave the game away—that, and his new safari clothing."

"I think it completely sensible to run away from lions," said Domenica. "If I encountered a lion, I should certainly run away."

Matthew laughed. "That would be a bad mistake, as it happens, Domenica. Lions are programmed—hardwired, so to speak—to chase after anything that runs away from them. No lion could forebear to chase you if you ran away. Look at the domestic cat—put something at the end of a piece of wool and drag it along in front of the cat—it chases it."

"I shall remember that, Matthew," said Domenica.

Matthew returned to authorship. "If people are able to detect gender, then how do authors get away with it when they claim to be . . ."

"Men . . ." prompted Angus.

". . . Or women," said Matthew. "And they're not." He paused. "If it's possible to tell whether you're reading a man or woman, then how do these people get away with it—sometimes indefinitely—or until somebody goes and looks up a birth certificate or something of the sort."

"That happens?" asked Angus. "I knew that it did in the past—when women had to claim to be men just in order to get published. But now?"

"It still goes on," said Matthew. "Apparently most men

are reluctant to read books by women. There's been market research that establishes that. Whereas women . . ."

"Are more open-minded?" suggested Domenica.

"Yes. Apparently women don't mind."

"There you are," said Domenica. "One of the differences I was talking about."

"I find it odd," said Angus. "I wouldn't care at all whether I was reading a book by a man or a woman."

"But lots of men do," said Matthew. "I saw something in the papers recently about an author who had a very wide readership of her male/male romances. She claimed to be a man, but she wasn't. She was a woman. She just used her initials and her surname. There was a major row."

"Assumption of voice," said Domenica. "Some people think you can only write about certain things if you're a member of the world you're writing about."

"It must be difficult to sustain that," mused Angus. "Shakespeare wasn't Danish, and yet he wrote *Hamlet*."

"Nor was he Scottish, and yet he wrote *Macbeth*," Domenica pointed out. "Of course, some contend there was a very anti-Scottish element in *Macbeth*. Had he written it today, Shakespeare would have been subjected to pretty strong abuse on the social media. People wouldn't have paid any attention to how well both Duncan and Malcolm came out of it."

"Our national shame," said Matthew. "Our open sore: the abusing and threatening of others."

"A London dramatist," said Angus, with a smile.

They sat in silence for a moment, and then Matthew said, "I have to talk to you about something. It's been preying on my mind."

Angus exchanged a glance with Domenica. Angus had told her that he felt Matthew was worried about something. Now, it seemed, it was about to be disclosed. Not a marriage problem, thought Angus; please may it not be a marriage problem.

It was as if Matthew had anticipated the question. "It's an artistic issue."

Angus heaved a sigh of relief. "Tell all," he said. "Is it a question of attribution?"

"No," said Matthew. "I think not. One of the paintings in question has been given very firmly to its painter, who just happens to be Vuillard."

Angus's eyes widened.

"I don't know about the others," said Matthew. "I'm at present trusting my own judgement. But the point is not that at all. The point is: do I own them?"

"If you bought them, you own them," said Angus. He paused. "They weren't looted, were they? There have been a lot of paintings coming onto the market that are being restituted to the heirs of owners who had them looted by the Nazis."

'Not that," said Matthew. "No, I found them in a secret room."

"How remarkable," said Domenica. "There are so few people who have secret rooms these days."

"That's what they may think," said Angus, with a smile. "By their very nature, there are more secret rooms than we might suspect."

37. Problems of Ownership

Angus and Domenica listened intently as Matthew told them about the discovery of the paintings. When he finished, Domenica sat back, stared at Matthew as if in disbelief, and said, "Well, I'm astounded. That just doesn't happen anymore."

"Oh, but it does," said Angus. "It happens far more often

than you'd imagine. There was that Caravaggio discovered in Dublin in a Jesuit parlour. And the Michelangelo found behind a sofa in Buffalo."

"A sofa!" exclaimed Domenica. "Shades of Lady Bracknell . . ."

"Those are the spectacular cases," Matthew went on, "but there are lots of more modest discoveries. For instance, paintings that have been attributed to the wrong artist and are then found to be by somebody far more significant."

"So finding a Vuillard in a hidden room is not unusual?" asked Angus.

"Unusual, but not impossible," replied Matthew. "The question, though, is this: the paintings in question were in a concealed room in a house I bought. Are they mine?"

Angus thought it depended on whether Matthew had bought the house *and* its contents. "Did you buy the furniture? The bits and pieces? The curtains?"

"Some things were specifically mentioned," said Matthew. "We bought those."

"And nothing else?" probed Angus.

Matthew frowned. "That's the problem. The Duke apologised for leaving a few items of furniture in various rooms. He said: 'Please help yourself to anything we've left behind. If you can't use it, Oxfam it.' Those were his words."

Angus reached a quick decision. "That's it, then: if he said that you could have whatever was left behind, then it's yours." He looked to Domenica for support. "Wouldn't you agree, Domenica?"

Domenica was not so sure. "Isn't it a question of intention? Isn't the test of whether somebody gives you something— or sells it to you, for that matter—whether they *intend* that ownership should pass?" She paused. "And in this case surely he couldn't intend to pass ownership of something that he didn't know was there."

Matthew saw a flaw in that. "But then how can you own something if you don't know it exists?"

"Quite easily," said Angus. "If Domenica gives me a present to pass on to you—it being your birthday, shall we say—and I set out to deliver it to you, then, until I actually hand it over, you don't know that you own whatever it is I have. Yet you do."

"Do I?" asked Matthew. "Or do I have a right to take ownership of it sometime in the future?"

They were silent as they contemplated this refinement.

"I think you own it," said Domenica. "But are we talking about the law here, or is it morality?"

"So," said Matthew, "you're going to ask whether the Duke has a moral right to the pictures?"

"Yes, actually I was," said Domenica. "You may have a moral right to something you don't know you have a moral right to—if I make myself sufficiently clear." She looked at Matthew. "I know that you're scrupulously honest, Matthew, and the last thing you would wish to do would be to deprive the Duke of something that would be his, if he just knew about it."

Matthew looked at the ground. "I find these things very complex," he said. "But I feel bad about holding on to these pictures. They were his, in my view—it's just that he didn't know they were his. But that doesn't make them any the less his."

"No," said Domenica. "I think that's right."

Angus thought of an objection. "But *were* they his?"

Matthew frowned. "What do you mean? If he owned the house—which he did—then he owned the things it contained."

"No," said Angus. "That's simply not true. The fact that you own the container doesn't mean you own the contents. Waverley Station doesn't own the things you leave in the left luggage lockers."

"Are there left luggage lockers in Waverley Station?" asked Domenica. "In these days of suspicion, do left luggage lockers still exist?"

"I don't know," said Matthew. "I can't remember when I put anything in a left luggage locker."

"I can," said Angus. "I visited the Ashmolean Museum in Oxford and they have left luggage lockers. I had bought a rather bulky book on Piero di Cosimo in the bookshop there and I didn't want to cart it round the museum, so I put it in one of their lockers and . . ." He became silent.

"And?" prompted Angus.

Angus looked at Domenica—a look of sheepishness. "Did I remember to pick it up when we left? Do you remember whether . . ." He faltered. "I didn't, you know. I didn't collect it. It'll still be there."

"How long ago was this?" asked Matthew.

"Four months ago, I think. I was in Oxford to see a friend. He invited me to a feast at All Souls."

"I'm surprised they still call them feasts," said Domenica. "I would have thought it more tactful to call them light suppers, or snacks, perhaps."

"Your book won't be there," said Matthew. "Sorry, Angus, but they'll clear out unopened lockers at the end of the day."

"So what will have happened to it?" Angus asked miserably. "It cost thirty-five pounds, as I recall. It had wonderful plates— di Cosimo's gorgeous work. Beautiful. You know that one of the man in the landscape with the dogs? You know that one?"

"It will have been put in their lost property department . . ."

Angus brightened. "Good, well . . ."

". . . and then sold," continued Matthew. "Still, it could have been worse. You could have put an actual di Cosimo in the locker."

"The point about all this," interrupted Domenica, "is what?"

Angus was emphatic. "The point is that you just don't know whether the Duke owned those paintings. They could have belonged to the person who owned the house before he had it."

"They'd had the house for a long time," Matthew pointed out.

"Even so, his father, or whoever," Angus went on, "could merely have been looking after them for somebody else. Somebody may have hidden them there, for all we know, because they were stolen."

"In which case they belong to the original owners—or their heirs," said Domenica. "You don't lose your right to things that are stolen from you."

"But what about acquirers in good faith?" asked Angus.

Domenica ignored the question. She had to think again about the di Cosimo book. What if Angus had simply lost it— left it on the train from Oxford to Edinburgh—a train journey so slow and tedious that one might easily forget what one had on one, or in an extreme case, where one was going. "Lost property," she said. "Who owns books about di Cosimo that are simply lost? Lost for a long time? So long that nobody knows who owns them?"

"Ultimately, the Queen," said Matthew. "Or at least I think she does. If something belongs to nobody else, she gets it. There's somebody called the Queen's and Lord Treasurer's Remembrancer who can claim things that belong to nobody."

"All those umbrellas," mused Domenica. "Thousands and thousands of them. And the Crown owns them all."

Matthew looked irritated. "I think I need to speak to him," he said. "In fact, I'm going to go and tell him."

"A very good idea," said Domenica. "And he'll say: 'Yes, of course, they're mine.' Who wouldn't?"

"We'll see," said Matthew. "At least my conscience will be clear."

"Even if his won't," said Domenica.

"Cynic," said Angus, but not rudely. Not every allegation of cynicism need be rude. One can accuse people of cynicism quite gently—as if it were, in fact, something of a virtue; which, of course, it is not.

38. Things Improve for Bertie

With Nicola established in the flat, life for the three members of the Pollock family then resident in Scotland Street improved beyond measure. Nobody was sure how Irene was at that time, although the general view was that she was doing rather well in the desert harem in which she found herself. A letter had been received by the British chargé d'affaires in the region that was unquestionably in her handwriting and appeared to be written free of duress. No mention was made in this message of any privations or suffering, and there were no pleas for release.

"I wouldn't be inclined to regard this as in any way distressed," pronounced the Foreign Office official who passed it on to Stuart. "In fact, your wife appears to be, well-settled, so to speak."

Stuart did not wish to appear disloyal. "I do hope they release her soon," he said. He did not sound convinced of his own words, though, and the conversation had been brought to an end.

"Mummy is still busy in the Gulf," Stuart said to Bertie that night. "I think she has a lot to do there."

Bertie did not appear at all concerned. "She shouldn't hurry back, Daddy. Write to her and tell her that everything's all right here and there's no hurry for her to come back to Scotland. Tell her that, Daddy, so that she doesn't worry."

Overhearing this conversation, Nicola suppressed a smile. She understood the situation perfectly well, and had already noticed how relaxed and happy both Bertie and Ulysses seemed to be. Over the two days that she had so far spent in Edinburgh, Ulysses, in particular, had become much more content and was bringing up his food much less frequently. He had settled to the bedtime she had imposed and slept all through the night, only wakening in the morning when the rest of the household was already up and about.

The patterns of her own day had quickly established themselves. After giving both boys their breakfast, she prepared Ulysses for the journey on the 23 bus that took Bertie up to Bruntsfield. From there they walked the short mile to the Steiner School, where she dropped Bertie off at the gate before making her way home.

There was plenty to fill the morning. She had found Big Lou's by chance and had decided that this was where she would regularly have her morning coffee. Big Lou prepared foamy milk for Ulysses, and this kept him occupied while Nicola tackled *The Scotsman* crossword over one of Big Lou's generous lattes. If there was company, she took advantage of it; she had already had one conversation with Angus Lordie, whom she had met briefly on the stairs, and she and Matthew had discovered a common interest in Robert Louis Stevenson and, to their mutual surprise and delight, the life and times of Robert the Bruce.

After coffee she wandered up to the National Portrait Gallery or into a bookshop—Ulysses was happy with both these destinations—before returning to the flat for a light lunch. While Ulysses had his after-lunch sleep, Nicola read or did the ironing until it was time for her to collect Bertie from school. It was not a demanding routine, but it had its occasional salience and she took great pleasure in the thought that not only was she helping Stuart in an almost impossible spot, but it was also giving her the time to get to know her grandchildren.

For Bertie, the arrangement was perfect: just as he had hoped she would do, Nicola had cancelled his psychotherapy sessions indefinitely, had contacted the yoga teacher to withdraw him from Yoga for Tots, and had suspended music lessons until further notice. Moreover, not a word of Italian had been spoken, although she had taught him the occasional Portuguese expression, mostly ones that could be used to express irritation or to put a curse on somebody one did not like. "Not that we should ever do that, Bertie," she had warned him. "But it's good to have these things up one's sleeve for an emergency, you know."

There were two highlights of the day, both of which occurred in the evening. One was the bath that Bertie always took after his supper and before bedtime. Under Irene, this had been a rather brisk experience, involving only a few inches of lukewarm water and not lasting very long; under Nicola it had been transformed by the addition to the water of a large quantity of Portuguese bubble-bath liquid that she had brought with her. This was so effective that it filled the bath to overflowing with foam, and Bertie was allowed to throw this foam around to his heart's content. "It's only foam," said Nicola. "Foam never harmed anything."

Ulysses was allowed to join in these baths, shrieking with delight and often disappearing under mountains of foam for several minutes until located again by Bertie. All this was allowed to happen while Nicola made herself a martini in the kitchen and listened to classic recordings of Italian opera. Bertie liked the sound of opera drifting through to the bathroom. "Puccini!" he would cry, tossing foam into the air. "Verdi! Rossini!" He amused himself by transposition: "Puverdi! Versini! Rosscini!" bringing gales of laughter from Ulysses, somewhere under the foam.

After the bath, which often lasted a good three-quarters of an hour, it was time for bed for both of them. Ulysses was settled first, and while this happened Bertie read in his room. *Scouting for Boys*, previously hidden under the bed to avoid Irene's censorship, was now openly perused, along with other literary contraband including unexpurgated Enid Blyton and the formerly banned *Just William* novels. But this literary fare, compelling though it was, paled beside the story that Nicola began for Bertie once the light was switched out. Sitting on his bed in the dark, she held his hand as she related a story that she had conjured up especially for him, the story of *Fersie MacPherson, the Scottish Person.*

Bertie listened entranced. Fersie MacPherson, the Scottish Person, lived in Lochaber and earned his living through prize money won at various Highland Games. He could toss a caber further than anybody in all Argyll, and was adept at other trials of strength conducted at Highland Games up and down the country.

"He was a good man too," said Nicola. "He would never tolerate any bad behaviour by anybody. If he saw any of that he put an immediate stop to it."

"How?" asked Bertie. He was thinking of Tofu, who behaved badly and presumably would never be tolerated by Fersie MacPherson.

"Oh," said Nicola. "He biffed them. Biff! And that put a stop to that."

Bertie listened open-mouthed and in silence. "I bet they respected him," he said at last.

"Oh they did," said Nicola. "Immensely."

39. *Do Something, Stuart*

The changes brought about by Nicola touched every area of Bertie's life, including those of diet and clothing. As far as diet was concerned, while Nicola subscribed to the general principles of healthy eating, she did not believe—as Irene did— that anything a child would naturally appreciate was suspect. So pizzas, never permitted under Irene, were now allowed—in moderation, and accompanied by something healthy. Bertie was quite content with this: broccoli or curly kale were perfectly palatable when served on the same plate as a slice of glutinous, cheesy pizza topped with pepperoni. Other foods were put on the table without any accompanying vegetables: macaroni, approved of by Irene as long as it was eaten either plain or with the merest hint of butter, was smothered by Nicola with melted cheese and copious quantities of tomato sauce, much to Bertie's delight.

But it was the wardrobe reforms that Bertie most welcomed. When Nicola first explored the cupboard in his room she had expressed shock at what she found.

"Are you sure that these are all the clothes you have, Bertie?" she asked. "Do you wear pink dungarees every day?"

Bertie nodded. "There are three pairs," he explained. "That means one pair can be in the wash and I still have two."

"Yes," said Nicola, "but surely you need other trousers. One can't wear dungarees all the time."

Bertie was silent. He agreed: one can't, but one did.

Nicola peered into the recesses of the cupboard. "You don't have any jeans," she said. "I thought that everybody had jeans."

Bertie looked down at the floor. His grandmother was right: everybody had jeans—except him. Even the Prime Minister had a pair of jeans: he had seen a photograph of him in the newspaper and he had clearly been wearing jeans.

Nicola reached out to touch her grandson's arm. "Would you like some jeans, Bertie?"

He nodded. He was close to tears. He did not want to be different from everybody else; he wanted to be the same.

"I think we should go shopping—you and I," said Nicola. "We could get some jeans. What colour would you like?"

"Blue," said Bertie, his voice barely audible. To talk about things like that too loudly—miraculous things like blue jeans—could be to invite disappointment.

"Then blue the jeans shall be," said Nicola.

She explored the cupboard once more. "And a kilt? Don't you have a kilt?"

Bertie caught his breath. In his mental list of wants, a kilt had always been second only to a Swiss Army penknife. "I'd love to have a kilt," he said, adding, "Ranald Braveheart MacPherson has a kilt."

Nicola smiled. "Ranald Braveheart MacPherson? He sounds like quite the boy."

"He's my friend," said Bertie. "He lives in Church Hill and his dad has tons of money. He has a safe where he keeps it. Ranald showed it to me."

"How interesting," said Nicola. "And he has a kilt?"

"Yes," said Bertie. "He gave me a shot of it once when I was at his house."

"And you liked it?"

"Yes. I liked it very much."

Nicola looked thoughtful. "Did you ever ask Mummy for a kilt?"

Bertie hesitated. Then he replied, "Yes. I asked her three times. But every time she said no. She said that she disagrees with tribalism, and kilts are all about tribalism."

"Oh really!" Nicola burst out. She checked herself immediately. "Does Daddy have a kilt? He used to have one, you know. When he was at school he wore a kilt quite often."

"Daddy had one," said Bertie. "But Mummy cut it up."

Nicola's eyes narrowed. "Mummy cut up Daddy's kilt?"

"Yes. She made it into cushions."

Nicola struggled to control herself. "And did Daddy mind?"

Bertie thought for a moment. "I think he may have minded, but I can't be sure."

"Why can't you be sure, Bertie?"

"Because I think Daddy's scared of Mummy. So I don't think he'd tell her he was cross when she made his kilt into cushion covers."

Nicola closed her eyes. You don't interfere in your child's marriage, she told herself—you just don't. Your child makes his bed and then he has to lie in it. And yet, and yet . . . how could Stuart tolerate all this? How could he live with this ghastly, overbearing woman with her absurd ideas and the tyranny . . . yes, the tyranny that went with them? How could he? Was Stuart *that* weak?

She opened her eyes again. Bertie was looking at her with that direct, innocent stare that she found so endearing. She wondered just how much of all this he picked up; he was a highly intelligent little boy—prodigiously intelligent, she thought—and surely he must understand at least a little of what was going on. And yet he was so loyal; he did not want to criticise his mother directly, in spite of what must be the most extreme provocation.

She realised that she would have to reach a decision. She had kept out of Stuart's marriage but now things were different: she was Bertie's grandmother and she was responsible for him, at least temporarily. That position gave her the standing, she felt, to do all that she thought was necessary for his welfare—and that was to give this poor child a life. It was as simple as that. He was being denied everything that a small boy might want. He was a victim of some bizarre theory of child-raising. That woman was . . . that woman was half-mad.

"Bertie," she said, "tomorrow you and I will go and buy some jeans—some blue jeans. Then we shall get you a kilt." She paused. "And is there anything else you want?"

Bertie's eyes widened. Nobody had ever asked him this before.

"A Swiss Army penknife," he said. And then added, "Please. If possible."

Nicola winced, and Bertie noticed. "No, not really," he said quickly. "I don't really want one. I've changed my mind."

Nicola watched him. This was extraordinary. What seven-year-old boy would have the sensitivity to see that his request had put her in a difficult position? It was one thing to buy one's grandson a pair of jeans and a kilt—it was another thing altogether to buy him a penknife.

"Well, in that case we'll concentrate on the jeans and the kilt," said Nicola. "You can talk to Daddy about the penknife."

Bertie shook his head. "I don't think I can talk to him about that," he said. "Daddy can't do anything about it."

Nicola turned away; she did not want Bertie to see her expression. She wondered whether there was anything she could do to give Stuart some backbone. He was her son, after all, and surely a mother could talk to her son about such things. Yes, she would talk to him and give him the advice that he needed. But what exactly was that? The words came into her mind unbidden: *Do something about this, Stuart—just do something. Anything. Anything at all.*

40. *The World According to Bruce*

Matthew had not seen Bruce for some months. The last time they met, which was by accident in George Street, Bruce had been about to enter a bar with people whom Matthew vaguely recognised but did not really know. He had acknowledged Bruce with a nod of the head and a halfhearted wave, but he did not want to get involved with the rowdy, exuberant crowd. They were, he knew, the friends with whom Bruce had worked in his days as a surveyor, and Matthew, now a father of three—*father of three!* he thought, with a sinking feeling of respectability—had neither the time nor inclination to prop up a bar with this group, discussing the fortunes of the various rugby clubs to which they almost certainly would belong. Those days, he said to himself, are past now, and in the past they must remain . . . He stopped. The words had entered his mind insidiously, the accompaniments of a musical meme, as some might call it. They were from *Flower of Scotland*, which Bruce and his friends would sing so volubly at Murrayfield Stadium as they watched poor Scotland go down to another defeat in the Six Nations Rugby Tournament; they referred, of course, to the Battle of Bannockburn which took place, in the minds of so many, only yesterday (1314). Edward II, a bully like his father, had no business interfering with Scotland, and had got his just desserts. Naturally one would not wish to be thought to be making too much of that enmity between England and Scotland today—hence the words of the song— *Those days are past now, and in the past they must remain*, although one could, so easily, mischievously add the line . . . *but we can still mention them—every now and again.* It scanned rather well and it fitted the tune too. Matthew smiled. He would sing those words next time and see if anybody noticed them; he might even start something; after all, folk songs had to start with somebody.

On that occasion, Matthew and Bruce had exchanged only a few words: "Must dash, sorry, let's catch up some time soon," and "Great idea. Cool. Why not?"

At the end of this brief and unimaginative conversation, Matthew had noticed that there was something unusual about

Bruce's appearance and, after a second or two, had realised that Bruce only had one eyebrow.

"What happened?"

"What do you mean what happened?"

"To your . . ." He pointed to his own, intact eyebrow.

Bruce shook his head. "Waxing accident," he muttered, and had broken off to join his friends inside the bar. "Can't tell you the whole story just now."

He had been puzzled, wondering how a whole eyebrow might be pulled off by mistake. Was the entire face covered with wax in some awful reenactment of the making of a death mask? Or was it merely a question of eyebrow-plucking that had gone awry, perhaps as a result of the overenthusiasm of the eyebrow-plucker?

Now, as Matthew met Bruce in the Cumberland Bar, he saw that the missing eyebrow had grown.

"So," said Bruce, as he came up to the table where Matthew was waiting for him. "How goes it, old fruit?"

Matthew did not like being addressed as old fruit, but he concealed his displeasure and gave Bruce a welcoming smile. "Not too bad." And then, to add cliché to cliché, to pile Pelion upon Ossa, he added, "Can't complain."

Bruce signalled to the barman to pour him a pint of beer, and then sat down opposite Matthew. "Fatherhood treating you all right? Any more, or is it still three?"

"That's it," said Matthew.

"Have you been to the vet?" asked Bruce. "You know what I mean? Snip, snip."

Matthew shook his head, grinning weakly. It was no business of Bruce's, or of anybody else.

"It's a real indignity," Bruce said. "The humiliation that we undergo for women. What we do for them . . ."

Matthew thought that that particular burden fell disproportionately on women. "But they're the ones who have to . . ." he began. He trailed off. "It's far more difficult for them . . ."

Bruce laughed. "Don't believe the propaganda, Matty-boy. Women have it easy—dead easy. Who does all the work round here? Who has to slave away every day to keep some woman at home, drinking coffee and exchanging the latest goss?" He reached across the table to tap Matthew on the chest. "We do, Matthieu—it's us. The chaps. We get a really raw deal."

Matthew's response was mild. "I don't think so," he said. "Most women work these days, don't they? My accountant's a woman. My lawyer's a woman. My hairdresser is a woman. My . . ."

Bruce interrupted him. "All of the things you mentioned are women's work," he said. "Soppy stuff. I'm talking about *real* work."

Matthew's eyes widened. "Soppy stuff? Are you serious?"

"Never more serious," said Bruce. "Girly stuff. Same difference. I'm talking about jobs that require a spot of the old testosterone. Flying a plane, for instance . . ."

Matthew remembered something he had read about women pilots. "But there are plenty of female pilots," he said. "I was reading the other day that they're actually safer, because they take fewer risks."

"Lies," said Bruce immediately. He laughed, as if he had just remembered something. "Imagine what they'd be like at parking planes? Or reversing them?"

Matthew looked at the floor. He could not look at Bruce directly—at the *en brosse* haircut with its clove-scented gel and the opinions that seemed to suit that haircut so very well. "You shouldn't say things like that," he muttered.

Bruce stared at him. "Shouldn't speak the truth? Is that what you're saying to me, Matteo? More PC speech control? Is that it?"

Matthew decided to let the matter slip. "You can say what you like," he said.

"Oh thank you!" said Bruce sarcastically. "Thanks for the permission." He paused. "You're like the rest of them, Matthew. You've been suppressed. You've let women run all over you, telling you what to do, what you can and cannot think. You may not have had the old two snips treatment but you're well and truly neutered, you know."

Matthew shook his head. "Let's move on," he said.

"You're a eunuch now," said Bruce. "God, it's depressing . . . Women stick their noses into everything we say or do."

Matthew saw his chance. "I was going to tell you about one of these women," he said.

41. The Ethics of Temptation

Matthew took a deep breath. He could not remember when he had last been quite this tense. He had always felt anxious when faced with examinations, and at the beginning of his university finals he had almost passed out at the entrance to the examination hall. Then, much more recently, he had felt full of trepidation immediately before Angus Lordie's wedding, when he had acted as best man and had tried to make up for all of his friend's oversights. And of course he had felt shell-shocked when Elspeth had given birth to triplets . . . but on all of these occasions his anxiety had had nothing to do with the fact that he was actually doing something wrong . . . and now he was.

What he was about to do was wrong because it involved deception, even if his motive was to help Pat and her father. He had agreed to approach Bruce with a view to proving that Dr. MacGregor's Czech fiancée was after his money. It was, then, an errand of mercy of a sort—but how many such errands were accompanied by something quite as . . . He searched for an adjective . . . quite as *low* as this?

He had tried to rationalise. Why, he asked himself, should people stand by when people showed themselves to be on the point of making a really bad decision? If you were walking along a path and you saw somebody on the point of taking a wrong turning—about to turn off onto a path that you knew went over a cliff—would you not be justified in doing something to prevent him, even if it involved grabbing him or bringing him down with a rugby tackle? The end justified the means, did it not? Or was the end/means point raised here by those who wanted to show that the end never justified the means? That possibility unsettled him.

The answer, he decided, lay in the relationship between ends and means, in the balance of evils. If you had to kill one person to save fifty, would you do it? A suicide bomber is walking down the street intent on reaching a group of innocent people at the other end. You have the suicide bomber in the sights of your high-powered rifle; all you need to do is to pull the trigger and the mortal danger facing the fifty is averted. Would I pull the trigger, Matthew asked himself. Of course I would; who wouldn't?

There were at least some who would say no, who would argue that the prohibition against taking life was absolute, that it would never be right to do something intrinsically wrong simply to prevent another doing something disastrous. That was the position of the pacifist, surely, and there were plenty of people who held those views, and held them strongly and sincerely. But would the pacifist witnessing the marching of innocent people into an execution pit not use force to overcome the guards and save the victims before the machine guns opened up? Perhaps not—but how could anybody with the slightest degree of moral imagination fail to be appalled by that failure?

He had thought this through and then felt vaguely ashamed of himself for even bringing up that particular analogy. This was not a matter of life and death—this was simply a matter of exploitation and dishonesty—if indeed it was that. Pat said that Anichka was mercenary, but was there any actual proof?

He thought of entrapment. Perhaps it was better to think of this as an attempt to recruit an agent provocateur. An agent provocateur offered people the chance to do something forbidden or illegal and then, when somebody did it, he or she was arrested. The police used to do this in the days in which they spent their time trapping people into making sexual advances and then arresting them for it. It was a tawdry old trick. Or they offered them illegal drugs and then, when the offer was accepted, pounced.

Was there anything wrong in that? Matthew was sure that it was wrong to persuade people to do something they would not otherwise have done, but what if you were quite willing to do something and were just waiting for an opportunity—which then materialised? All that the agent provocateur was doing in such circumstances was revealing that you were, indeed, the sort of person who would buy drugs if given the chance, or who would deal in illegal weapons if somebody claimed to have a consignment, or would engage in any other illegal pleasures if somebody were kind enough to offer you them.

If Anichka fell for Bruce, then that showed that she was not prepared to be faithful to Dr. MacGregor. It was entrapment, yes, but Bruce could be told not to persuade her actively but simply to present an opportunity. There was a big moral distinction there, thought Matthew.

"Right," said Bruce. "What's this about a woman? Have you been misbehaving, Matsworth? Tut, tut—and you a father of three—so far, and presumably more in due course."

Matthew blushed. He did not like Bruce. He had never liked him. He had no idea why he should continue to consider him a friend.

"Not me," he said. "I'm married."

"Hah!" said Bruce. "So was Casanova."

"I'm telling you—it's not about me. It's about a woman who's planning to rip off Pat's father."

Bruce put down his glass of beer. "Pat MacGregor?"

"Yes."

Bruce looked serious. "Her old man was quite nice. I liked him. A shrink, isn't he? Up at the loony bin?"

"Yes," said Matthew. "Except that's not what they call it these days."

Bruce made a dismissive gesture. "Okay, funny farm then. Anyway, who's this broad and what's her angle?"

Matthew wanted to laugh at the Runyonesque expression. *Who's this broad* . . . "She's a Czech lady."

"From Czechoslovakia?"

"That doesn't exist any more. You've got two countries . . ."

Bruce brushed him aside. "Yeah, yeah. Your actual Czech whatever and your actual Slovenia."

"Slovakia."

"Slovenia, Slovakia, Slobonia . . . what's the difference? Anyway, who is she?"

"She's called Anichka and she's engaged to Pat's father."

Bruce whistled. "There's life in him yet. I really like it when oldies get hitched. Life doesn't stop at forty, it seems. There are pills that can keep you going."

Matthew bit his tongue. Hateful creep, he thought. Ghastly Bruce. You don't *deserve* to have two eyebrows.

42. *The Canny Man's Plan*

Bruce stared at Matthew. Very slowly, he started to smile. The smile was a smug one.

"I think I know what you're going to ask me," he said. "Am I right, or am I right?"

Matthew's irritation at Bruce's turn of phrase was mollified by the sudden realisation that he might not have to spell out what he and Pat wanted of him. "You're probably right," he replied.

Bruce sat back in his chair. "So," he said, "you want me to . . . how shall I put it? You want me to distract this woman."

Distract, thought Matthew. *Yes, that was one way of putting it.*

Bruce looked triumphant. "You're pretty transparent, Matt, you know. I could see what you had on your mind, nae bother." His smile became an enthusiastic grin. "So you want me to meet this chick. She takes one look at me and goes weak at the knees. MacGregor *père* sees what's going on and puts two and two together. Gives her her papers. Problem solved." He paused. "That's what you had in mind, right?"

Matthew was surprised by his own sense of relief. For some reason it seemed to make a major difference that Bruce should articulate the plot for himself; it was as if it were his own idea, which made a moral difference, didn't it? If somebody does something without its being actually suggested, then does the person who *would have* suggested it, had he had the opportunity, bear any responsibility for what happens? Matthew thought not; or, if there were some responsibility, then it would be considerably less than the responsibility that flowed from a suggestion actually made.

"Not a bad idea," said Matthew, as if it were Bruce who had come up with the scheme.

The disingenuousness was blatant, and most people would have disclaimed credit for the plan, attributing it, quite rightly, to those who first thought of it—Pat and Matthew. But Matthew knew that Bruce would never resist basking in any credit on offer.

"Thanks, Matt." He frowned, adding, after some hesitation, "What's she like?"

"I haven't actually met her," said Matthew. "But I gather she's attractive enough. She's much younger than Dr. Mac-Gregor."

Bruce seemed reassured. "Not that it matters to me, of course. Sense of duty, you see. Anything for the cause."

"Of course," said Matthew. "It's really good of you, Bruce."

Bruce made an airy gesture. "No sweat," he said, and then added, "Where and when?"

Matthew and Pat had already discussed this. Now he explained to Bruce that Pat would have a dinner party in her flat and would ask her father and Anichka. Bruce would be invited, along with one or two others, and Pat would make sure to seat Anichka next to him at the table. "Thereafter, it's up to you. Maybe you could arrange to meet her in a bar somewhere. Then, once you've set up the date and she's accepted . . ."

". . . Which is likely," interjected Bruce.

Matthew tried to conceal his feelings. What was it like, he wondered, to be so utterly and completely pleased with yourself, to be so sure that others would like you as much as you liked yourself? It was a gift possessed by infants, puppies, and young men like Bruce.

"You've set up the date," Matthew continued. "You tell Pat where and when . . ."

"The Canny Man's," interrupted Bruce. "They have this dining section at the back."

"All right. You book the table for a certain time and you let Pat know. She asks her dad to a film at the Dominion. Then she suggests getting a bite to eat afterwards. Carefully timed, of course."

Bruce was enjoying himself. "They come in and find that what's-her-name . . ."

"Anichka."

"All right, they see Anichka sitting with me looking at me with mute adoration . . ."

Matthew could not stop himself from bursting out laughing. There was no end, it seemed, to Bruce's self-regard.

Bruce looked puzzled. "I said something funny?"

Matthew adopted a straight face. "No, I was just thinking of their reaction—that's all."

"Oh yes," said Bruce. "She sort of jumps back—you know, like this—and acts all innocent. But of course Pat's old man, being a shrink, is too switched-on to be fooled."

"That's right."

"So he does the mathematics and he realises that this Annetta . . ."

"Anichka."

". . . that this Anichka is bad news. End of engagement."

Matthew nodded.

Bruce rubbed his hands. "Very funny. Serves her right."

It occurred to Matthew then that Bruce actually did not like women. He was a misogynist—of course he was! He should have seen it before, but now he understood perfectly. Like all great lady-killers, he did not like women. And it was not that he liked men—not in that way: his sexual tastes were as they were advertised to be, but they were not accompanied by any feeling for women as people.

Now Bruce looked thoughtful. "One thing," he said. "What's in it for me?"

Matthew was momentarily at a loss for a response. But then something within him rebelled. "Why do you even ask that?" he snapped. "Hasn't it occurred to you that you might do this just to help Pat—and Dr. MacGregor too? Isn't that enough?"

Bruce flinched. "Okay, okay, keep your hair on, Matthieu! I was just asking. We can't all be St. Francis."

Matthew swallowed. "Sorry, I didn't mean to bite your head off. It's just that Pat's worried sick about this."

Bruce smiled. "You care for her, don't you?"

"Yes, I do. She's a nice girl."

Bruce continued to smile. "Yes, she is. I wish she'd be nice to me." He paused. "I mean, nice in a nice sort of way."

Matthew closed his eyes. He could not believe that Bruce would be expecting . . .

Bruce laughed. "Only joking. No, I'm happy to be able to help her," Bruce continued, "for nothing. Pro bono."

"Yes," said Matthew. "Pro bono, just as you say."

"Virtue is its own reward, isn't it, Mathsbury?"

Matthew reached for his glass of beer and took a sip. "What exactly are you doing these days, Bruce? I've lost track, I'm afraid."

Bruce pointed to the ceiling. "My career's taking off big time," he said.

"Doing what?"

"I've bought a wine bar."

"Oh?"

"Yes. There's this guy I was at school with—at Morrison's. His uncle owned a wine bar in Dundee and one in Edinburgh. The uncle wanted to retire and he said he'd sell the Edinburgh one to his nephew. He had another buyer for the Dundee place."

"So your friend bought it?"

"He had no cash and that's where I came in. I had a bit of dosh to invest, and so I bought most of it. I own eighty percent and he has twenty. We split the profits fifty-fifty, but he has to do all the work."

"Very satisfactory," said Matthew. "For you, that is."

"Too true," said Bruce. "But then that's the way things are, isn't it? You have to look after *numero uno*, in this case *moi*."

Matthew did not answer. What's the point? he asked himself. And the answer, of course, was: none. But then he turned to Bruce and said, "What's this place called?"

"Bruce's," said Bruce. "Natch."

43. *Tiny Slivers of Favour*

The invitation was addressed to both Angus and Domenica. *The Lord Provost requests the pleasure of your company at a reception to mark the appointment of this year's Artist in Residence, at the City Chambers, the High Street, Edinburgh.*

Domenica held it up to the light, and smiled. "Seems genuine enough."

"But I don't know him," said Angus. "Do you?"

She did, but not particularly well. "He's good news—I rather approve of him." She looked thoughtful. "We've been lucky with civic leaders. The last two—the woman and the tall man—both did a good job. And now the current one is good as well. We've been fortunate." She paused. "Look at London. Look at some of their local politicians."

"The one with the hair? Or the one who kept newts?"

"I wasn't necessarily thinking of them. They're all right. I was thinking of some of the rotten boroughs."

"Local politics is not about point-scoring against the other side," said Angus. "That's why it's better than Westminster politics."

Domenica raised an eyebrow. "Or Holyrood?"

"Oh, I don't know . . ."

She frowned. "A country that ignores the advice of its own judges should ask itself some searching questions . . . We Scots love to boast about how marvellous we are but we don't sit down and look at ourselves critically. We think we do, but we don't. We prefer, you see, the security of our preconceptions, our prejudices."

"If we have problems with the Scottish Parliament," said Angus, "I think it's something to do with the way Holyrood's debating chamber is laid out. It's a sort of semicircle, isn't it? That's not ideal."

Domenica looked surprised. "You're not suggesting that the Westminster layout is better? Two sides facing each other and shouting and waving order-papers in each other's face. Surely not."

"Well, you might just be surprised," said Angus. "It's fashionable to say that system is dysfunctional, but are the alternatives any better? Is our standard of debate higher? Is our committee system more effective?"

He waited for an answer that was not forthcoming. "Whatever view one takes on that," he continued, "people thought it would be helpful to have a different system."

"Really? I don't see why."

"Because people can't relate to one another if they are sitting in a line. They just can't. And the arrangement there consists of rows of people, shoulder to shoulder—to all intents and purposes."

She waited for this to continue. Angus was unpredictable in his views, and this was not one she had heard before.

Angus sucked air through his teeth. It was a habit of his, and Domenica was going to speak to him about it—but not just yet. Some habits are best left uncommented upon until at least one's fifth wedding anniversary; they had been married for barely a year. The sucking of air through the teeth, it appeared, was an aid to deliberation.

"Look at how uneasy people are when they live on long streets," he said. "They don't relate to their neighbours; they don't even know their names, in many cases. But put them in a courtyard—a square—and everybody knows everybody else—and looks out for them. That architect I've talked to you about . . ."

"Christopher Alexander?"

"Yes, him. He explains all this in his *Pattern Language* book. He very specifically says that happiness and courtyards go together. It's the same as having light come into a room from two sources." He looked intensely at Domenica, as if he wanted to convince her of something. "It's all related, you see, Domenica. How we behave towards one another is mediated by our environment, by what we see about us."

"And good debating chambers lead to good government? Is that what you're saying?"

Angus nodded. "They play a role. Yes. A square or a rectangle is a comfortable shape for people. A long line has no resolution."

"No resolution?"

"A long line goes nowhere. It doesn't resolve." He paused. "That's why a meeting always goes better if people are sitting round a square table—looking at one another. You can talk to somebody you're looking at. You can talk to people on either side of you—or you can, but it doesn't lead to comfortable exchanges."

Angus picked up the invitation again. "Why do you think he's asking us?"

"Well, you have a reputation as a portrait painter," said Domenica. "Perhaps this new artist in residence is interested in portraiture."

Angus shook his head. "Highly unlikely. Nobody's interested in portraiture anymore. Nobody."

"But they are," protested Domenica. "Look at Lucien Freud. And Hockney."

"They're both considered to belong to an earlier generation," said Angus despondently. "No, it's all conceptual now."

"Shall we go?"

Angus hesitated. He received few invitations, and this was, after all, a reception in the City Chambers. It was not quite an invitation to the Garden Party at the Palace of Holyroodhouse, but it was the next best thing. Indeed, it might even be considered rather better than the Royal Garden Party, at which all that the guests received was a cup of tea, a slice of cake, and a couple of cucumber sandwiches. Not that this was indicative of parsimony on the part of the monarchy: it spent a fortune on tea and sandwiches each year, and Angus had seen the figures. Twenty thousand sandwiches at each garden party; twenty thousand slices of cake; twenty-seven thousand cups of tea—that was hospitality on a grand scale, dispensed to citizens whose good works had attracted attention.

So might a lifetime spent manning a lifeboat or running girl guide camps be rewarded with an afternoon of glory at Holyroodhouse, with a heavy card invitation commanding attendance and a sticker to put on your car allowing you to park in the royal car park. The card invitation was of a thickness specially chosen to allow it to be displayed on a mantelpiece for a good twelve years, and the car sticker, although by the nature of things flimsier, could be left on display for several weeks after the day of the Garden Party.

These were small things—tiny slivers of favour and privilege—but they were enough to turn at least some heads. One man had been seen driving up and down the High Street with a Garden Party sticker eight or nine times day, enjoying the admiring and envious stares of visitors and locals alike, and the sticker had remained in place for weeks thereafter.

"I see you're having trouble getting your parking sticker off," remarked a colleague of the offender. "Soap and water works, you know."

That was an unkind remark, even if amusing to those who heard it. We all wish to feel just a little bit important, to be recognised, to be singled out for attention, and for some of us a parking sticker may be all we have to cling to.

44. *The Decline of the Dinner Party*

In the taxi, on the way to the Lord Provost's reception in the City Chambers, Angus said, "I know we said we'd go. I know we've sent in our RSVP, but I'm not sure that I want to go after all."

"Come, come, Angus," said Domenica lightly. "You'll enjoy yourself once you're there—you always do."

She was concerned that Angus was becoming a stick-in-the-mud. She liked parties and hoped that now that they were married they might get a few more invitations. Say what people might, a woman on her own was often left out of things; many felt excluded, particularly widows and divorcées, who frequently felt uncertain as to where they fitted in. Domenica, although of independent mind, had thought that keenly; now, though, that there was a new entity, *Domenica and Angus*, she hoped that invitations that previously did not arrive would soon start to flood in.

Of course, there were all sorts of reasons for a paucity of invitations. One of these sprang from a change in people's social habits. Dinner parties, a staple of the social scene for those over forty, had become rarer with each year that passed. Domenica realised that this might be simply an instance of observer bias or even ignorance of all the facts; Aristotle had suffered from this, having said that moles were blind—which is not completely true—only because he never succeeded in finding their minute eyes. For this reason you might have to be careful about saying that there were fewer dinner parties; there might be just as many as before, but you might not be invited and therefore would not know about them.

But no, she was sure that an entirely objective observer would conclude that dinner parties were on the decline, and once that fact was accepted, the interesting issue arose as to why this should be so.

She and Angus had discussed this only a few weeks earlier.

"People are just a whole lot busier," Angus ventured. "They're tired at the end of the week. They want to put their feet up."

"Yes," said Domenica. "And holding a dinner party involves a lot of work. You have to plan. You have to go to Valvona & Crolla to get food. You have to cook. And then you have to wash up. That all takes time."

"Yes, it does. A lot of time."

"And more women these days tend to have jobs. They have to work *and* they have to run a household." She paused, looking at Angus as the taxi chugged its way up Hanover Street. It was an older Edinburgh taxi and the seats were slightly uncomfortable; newer taxis believed in padded seats, while the earlier models were made of sterner stuff.

She caught the driver's eye in the mirror. There was a brief moment of understanding: the driver was a woman and had overheard the conversation.

"Of course," Domenica continued, "there's no reason why men shouldn't do all the cooking."

The taxi driver glanced in the mirror again.

"Don't you agree?" Domenica said to the back of the other woman's head.

"Oh, I do," said the driver. "My man does nothing in the kitchen. Nothing."

"You cook everything?" asked Domenica.

Angus squirmed.

"Aye, I do. And I hold down this driving job. And I've got three kids."

Domenica pursed her lips before making her next remark. "Well, there you are," she said.

Angus sought to lead the conversation onto less awkward ground. "Money may play a part too," he said. "Having a dinner party is expensive."

Domenica agreed that this was so. "But it's not just time and money," she said. "I think there's something else going on."

"Namely?"

"It's to do with conversation," said Domenica. "Dinner parties are about conversation. You don't go to dinner with somebody to sit there and eat your meal silently. You go to a dinner party to converse."

"That's right," said Angus.

"And structured conversation is becoming rarer," Domenica continued. "People are talking to one another in a different way. Our conversations have become less formal."

"And isn't that a good thing?"

"Yes and no. There's obviously a role for informal conversation, but talk pretty quickly becomes superficial if there's no structure to it. A proper conversation is an exchange of ideas, and gets through the business in the same way as a well-run meeting. More is said, or rather, more of substance is said."

Angus thought about this. It was probably true. You had to have structure if elevated, intelligent speech was to occur. He thought of Dr. Johnson and his friend, Samuel Boswell, on their trip into Scotland.

"Dr. Johnson was your man for that, wasn't he? And Oscar Wilde."

"They were both good," said Domenica. "Though Wilde, I suspect, liked to hold court, dropping his aperçus very carefully at just the right moment, and watching their effect. Having a conversation with him might have been a bit one-sided, I think."

"Whereas Johnson?"

"He was prepared to listen. He was curious about what people had to say. Look at what Boswell wrote. Johnson was sometimes rude about Scotland, but he could not be accused of being uninterested. Nor could he be accused of not allowing others to have their say."

"Whereas most people don't?"

"I'm not sure that I would say that most people don't. I think, though, that many don't listen. A good conversation requires that both sides listen. It's like a game of tennis. The serve is returned and the points go backwards and forwards. That's what a conversation should be."

"But without the backhand?"

Domenica liked that. "Very clever, Angus. Wilde himself would have been proud. But, no, one probably doesn't want a backhanded remark in a good conversation. It's nasty, and it destroys the courtesy that good conversation requires. You shouldn't insult the person with whom you're exchanging ideas. You just shouldn't. Did you ever see William F. Buckley in action?"

Angus was unsure. He thought he might have seen him discussing something or other on television, but the memory was vague.

"He was famous for his television conversations," Domenica continued. "And although there was an exchange of views, he actually seemed to sneer. There was something about his mouth, his teeth, that gave one the impression of sneering at the people with whom he spoke."

"I can't stand sneering," said Angus.

Domenica was of the same view. "He met his match in Noam Chomsky, though. Chomsky was very courteous and just refuted Buckley's points, one by one. You can disagree in a conversation—you can disagree very strongly—but you must be courteous."

Angus thought about this. She was right. That was why our national conversation was so bad. Courtesy had been abandoned in favour of the put-down, the attack, the calculated sound bite. What sort of national conversation was that? The answer came to him immediately: none.

45. The Symbolism of the Sphinx

At the foot of Hanover Street, directly opposite the neo-classical Royal Scottish Academy with its honey-coloured array of columns, their taxi stopped at a red light.

"The thing about Edinburgh," Angus observed, "is that the gaze must be raised. If you walk about this city with your eyes downcast, you miss the point. Our skyline is so important."

Domenica had been looking down Princes Street, watching the crowds of evening shoppers on the pavements. Now she looked up.

"Queen Victoria," she said.

"Yes, there she is," said Angus. "Seated on top of the Academy, and flanked for some reason by sphinxes. Playfair added her—and the sphinxes—afterwards, I believe. I imagine he said to himself, *How about a few sphinxes?* Very strange. Have you given much thought to the sphinx symbolism, Domenica?"

She shook her head. "Never," she said. "We take the sphinx for granted, I suppose. We see a sphinx and think *Oh, there's a sphinx*, but we never ask what it's doing there. They're rather like cats, I've always thought. Rather agreeable creatures."

"Oh, don't get too close to a sphinx," said Angus, adopting a tone of mock warning. "Remember what the Sphinx got up to in Greek mythology. She asked people riddles and if they couldn't answer, she ate them. Oedipus came up against her at Thebes, did he not? He, of course answered the riddle and the Sphinx took frightful offence and self-destructed. A bit of an overreaction, but then if one is a sphinx I suppose one looks at things a bit differently."

"I suppose one does," agreed Domenica. "But why did Playfair put those stone sphinxes on top of the Royal Scottish Academy?"

"*Faute de mieux*," said Angus. "Or they may represent

something other than sphinxdom. I gather they were thought to represent wisdom and learning."

"Or they could have been put up there to scare the seagulls," suggested Domenica. "You know how people these days put plastic owls on their roof to keep seagulls from nesting? This may have been an early example of just that. A sphinx looks rather like a cat, doesn't it? So if you put two massive stone cats on top of the Royal Scottish Academy you'd have no trouble with seagulls, would you?"

Angus laughed. "Possibly."

The taxi began to move again, but stopped immediately to allow a man to complete his crossing of the road. Angus noticed that the man had a tattoo across the back of his neck—a tattoo that was given full exposure by the low cut of the T-shirt he was wearing. Angus noticed it, and gave a start.

Domenica looked round. "What?"

"That man. Look."

She followed his gaze. The man had reached the side of the road; shortly he would be swallowed up into the crowd of shoppers.

Domenica uttered a small cry of surprise. "My goodness! A sphinx!"

Angus craned his neck to get a final glimpse of the man and his extraordinary tattoo. He had only that glimpse, and it was a short-lived one. Now the taxi had started to move again and they were sweeping round the bend in the road that took them onto the foot of the Mound. He turned to face Domenica.

"What an amazing thing," he said. "There we were talking about sphinxes and that man . . ."

". . . had a large sphinx tattooed on his neck," she supplied.

"I feel quite unsettled by that," said Angus. "I know it's only a coincidence, but still . . ."

"I wouldn't read anything more into it," said Domenica.

He nodded. "And yet, I wonder why he chose the sphinx."

"Genre theory might throw some light on it," said Angus. "If there is a lot of something—images or ideas or whatever— it's often because they were expected within the genre."

Domenica looked puzzled.

"Take Chinese poetry," said Angus. "Scholars used to wonder why there were so many poems from certain periods— you know, ages ago, Tang Dynasty and so on—that all dealt with the same subject. There were poems about finding a strand of a mistress's hair on a pillow, or poems about losing a favourite apricot tree to frost. Hundreds of them, apparently. Was this because lots of poets had these experiences?"

Domenica looked thoughtful. "Possibly. I suppose Chinese poets had mistresses and mistresses do occasionally leave a strand of their hair on the pillow—that being the sort of thing mistresses like to do. Almost like establishing a territorial claim. My hair, my pillow, my poet . . ."

"No," said Angus. "It was because poets were required to write poems on certain subjects as part of their exams for the imperial civil service. They were exam or competition pieces."

"Ah!"

Angus warmed to his theme. "And there were genres, too, in Greek and Latin poetry. There were certain subjects that came up time and time again. And in art." He paused. "So in this case, you might well find the answer to your question in the design books of tattoo artists. There's probably a sphinx."

Domenica smiled. "Along with all the intertwined hearts and skulls?"

"Exactly. You'd like a sphinx? No problem. How's this sphinx here?"

Domenica looked out of the window. They were now level with the Old Sheriff Court and the statue of David Hume. "Why do people have tattoos?" she asked.

"Because, like all of us, they're searching for beauty."

"An odd way of doing that."

"In your view," said Angus. "But not in theirs. Remember we are the heirs of the Picts, and the Picts were so called because they were painted all over. Painted people. So that's where all this comes from. We're merely reverting to our previous enthusiasm for being painted."

"Beauty," mused Domenica.

"Yes," said Angus. "The search for beauty. It carries on, you know. We're all searching for beauty except for . . ."

"Yes? Except for?"

"Conceptual artists," said Angus. "That's why the Turner Prize is so absurd. It has nothing to do with the cultivation of the beautiful—which is what art should concern itself with. It's all about posturing and banality."

"Oh," said Domenica.

They were now outside the City Chambers and the conversation came to an end. Within the City Chambers, the Lord Provost awaited his guests for his little party.

46. *A Moment of Insight*

The room in which the reception was being held was already crowded by the time that Angus and Domenica arrived. Angus hesitated at the doorway, as if reluctant to enter the crowd of people, momentarily repelled by the wave of noise that greeted him. This was the sound of the conversations that were taking place across the room, each intelligible within a few feet of its occurrence but collectively a hubbub as opaque to the human ear as the sound of a flock of squabbling birds. Here and there a word or two achieved salience—*shocked rigid, European Parliament, corruption, barefaced lies, his birthday, drunk* . . . tags, in a sense, to hinterlands of exchange covering the concerns and preoccupations of those present.

What daunted Angus was the fact that everybody in the room seemed already to have found old friends. In groups of three or four they stood about, seemingly completely at ease, listening, smiling, laughing, expostulating on this and that. He had never understood how this happened. How could it be that the one hundred and twenty people present in the room should appear to know if not everybody else then at least a fair number of them? He considered himself sociable, and had even been for a brief time on the social committee of the Scottish Arts Club in Rutland Square, but when it came to gatherings such as this he felt as one might feel in an unfamiliar town where everybody was a stranger.

Domenica, who was unusually sensitive to the moods of others, felt his unease. "It's all right," she whispered. "There are bound to be people you know."

"There aren't," Angus replied. "There isn't a single soul here. Not one."

Her reply was brisk. "Nonsense, Angus. Look over there. There's Richard Neville-Towle, the conductor. See, over there. You know him. And there's James Holloway. And there's . . ." As she ran her eye round the room she recognised and identified guest after guest. Tam Dalyell. David Steel. Edward and Maryla Green. Duncan Macmillan. She reeled off the names, and as she did so, Angus's nervousness lifted like morning mist off a field.

"Oh well," he said. "We'll find somebody to talk to after all. What about a drink?"

"You go and find somebody," said Domenica. "I'll get us each a glass of wine."

Encouraged, Angus began to make his way through the throng that had developed at the door. On the other side of the room, from the windows facing north, a view of the city revealed itself: spiky rooftops, stone crenellations, angled expanses of dark grey slate, all touched with gold by the evening sun. His artist's eye caught the view and made him stop for a moment where he was, halfway across the room, and stare at what he saw. And for a moment he felt a strong sense of delight in belonging to this place, this city that vouchsafed to those who lived there, and to those who came in pilgrimage, sudden visions of such exquisite fragile beauty that the heart might feel it must stop. And it was his; it was his place, his home, and these people about him were no longer strangers but were bound to him in a brotherhood of place, sharers in the mystery celebrated there, right there, in the City Chambers on that summer evening.

Domenica returned with the glasses of wine.

"I bumped into the Lord Provost," she said. "I thanked him for the invitation."

"Good."

She gave him a sideways glance. "Are you all right?"

He turned to her, raising his glass half in toast to her, half to take a sip of wine. "I had an extraordinary experience," he said.

She frowned. "Right now? Here?"

He nodded. "I was walking over towards the window and my eye caught the view."

She glanced towards the window. "Edinburgh."

"Yes," he said. "But it was more than that. It was more than just a view of the city from up here. It was . . . How shall I put it? I felt as if I was being filled with something. I felt an extraordinary current pass through me."

He looked at her, embarrassed by what he had just said. But there was nothing mocking in her expression. "A mystical experience," she said.

"I don't know . . ."

She brushed aside his diffidence. "But of course it was, Angus. It was a moment of mystical insight."

"I'm not sure . . ."

"It can happen at any time," she went on. "We can be anywhere—out in the street, at home, climbing Ben Lawers, anywhere . . . and suddenly it comes to us, a sense of being at one with the world. Or it can be a sense of suddenly feeling a current of life that simply fills us with delight or warmth or . . . It can be anything, really."

He took another sip of his wine. Had he felt that? Had he suddenly felt at one with the world?

He felt prosaic once more. If he had indeed experienced a feeling of unity with the world, then the feeling had not lasted. "Are you sure?"

"Absolutely," she said. "You know that Auden had just such an experience? He uses it in his poem *A Summer Night*, but he described it later, in prose. It was when he was teaching at a school. He went to sit outside with a small group of colleagues, under the night sky, and suddenly he felt just what I think you felt a few moments ago. He had what amounted to a vision of *agape*, that pure disinterested love of one's fellow man that so many of us would love to find, but never do. And he said that the glow of this stayed with him for some days. Imagine that, Angus, you're sitting in a deckchair under the night sky and you suddenly realise that you love humanity. Imagine that."

He could. Now he could.

"Those lovely lines," said Domenica. "Those lines he wrote in that poem about those whom he loved lying down to rest." She paused. "Why are people so unkind to one another, Angus?"

He looked into his glass. "Because they don't open themselves to the feelings that banish unkindness. Because when a vision of *agape* comes to their door they keep it closed."

"Yes," she whispered. "Exactly."

She might have said more, but was interrupted by the arrival at their side of a fellow guest.

"Duke of Johannesburg," he said with a smile. Then turning to Angus he said, "You remember me, perhaps. Or perhaps not; it's so easy to forget that although we're at the centre of our own world we are often only on the periphery of the world of others."

47. A Cocktail Party in Moray Place Gardens

On the same evening that the Lord Provost was holding his party in the City Chambers, in another part of Edinburgh— Moray Place—a gathering of a very different nature was taking place. This was the summer cocktail party of the Association of Scottish Nudists, an event that was keenly anticipated by the members, even if the gathering was a clothed one. If the Association had its way, it would have opted to make it a naturist function—one in which no clothes were worn—but the committee that ran the gardens had, after some swithering, ruled that clothes should be worn because of complaints received from neighbouring streets. At the last occasion on which normal nudist rules had applied, a small group of jeering onlookers—described by one neighbour as "thoroughly undesirable types" and by another as "the keelies of the town"—had arrived to shout ribald and unflattering comments at the members of the Association. This had brought people to their windows, and one or two of the residents, who had not previously witnessed any of the Association's functions, had been unprepared for what they saw.

For the most part the members simply wore the clothes they would wear to any normal cocktail party, although one or two of the women wore shifts made of diaphanous voile that, in the right conditions, favoured translucence over opacity. Some of the men, moved by the same spirit of compromise, wore Bermuda shorts that exposed at least their knees and several inches below that until the long blue hose that complemented Bermuda shorts so well took over. But in spite of these nods in the direction of the flesh, the gathering was in no way different from any group of people meeting to discuss common interests and to share a glass of wine on a fine summer evening.

This was the first summer party to be held after the restructuring of the Association and the election of a new committee. The new chairman and secretary had made much of the changeover and had insisted on a complete revision of the order of proceedings and the menu of canapés. The wider membership, pleased at the ousting of the self-perpetuating Edinburgh clique that had run the Association since the nineteen-thirties, was pleased at this symbolic reordering. "Even the cocktail party needed change," a new committee member said. "This is all so much better, isn't it?"

That was not the view of the ousted Edinburgh committee.

Its members had seen no need for change, and felt insulted that their careful stewardship of the Association should now be portrayed as a selfish hanging on to power.

"They're not the most sophisticated people in the world," said one Edinburgh member. "Their horizons are distinctly limited, you know. I happened to mention the other day that the World Naturist Federation would be having its meeting in Croatia this year and one of them—one of these backwoodsmen—thought that Croatia was in the Caribbean."

"No!"

"Yes. And when something was said about the new *Ring Cycle* being done at Santa Fe—that new nudist version—one of them thought that the *Ring Cycle* was a bicycle race! Can you imagine that? A sort of *Tour de France sans pantalons*, so to speak."

"Hah! What a bunch of *ignorami*!"

"Yes indeed. But that's what we're up against."

There were other complaints voiced—privately at least—by the Edinburgh membership. One of these was the argument over the Association's name; the new committee had indicated that it was in favour of a name change at some point, although the precise nature of that name change had yet to be decided. The suggestion of Nudism Scotland had been briefly raised, but had not met with wide enough approval. More popular, though, had been the suggestion that the Association should be known as the Scottish Association of Nudists rather than the Association of Scottish Nudists, and this change had duly been set in motion.

"There is a difference," said one of the proponents of change. "The current name—the Association of Scottish Nudists—implies that the members are all Scots. That, I think, is too exclusive. There are members who are not Scottish by background but who live in Scotland and may wish to participate in the movement while here. If we call ourselves the Scottish Association of Nudists that means that we are a Scotland-based association of people who are nudists, but who may be of a different nationality. There could well be French nudists, say, in a Scottish Association of Nudists; they are not Scots—because they are French—but they are still members of an association that is Scottish in its domicile and outlook."

"There they go again," said the former secretary. "A perfectly good name sacrificed on the altar of political correctness."

This remark, delivered with a sigh of acceptance, was made at the cocktail party, as the former secretary and the former chairman gathered together a small huddle of Edinburgh members to share regrets over what had happened. When the former chairman finished his first glass of Cava, he felt emboldened to reveal the plan that he and the former secretary had already discussed privately.

"We need to keep this absolutely under wraps," he said. "But the time has come to act, and I need to let you in on the secret."

The huddle became tighter. One of its members cast an eye over his shoulder to make sure that no members of the new committee were approaching or were within earshot. "The coast's clear," he said.

"Right," said the former chairman. "This is the plan. Aberdeen is the key."

They looked at him blankly.

"In what respect?" asked one, a thin, rather mousy-looking woman from Silverknowes.

"At present there are very few members from Aberdeen," began the former chairman. "Barely more than ten."

"I think it's twelve," said the former secretary. "That's counting Huntly and Inverurie."

"Very few," said the former chairman. "But we could change that. We could try to swell the membership from Aberdeenshire. We could make it fifty or sixty—maybe even one hundred."

This brought looks of incredulity. "I doubt it," said a man who in his ordinary life was a senior fund manager.

The former chairman turned to smile at him. "But I think you're wrong, Jock," he said. "And I suggest we put it to the test. There's one of the Aberdeen members over there. I'm going to ask him to join us and we can put something to him."

He moved away to intercept the Aberdeen member, who was on his way to the drinks table.

"Could we have a word with you, William," he said. "Just a little idea we have."

48. *The Dastardly Plot is Revealed*

"Well, William, how are things up in Aberdeen?" asked the former chairman. "In the movement, that is?"

William Macdonald, the chairman of the Aberdeen branch, was a thickset man with a fresh, ruddy complexion. It was a face that seemed to have been buffeted by winds of the North Sea and in its directness of expression and equanimity it was one that inspired trust. It was the ideal face for the plan that the former chairman had in mind, provided that . . . the former chairman stopped to think. What he proposed to do was not exactly dishonest—at least in his view; it was more of a defensive move designed to rectify an entirely unjustifiable capture of power by a calculating and ruthless faction. They had been prepared to use extreme methods to secure their goal; he and his allies in Edinburgh were fully entitled, he thought, to use similar methods to fight back. The only question was this: would Aberdeen see things in the same way as Edinburgh?

The former chairman was something of a psychologist. Years ago, as an undergraduate at the University of St.

Andrews, he had included psychology in his studies for his MA degree. Since then he had maintained a dilettante's interest in the subject, fancying his ability to see through both clients and competitors in his small private-client legal practice.

He felt that he understood Aberdeen, which was not the same as Edinburgh or Glasgow, or indeed any other Scottish city. Aberdeen was canny. Aberdeen did not believe in showiness or waste. Aberdeen was modest in the conduct of business. Aberdeen did not waste words. Aberdeen was good at engineering, farming, and sheer hard work. Aberdeen, in short, was everything that Scotland used to be.

Now, in his conversation with William Macdonald, his shrewd understanding of Aberdeen came into play.

"Jist tchyaving awa," said William in answer to the former chairman's questions. "It's been waar."

This was what the former chairman had expected and wanted, as this gave him his cue.

"Well, I've had an idea, William, about how we can deal with a little problem that's cropped up in the Association. This business of the takeover . . ."

"I wisnae afa pleased wi that," said William. "Glasgow chiels are afa ill to deal wi."

The former chairman smiled—he could not have chosen better words himself.

"Yes," he said. "Showy bunch."

"We're nae impressed wi that in Aiberdeen."

"No, of course not. So perhaps you might like to join me in a little plan to . . . to get rid of them."

"Aye, fairly that," said William.

"Good, all that's required is that we expand the membership a bit . . . well, a great deal, actually, and then in the background we set up a new Association—one with the old name that they're so casually about to abandon." He paused. "You with me?"

"Aye, am I."

"Then," continued the former chairman, "once we have our new members enrolled in the current association we call an extraordinary meeting—at a time that might be difficult for our Weegie friends . . ."

"When they've all gone doon the watter, or something like that," said one of the others, to general laughter.

"A meeting sounds afa dear," said William.

"Don't worry, we'll pay," said the former chairman quickly before resuming his explanation. "Well, we call that meeting and we unseat the current committee and we put the old one back in—with you on that, of course, William, representing the fine city of Aberdeen, and then . . ." He paused for effect. "And then we sell the property in Moray Place to the new association we'd set up—it will use the old name, of course. Then we all resign and transfer our allegiance to the Association of Scottish Nudists—our old name, of course. We'll let the Glasgow crowd and their pals in the Scottish Association of Nudists keep the flat in Ainslie Place and a bit of the money, but we'll have the major asset, namely, the Moray Place premises. We'll sell the basement and use the proceeds to fund the Association. We'll be home and dry."

William considered this. "Div ye ken foo y'ere gan tae get aa these members?" he asked.

The former chairman smiled as he revealed his master stroke. "We'll advertise three years of free membership, only up north," he said. "No Aberdonian will be able to resist an offer like that—even if they have no intention of practising nudism."

William agreed. "Mercy, aye, they'd like that fine even if they aye haud on tae their claes!" Then he added, "I'll put a small ad in the *P&J*."

"Which of course we'll pay for," said the former chairman.

The matter was settled there and then.

"It's going to work," whispered the former chairman to the former secretary. "I was worried that he'd get on his moral high horse about it, but no sign of that."

"They're very pragmatic up there," said the former secretary.

"I do so love pragmatism," said the former chairman.

With the plot settled, they went their separate ways. The party was now in full swing, with a small jazz band striking up in one of the corners of the gardens and the Association's numerous bottles of Cava being circulated by the students hired to act as waiting staff. These students, who earned a bit of pin money working for a catering firm, were used to serving at various Edinburgh functions, but never before at a party of the Association of Scottish Nudists. Two of them, a young man and a young woman, both nineteen, took a short break from their waiting duties (they were allowed the occasional ten minutes to get their breath back) and did so behind some bushes at the edge of the gardens.

"Do you realise who these people are?" said the girl. "Would you have believed it?"

"I know," said the boy. "Seriously weird."

They were both silent for a few moments. Then the boy said, "Should we pretend we're members? Prance around. Just for a few minutes? Right here?"

Time seemed to stand still. A shaft of sunlight, filtered through the green of an overhanging branch of a tree, fell upon the boy's face, and upon the girl's forearm. Somewhere in a rhododendron bush a thrush burst into song, but briefly.

The girl smiled. "I don't think we've got time. And we might be caught before we had time to get our clothes back on."

"Yes," said the boy, with regret. In fact he would have a lifetime to regret this—as we all have a lifetime to regret that which we would have wished to do but did not do.

49. *Macbeth and Proportional Representation*

Bertie's grandmother had arranged that the promised purchase of his kilt should take place on a Saturday morning, as that would mean that Stuart could look after Ulysses while she and Bertie went to a kilt-maker on the High Street. Ulysses could have accompanied them in his pushchair, but Nicola understood that for Bertie this was a very significant trip and he would feel much more important were he to make it in her company alone. From her point of view, she was looking forward to the opportunity to get away from Ulysses for a short time, not that she disliked her younger grandson—well, when she came to think about it, she was not overly fond of him.

He could not help his tendency to bring up his food, of course; nor could he be blamed for his prolonged attacks of wind; it was just that there was a limit to the amount of time and energy one had and Ulysses somehow succeeded in using up much of that. Nicola did not complain about grandparental responsibilities—and indeed handled them rather well—but if given the chance to spend some time other than in the company of Ulysses she tended to take it.

Bertie's excitement over the expedition meant that he had got himself out of bed, had helped himself to breakfast, dressed, brushed his teeth and done his morning music practice by half past six. It was at that point that he took it upon himself to take his grandmother a cup of tea in her bedroom.

"My goodness," said Nicola, as she emerged from sleep. "Is that a cup of tea I see before me?"

"Macbeth asked whether it was a dagger," said Bertie. "It might have been better for him—and for Scotland—had it been a cup of tea."

Nicola sat up in bed, rubbing her eyes. She had not yet become used to just how advanced Bertie was, and she was still astonished when he made this sort of pronouncement.

"Have you read *Macbeth*?" she asked, as he handed her the teacup.

"Yes," said Bertie. "Mummy got it for me out of the library, and I read it all."

"Do you study Shakespeare at school?" asked Nicola, as she took a sip of her tea.

"No," said Bertie. "I do it by myself. Most of the people I know can't read yet. Tofu certainly can't. He says reading's rubbish."

"That's not true at all," said Nicola. "Tofu's going to grow up very ignorant, I fear."

"He's already ignorant," said Bertie.

"So it would seem," said Nicola. "And he does have a

very unusual name, doesn't he? Do you know any other boys called Tofu?"

Bertie shook his head. "Not at Steiner's," he said. "We've got a Sirius in my class. There's a girl called Quinoa in one of the senior classes. She lives in Stockbridge. Quinoa's a sort of grain, isn't it?"

"Yes," said Nicola. "But do you know why Tofu's called Tofu?"

"His dad is a very famous vegan," said Bertie. "He's written a book about nuts and he's converted his car to run on olive oil. Sometimes you can see him parked outside Valvona & Crolla filling the car up with olive oil."

"Very strange," said Nicola. "But back to *Macbeth*, Bertie, what did you think of it? Did you enjoy it?"

Bertie nodded. "I felt sorry for Macbeth," he said. "I think that Lady Macbeth made him kill King Duncan."

Nicola agreed. "She was a very manipulative woman, a bit like . . ." She stopped herself in time. She had almost said *like Mummy*, which would have been a tactless thing to say. But it is absolutely true, she thought; Irene *is* Lady Macbeth. Stuart had married Lady Macbeth.

"You know, Bertie," she went on, "Macbeth was probably quite a good king in real life. We're told that Scotland prospered under him. It was still a dangerous place, though. There was a lot of rivalry between the different factions—that's always been a big problem in Scotland. We fight with one another." She paused, thinking of the discourtesy that marred Scottish politics. "We do not have a particularly edifying political culture, Bertie, but at least we don't use claymores any more."

"Ranald's daddy went to a re-creation of the Battle of Bannockburn last year," said Bertie. "He said that there were people dressed up in armour. They had swords and lances too. He said that he didn't think they had proportional representation in those days, Granny."

"No indeed," said Nicola. "Now, Bertie, it's far too early to set off for the kilt-maker. They don't open until nine, you see. So I suggest that you sit quietly and read while I get up and get myself organised."

There was a small bedroom chair in Nicola's room and Bertie sat himself down on that. The book that Nicola had been reading lay on the floor beside the chair, and Bertie picked this up, examined the title and began to read.

"This is very sad," he said after a while.

"What's sad, Bertie?" asked Nicola, from behind her make-up mirror.

Bertie held up the book: Jean Findlay's biography of Charles Scott Moncrieff. "Mr. Scott Moncrieff went off to war in France and then he became sick and died. That's very sad."

"Well, he managed to do quite a lot in between going off to war and dying," said Nicola. "He translated Proust into English, for instance."

Bertie laid down the book. "Who's Proust?"

"Proust was a French writer," said Nicola. "He wrote about . . . well, he wrote about a lot of things. He paid great attention to the small details of life."

"Did he write about pirates?" asked Bertie.

Nicola smiled. "No, I don't think Proust wrote about pirates. He wrote about cakes, though—Madeleine cakes." She remembered something else. "He may not have written about pirates, but he did write about boats sometimes. He said something about steamships, as I recall."

Bertie's attention was engaged. "I like steamships a lot," he said. "Did Mr. Proust like them?"

"No," said Nicola. "He said that steamships insulted the dignity of distance."

"That's a very odd thing to say," said Bertie. Then he changed the subject. "Do you like martinis, Granny?"

Nicola looked sideways at her grandson. She did like martinis, but what had possessed him to ask?

It was as if Bertie had intercepted her unexpressed question. "Because Mummy says you have a weakness for them. She says that you probably have them for breakfast—but I've never seen you eating martinis for breakfast."

"You don't eat martinis, Bertie," said Nicola indulgently. "You drink them."

"Then you do have them for breakfast," said Bertie, quite politely. "I've seen you."

50. *On the Way to the Kilt-Maker*

They walked to the kilt-maker's shop, which was in a small close off the High Street. Their route took them up Dublin Street, where Bertie explained to his grandmother about the importance of not stepping on cracks in the pavement.

Nicola laughed. "I remember that so well," she said. "When I was your age, Bertie, we used to think that bears would get you if you trod on a crack. I remember really believing that, you know."

"There are no bears, Granny. I don't think you need to worry."

"Oh. I'm not worried, Bertie."

Bertie frowned. "But you should still be careful not to step on a crack."

"But if there are no bears," said Nicola, "then why should you be careful?"

"Because stepping on a crack harms the immune system," answered Bertie.

Nicola looked at him with astonishment. He had been quite

serious. Where on earth did her grandson, this remarkable little boy, get ideas like that—and the words to express them?

"Mind you," continued Bertie, "sometimes you can't help stepping on the cracks in Edinburgh. There are so many, you see. The Government has run out of money, I think. They've kept saying there's lots and lots of money, but I think when they went to look in the safe there wasn't very much. None, in fact."

Nicola smiled. "How interesting. Did Daddy tell you that?" Bertie nodded.

"Well, well!" said Nicola. "What an interesting insight to get."

They reached the top of Dublin Street. "This is where Queen Street starts," said Bertie. "I used to go to psychotherapy down at the other end. I used to have a psychotherapist called Dr. Fairbairn. He's the one who looks like Ulysses—or rather, Ulysses looks just like him."

"Even more interesting," muttered Nicola. "Did Mummy like Dr. Fairbairn, Bertie?"

"Oh yes," replied Bertie. "She used to talk to him for ages while I sat in the waiting room. Sometimes when I went for my psychotherapy Mummy used up all the appointment and I only had five minutes at the end. I didn't mind."

"What was this Dr. Fairbairn like, Bertie? Did you like him?"

Bertie was slow to answer. "I liked him a bit," he said at last. "Not very much—just a bit. He was mad, you know, and everybody says it's not your fault if you're mad. So I didn't blame him for being mad."

"Why do you think he was mad, Bertie?"

"Because he had very strange eyes," said Bertie. "Just like Ulysses' eyes, actually. And also because he said very peculiar things. I think that was why the Government knew he was mad—they'd heard some of the things he said and they decided to send him to Carstairs. I think they had a room ready for him there. He said that he was going to Aberdeen, but I think he was really going to Carstairs."

Nicola was having difficulty keeping a straight face. "And tell me, Bertie, have you mentioned to anybody that Ulysses looks like Dr. Fairbairn? What does Mummy think about that, I wonder?"

"Oh, I told Mummy," said Bertie.

Nicola waited.

"I told her a long time ago."

Nicola hardly dared ask. "And what did Mummy say? Was she pleased?"

Bertie hesitated. "I . . . I don't think so."

"What did she say?"

"At first she said nothing. So I told her again and that's when she started screaming at me."

"She screamed?"

"Yes, she was jolly cross. She told me to keep quiet." He paused. "I think it's because she didn't like the thought of

Ulysses looking like anybody. I can't see why anybody should mind that, can you, Granny?"

"That depends," said Nicola. "Sometimes people can be a bit sensitive about these things. And what about Daddy? Did you tell Daddy?"

"Yes," said Bertie. "Daddy just became very quiet. He didn't scream at me or anything. He just stopped talking for a while."

"It might have been a surprise for him," said Nicola. "These things can take people by surprise."

They crossed Queen Street and continued their journey. Both were silent now—Bertie because he was thinking of the kilt that awaited him, and Nicola because she was pondering what Bertie had just said. It was glaringly obvious: that woman had been having an affair with the psychotherapist. And Stuart—poor Stuart—had obviously come to hear of it through Bertie and had either decided to condone it or had simply suffered in silence—which had always been his response to trying circumstances.

The knowledge that Irene had been seeing somebody else made it easier for Nicola. She would not interfere in the marriage—not directly—but she owed it to her son to persuade him to look after himself. She would sit down and talk to him. She would encourage him to consider his future. "It's patently obvious to me," she would say, "that you are happier without her. Look at you: you needed to put on a bit of weight, and you've done that. Your skin tone is better. You're smiling more. Why, may I ask? Well, it's obvious, isn't it? She's the problem, Stuart—it's so clear to me, it really is."

She allowed herself some time to contemplate this scene and this imagined conversation, and then she realised that they were already on the North Bridge, looking up at the old offices of *The Scotsman* and the craggy skyline of the Old Town tenements.

"Have they made the kilt specially for me?" Bertie asked, his voice filled with pride.

"Yes," said Nicola. "I gave them your height, told them which tartan you wore, and they've done the rest. Ancient Pollock, I believe. It's very like the Maxwell tartan because I think Pollocks and Maxwells were all mixed up together."

"And our clan symbol is a pig, I think."

Nicola corrected him. "Actually, it's a boar, Bertie. A boar sounds a bit better than a pig."

"I bet they were brave," said Bertie. "All those old Pollocks—I bet they were brave."

"Oh, they were," agreed Nicola. And she thought: no ancient Pollock, no scion of an early Pollock, would have tolerated Irene for more than a couple of days. Those hairy early Scotsmen would not have put up with being lectured about Melanie Klein. And none of their hairy sons—and she imagined that all early Scots were somewhat hairy—would have allowed themselves to be sent off to yoga lessons and psychotherapy. *Oh Scotland,* she thought, *what has become of you?*

51. *More about Fersie MacPherson*

Proudly clad in Ancient Pollock tartan, Bertie made his way back down Dublin Street with his grandmother, the folds of his new kilt swinging with all the jauntiness of its seven-year-old owner. Both had enjoyed the outing—Bertie because his long-held wish to own a kilt had been fulfilled; Nicola because she had seen the expression of unqualified delight on her grandson's face as the kilt had been extracted from its wrapping of tissue paper and handed over to him, to be donned immediately, adjusted by the kilt-maker, and then given the final nod of approval. Nicola had asked about a boy's sporran, but had been told that these would not be coming into stock for a few weeks yet.

"We shall notify you immediately we get them," said the kilt-maker. "But in the meantime, I'd suggest just wearing it without a sporran. Anything goes these days, you know. People wear kilts with boots, for instance, and lots of people forget about the *sgian dubh*." He sighed. "To such a pass have things come . . ."

"That's the little knife people tuck into their stockings," Nicola explained.

Bertie's eyes widened as he saw his chance. "Couldn't I wear a Swiss Army knife instead, Granny? I don't mind."

The kilt-maker exchanged glances with Nicola, and smiled. "I'm afraid not, young man," he said. "But when you're a bit older, come back and we'll fix you up with a real *sgian dubh*."

At length they left the shop with Bertie's dungarees neatly wrapped up in a brown paper parcel and tied up with string. "We could leave the dungarees here in the shop," he suggested. "Then we could pick them up some other time."

"I don't think so," said Nicola. "Mummy might wonder where they are." And she thought: *I can just imagine it: 'Where, may I ask, are Bertie's secondary dungarees?' What a cow that woman is.*

"But she'd never know," said Bertie. "She's going to be away for years, I think. She really likes it in the desert."

Nicola thought: *Oh, if only! But that Bedouin sheikh in his desert fastness is not going to be able to tolerate her for much longer; poor man, who can blame him? And there's one thing you can be quite certain of—sheikhs, for all their undoubted talents, are not exactly new men.*

The kilt-maker raised an eyebrow.

"It's a complicated story," Nicola explained. "The mother is . . ." She leaned forward to whisper something to the kilt-maker. "Actually, the poor woman's in a harem somewhere on the Persian Gulf. Terribly sad, but there we are—we soldier on." She did not mention the fact that Irene appeared to be enjoying herself and had started a harem book club in which the latest novels (reviewed in *The Guardian*) were discussed with great interest by the members.

The kilt-maker looked shocked. "Poor wee fellow," he said. "How's he bearing up?"

"Oh, actually he rather likes the situation," said Nicola. "As I said, it's a complicated story."

Now, as they approached Scotland Street, Bertie's heart was close to bursting. Remembering the story his grandmother had begun for him, the story of *Fersie MacPherson, the Scottish Person*, he asked, "Do you think that Fersie MacPherson had a kilt like this when he was my age, Granny?"

Nicola assured him that he did. "Fersie MacPherson had tartan nappies when he was a baby," she said. "Ancient MacPherson tartan. Then, when he was a bit older, maybe one and a half, he got his first kilt. They went into Oban to buy it and he never took it off until he was three, and got his next kilt."

"Except in the bath," said Bertie.

"Of course. Mind you, he played a lot outside when he was very small. He was mostly washed by the rain. There's a lot of rain over there in Lochaber and they would just put Fersie outside to get him clean. It toughened him up too."

"He was jolly strong, wasn't he?"

"Yes. He started to toss the caber when he was only five, Bertie—a couple of years younger than you. He threw his first telephone pole then. Everybody was astonished. He tossed it at least five feet. It was amazing. There was an article about it in the *Oban Times*."

"I bet he had a Swiss Army penknife," muttered Bertie.

Nicola did not reply to that. "Remember that he was a kind

boy, Bertie. Very strong people are usually kind. It's only the weaklings who are unkind to other people."

"I know that," said Bertie. "I'll try to be kind too, Granny— now that I have a kilt."

Nicola looked down at the little boy walking beside her. She wanted to lift him up and hug him. She wanted him to stay like this forever. She wanted him to have the fun he had been missing, to get some enjoyment out of life, to set out on any one of the glorious paths that lay before him before, one by one, life closed them off.

They reached Number 44 and Nicola opened the door to the stair. Bertie began to bound up, as he usually did, but stopped halfway up to see who was coming downstairs towards them. There was a snuffling sound and then a familiar bark as Cyril, accompanied by his owner, Angus Lordie, came into view.

"Well, well," said Angus as he saw Bertie. "You're wearing the kilt, Bertie. That's a fine thing."

Bertie beamed as Angus admired his new kilt. Bending down, he patted Cyril on the head and the dog, famous for his gold tooth, gave him a broad smile of welcome.

"Is Cyril going for a walk, Mr. Lordie?" asked Bertie.

"He is indeed, Bertie," said Angus. "We're having a bit of an issue about dogs in the Drummond Place Gardens, but I take the view that regulations do not apply to Cyril. He's a special case in my view." He paused as Nicola caught up with them. "And good morning to you, Nicola. I was complimenting your grandson on his very fine kilt. And let's see . . ." He broke off and looked at Bertie with dismay. "No sporran, Bertie?"

"They didn't have one," explained Bertie.

Angus frowned. "I think we might be able to do something about that. I still have the sporran I wore as a boy and . . . well, sporrans in cupboards are of no use to anybody. A sporran on a boy is another matter altogether."

Bertie held his breath. He thought he understood, but he hardly dared hope.

"Nicola?" Angus went on. "Why don't the two of you join me within? Domenica has gone shopping and so whatever coffee is served will be made by me, although . . ." He looked at his watch. "A martini, perhaps?"

52. *Bertie's Sporran*

Angus Lordie led the way into the kitchen of his flat in Scotland Street. He was only just getting used to the fact that what he had always seen as Domenica's flat was now his as well, and that by the same token she had become the owner of half of his own flat and studio in Drummond Place. The change, though, had not been a difficult one, as the Scotland Street flat was ample enough for both of them to spread out; this was the result of Domenica's acquisition of the next-door flat and the removal of the wall dividing the two.

That flat had been the property of Antonia Collie, author of an unpublished work on the lives of the Scottish saints and now a lay member of a community of nuns in Italy. Antonia had recently been in Scotland but had gone back to Italy, leaving behind her friend, the enigmatic nun, Sister Maria-Fiore dei Fiori di Montagna. Sister Maria-Fiore, whose liking for an aphorism appeared to have a hypnotic effect on many of those who met her, had been something of a social success in Scotland, having been invited to all the major parties, gallery openings, and Holyrood receptions that enlivened the social life of the capital. After Antonia's return to Italy, the nun had remained in Scotland, and was last heard of staying on a Perthshire estate, where she was successfully holding court. Not everyone was well-disposed to the nun, of course, and various people had expressed views that were distinctly less than charitable. "A cliché in black and white," one Perthshire hostess had remarked, referring to the black and white habit Sister Maria-Fiore dei Fiori di Montagna wore. "Rasputina," said another, adding, "Oh, for another Prince Yusupov!"

There was enough room to entertain in the drawing room, but Domenica and Angus habitually received visitors in the kitchen, a homely room dominated by a large cooking range and a line of copper-bottomed saucepans hanging against one wall. It was here that Angus read the morning paper while Domenica answered correspondence or perused the various anthropological journals to which she subscribed.

Angus invited Nicola and Bertie to take a seat around the large pine table while he went into the room where he stored his clothes in the generously proportioned Edwardian wardrobe Domenica had bought for him at a Lyon & Turnbull auction. After a minute or two, he returned with an old cardboard box out of which he extracted a small sporran. Dusting the sporran with the cuff of his shirtsleeve, Angus handed it over to Bertie with a flourish.

"There, young man," he said. "A very smart boy's sporran, *circa* 1965, previously the property of one Angus Lordie, RSA (rejected), DA (Edinburgh School of Art, with distinction), now in the possession of Master Bertie Pollock. How about that?"

Bertie took the sporran as one might take a revered religious object. "Is it for me?" he asked, his voice so small and overawed as to be almost inaudible.

"It is," said Angus. "And if you look at the plate at the top, Bertie—that silver bit—you'll see that it has the most beautiful Celtic designs. I think they might be by George Bain himself—he was the greatest of our modern Celtic artists. He did those lovely swirling illustrations you see here and there. Look at that."

He reached over to touch the design etched into the silver, tracing one of the whorls with the tip of his finger.

"I remember one of George Bain's designs that really moved me," he said. "It was a picture of a figure of modern Scotland, represented by a boy, being comforted by the encompassing arms of a seated woman. It was so touching."

Nicola swallowed. She had been looking at Bertie's face; at the joy of his expression. "I can imagine," she said quietly.

"Your own design there is a bit different, Bertie," Angus continued. "But it is beautiful nonetheless."

While Bertie prepared to put the strap and chain of the sporran round his waist, Angus turned to Nicola. "I mentioned a martini," he said. "Shall I?"

"Most kind of you," said Nicola.

He went to fetch the drinks, fetching at the same time a glass of Irn Bru for Bertie.

"Irn Bru is just what you need," said Angus, handing Bertie the drink. "*Slàinte*, Bertie!"

Bertie raised his glass to the Gaelic toast. "Thank you so much, Mr. Lordie," he said.

"Not at all, Bertie," replied Angus. "I'm delighted that my sporran will see the light of day again." To Nicola, he said, "Do I detect a certain, how shall I put it? A certain lightening of the mood upstairs since . . ."

Nicola glanced at Bertie, but he was not paying attention, being absorbed in the investigation of his new sporran. "Yes," she said quietly. "The mood music is very different."

Angus nodded. "Frankly, I'm surprised that a certain young person hasn't absented himself before this—such is the provocation he's received from a now enGulfed party."

"You mean . . ." Again Nicola checked to see that Bertie was not listening. "You mean . . . run away?"

"Exactly," said Angus. "I had a friend who ran away, you know. He ran away from the boarding school we were sent to. He was at odds with the whole ethos at the time—the insistence on sports, the Philistinism, the cold showers, the whole lot. He was sixteen. He went to Glasgow and was apprehended there within hours by a policeman who recognised him from his circulated description."

"And he was sent back to the same school?"

"No," said Angus. "His father consulted a firm of educational consultants that he saw advertised in *The Times*. They recommended that he be sent to school abroad. His father was quite well off and so he was able to comply with their advice. He wanted his son to learn French, and so he thought their recommendation was spot-on. He was sent to a school in France."

"How interesting," said Nicola.

"Unfortunately, the educational agency was very badly informed. They were very slack, in fact. They had not done their research properly and the school he was sent to was actually a finishing school for girls!"

"Oh, my," exclaimed Nicola "What a mistake!"

"The school, it transpired, was having a bit of a tough time filling its places, and so they wanted him to stay—in order to get the fees. And he was perfectly happy to comply. He had a whale of a time. The girls were all studying cookery and deportment, but he was allowed to go into the village, drink coffee, and smoke Gauloises. They—the girls—were very pleased to have a boy about the place, and when he wrote home to his father he simply referred to what 'the other chaps' were doing—the other chaps being, in fact, all girls. It was no more than a white lie, I feel.

"He told me it was the best year in his life," concluded Angus. "He remembers it with such pleasure, he really does."

53. *The Trap is About to be Sprung*

Pat replaced the telephone receiver on the hook and immediately sank her head in her hands. She felt terrible. She had made the call to her father, inviting him to dinner at her flat, with Anichka, and he had sounded pleased; he had sounded cheerful and trusting *as he walked right into her trap*. How could she have done it? How could she have deceived her father, of all people, the man who had stood by her all her life, who had supported and encouraged her, who would never—in any circumstances—mislead or betray her? Now she had done precisely that to him.

But then she thought of the alternative. If she did nothing, then he would marry Anichka, who would make off with as much of his money as she could get her hands on, and he would find himself deserted and considerably poorer. If she were letting him down now, it was as nothing to what Anichka was planning to do.

"What a nice idea," he said over the telephone. "Saturday? Yes, we're free as it happens. And Anichka will be very interested to see your flat."

Pat closed her eyes. Yes, Anichka would be very interested to see her flat—and to ask about how much it cost, which is what she always asked about everything.

"Can we bring anything?" asked her father. "Wine? My cellar's a bit depleted at the moment, but I could find something no doubt."

Pat opened her eyes—wide. Why, she wondered, was his cellar depleted? Her father was a modest drinker and he usually replaced bottles as he used them. Had he been entertaining more than usual, or had Anichka been working her way through them? Or stealing them, perhaps?

"Sorry to hear that the cupboard's almost bare," she said, trying to sound lighthearted. "Old Mother Hubbard and all that . . ."

"Oh, there are a couple of bottles," said her father. "Don't worry."

"How's it happening?" asked Pat. "Having lots of parties?"

There was a moment's hesitation at the other end of the line. "Oh, you know how it is," said Dr. MacGregor.

Pat felt her heart pounding with her. "Does Anichka like a glass of wine?" she asked.

"Now and then," replied her father.

She did not pursue the point, but Pat was sure that her suspicions were well-founded. The conversation was concluded and she rang off. Now, more than ever, she was determined to foil this woman, but she was not prepared for the flood of guilt that overcame her. "Be strong," she whispered to herself. "Just do it."

Her next phone call was to Bruce, to tell him that the dinner had been arranged. "I'll be there, Pat baby," he said. "What would you like me to wear? Something seductive?" He laughed.

Pat gritted her teeth. "You're the one with the experience," she said. "You're the professional."

For a few moments Bruce was silent. "Are you suggesting I'm a gigolo?"

"Of course not," said Pat quickly. "What I meant to say

is that you're the one who knows what turns women on—clothes-wise, I mean."

The note of resentment left Bruce's voice. "You're right there," he said. "I think I'm going to wear black. Black is it this year. And a bit of grey. Women are heavily into grey these days, you know. It's that book they've all been reading. You read it yet, Patsy?"

"No. Definitely not."

"Come on," said Bruce. "You can admit it. You've read it, Pat. I know."

"I have not read it," she said, chiselling out the words. "I have not."

"Well, I bet this Polish woman will have read it. Totally sure."

"She's Czech."

"Same difference. They're all reading that book. Poles, Czechs, Russians. It's answering a need that all women have—obviously. They're not reading *Winnie the Pooh*, they're reading *the* book."

"Let's get back to what you're going to wear," said Pat.

"Okay: black and grey. Jeans and a Jermyn Street shirt—grey. Linen jacket with two buttons in the front, both undone. Friendship bracelet—elephant hair. That's should do the business for this old Czech chick."

Pat winced. "I hope so. But look, Bruce, don't overdo it. Be subtle."

"Have I ever been anything but?

"Well . . ."

"See you," he said breezily. "Got to go."

That conversation took place on a Monday and the dinner party was due to be held the following Saturday. Pat asked Matthew and Elspeth to the dinner as well; this was better than inviting people who would not be parties to the plot.

"I suppose it means having dinner with Bruce," said

Matthew, "and that is not exactly appealing, but duty calls—so the answer is yes, we'll come along."

Now, with the guest list complete, Pat planned her meal. She would serve borscht as the first course, a vague nod in the direction of Eastern Europe (they did eat borscht, she imagined, or was it an exclusively Russian soup?). That would be followed by salmon steaks, broccoli, Puy lentils and potatoes. The final course—by which time she hoped Bruce's magic would have had its effect—would be a lemon sorbet made in the ice-cream maker her father had given her for Christmas.

By six o'clock on Saturday evening she had the borscht and the sorbet prepared, the wine in the fridge, and the table laid for six. She had planned the *placement* carefully; she would sit at the head of the table, with Bruce on her right and Anichka on the other side of him. Her father would be at the other end of the table, so that if Bruce were to be indiscreet in his flirting he would not see it: it was not part of the plan that Dr. MacGregor should suspect anything at this stage. It was to be on the discovery of the two of them in the Canny Man's that the scales would fall from his eyes.

Poor Daddy, she thought; to have scales on your eyes at fifty-eight was extremely unfortunate; how lucky, though, he was to have a daughter who could see those scales and who was prepared to do something about it. That slightly self-congratulatory thought made her feel a great deal better—as slightly self-congratulatory thoughts so often do.

54. What to Take to a Dinner Party

Matthew and Elspeth arrived first. They brought with them a box of chocolates (regifted) and two bottles of South Australian Shiraz. This, Matthew said, was exactly the right combination. "There are rules about these things," he explained to Elspeth. "And these rules are quite clear."

"That's the first I've heard of them," said Elspeth.

"Well, the fact that one hasn't heard of a set of rules doesn't mean they don't exist," said Matthew patiently. "*Ignorantia iuris neminem excusat*, as you well know."

"You're trying to intimidate me with Latin," said Elspeth.

Matthew smiled. "Remember what Jean Brodie said of the headmistress, who'd summoned her for four-fifteen, or something like that? 'She's trying to intimidate me by the use of quarter-hours.' What a wonderful thing to say—or write; I think Muriel Spark got Edinburgh better than anybody else. Captured the essential . . ."

"Brittleness?"

"Perhaps."

Elspeth sighed. "Back to the issue of offerings for dinner. I can understand one bottle of wine, but why two?"

Matthew looked serious. "Because this is to help Pat in a bit of a spot—and I'm her employer, after all. However, there may be circumstances in which you wouldn't take even one bottle of wine. It depends on the hosts, you see."

Elspeth clearly found this abstruse. "I'm not with you."

"Well, here are the rules," said Matthew. "Let's start with students. Students invite other students to a meal in their flat: the guests must take a bottle of wine each—no exceptions. It needn't be expensive—but it would be socially unacceptable for them to arrive empty-handed."

"Even if they're owed an invitation?"

Matthew nodded. "Even if."

"That seems fair enough."

Matthew agreed. "Oh, these rules are very fair. Now let's say that it's people—no longer students—but actual people . . ."

"A strange way of putting it."

"Well," continued Matthew. "There is a transition, you know.

The student life is very different from the life led by the rest of us. So, people in their first job, say: twenty-something . . ."

"Twenty-six."

"All right," said Matthew. "Twenty-six. Going for dinner with other twenty-six-year-olds. The same rule applies, but now the quality will be slightly better. Eight pounds is the current minimum. The important thing is it isn't just any old bottle that was lying around. Chocolates, though, are optional. However, there are qualifications to this general rule."

"Such as?"

"Where the invitation comes from somebody much older. So let's say that a young couple . . ."

"Aged twenty-six?"

"Yes, aged twenty-six, are . . ."

"Is . . . couple is singular." Elspeth paused. "I was a teacher, remember."

Matthew smiled. He loved Elspeth for all her attributes, but particularly for having been what she was in life—a teacher of children.

"All right: a young couple is invited to dinner with the boss of one of them—let's say hers. So the invitation comes in. Dinner in Nile Grove—deep Morningside. Let's say the boss is a partner in a legal firm—something like that. They don't have to take a bottle of wine. In fact, they shouldn't—it would embarrass the host because he's not going to serve what they bring. He'll have made his own choice. And the rule then is: no wine, but flowers."

"Not chocolates?"

"No, because chocolates fall into the category of presents that people may not want. Think of the chocolates you received when you were a teacher. Did you ever think *Oh, good! Chocolates!* Did you ever eat them?"

"No. But then I taught at the Steiner School. I loved it, but

I didn't get chocolates. I was given organic carrots sometimes, or soap from Mull—not chocolates."

Matthew returned to the rules. "Now, if you're going to dinner in later life—and for these purposes later life starts at thirty-five, and your host is younger—say . . ."

"Twenty-six?"

"Yes, twenty-six—then you must take a bottle of wine. It's obligatory. And it must be of a quality that your host could not normally afford. And if you're going to dinner with some other person in later life . . ."

"Thirty-five and above?"

"Yes, then you can discuss in advance whether you bring anything. So you say: 'Shall I bring a bottle of something nice?' And they say, 'Oh, that would be great. Don't go to any trouble, though,' which means that they hope you will go to considerable trouble. Now the difference here is that anything you bring in such circumstances will be drunk at that dinner. It would then be rude for the host to accept the gift and not serve it, unless . . . unless you say right at the beginning, as you present the bottle, 'I've brought something for the cellar.' In that case the wine can be put in the host's wine rack—the cellar being metaphorical, you see."

Elspeth considered this. "But what about chocolates? What if somebody brings you chocolates and you don't like them? Can you give them away? Can you take them to the next dinner party you're invited to?"

"Definitely," said Matthew. "The rules are quite clear about that. Chocolates can be passed on—provided, of course, the box hasn't been opened."

Elspeth laughed. "But naturally!"

"You may laugh," said Matthew. "But there is a recorded case of somebody passing on a box of chocolates from which she had eaten all the soft-centre ones."

"How odd."

"More than that," went on Matthew, "there were one or two that she'd tried, discovered they were hard, and then replaced in the box."

"Unbelievable," said Elspeth.

"And here's another thing," said Matthew. "There's a box of regifted After Eights doing the rounds in Edinburgh circles that has been passed on from guest to host for—believe it or not—eighteen years! There are people who actually recognize it. And if you look on the bottom it says: *À consommer avant 1998*, which means that it actually came from France in the first place. It must have done the rounds of Parisian dinner parties before being brought to Edinburgh."

"The Auld Alliance," mused Elspeth.

"The Auld Box of Chocolates," said Matthew.

"I rather like *Après Huits*," said Elspeth.

55. Celebs, Popes, Tattoos

Bruce arrived next, and the moment she opened the door of her Marchmont flat to him Pat saw that he had made an effort. He was wearing exactly what he had promised to wear, but he looked very well-groomed.

He took her hand and pressed it to his cheek. "Feel this," he said. "A Turkish hot shave. There's this barber guy near Tollcross who pushes you back in the chair and applies his cut-throat. You feel really vulnerable, of course—one slip and you're a goner—but this guy's amazing. Like the feel?"

Pat blushed. At one level she was appalled, but at another she felt the sheer physical power of Bruce's presence. What exactly was it about him? Was it that he had the disarming naivety of the little boy? Was that what made him irresistible to women?

Bruce dropped her hand and leaned forward to kiss her. He rubbed his cheek against hers. "Nice, isn't it?"

Her blush deepened—a combination of anger, disgust, and discomfort over uninvited physical proximity.

"Anyway," said Bruce, straightening up. "Who's here? Has your old man and What's-her-face arrived?"

"Anichka. She's called Anichka." Pat nodded in the direction of the kitchen. "Just Matthew and Elspeth."

"Good," said Bruce. "Time for a quick smooch . . ." He laughed. "Only joking, Pat. Sorry to disappoint. You know, this barber guy was telling me his story while he did the shave. He's got five kids back in Turkey, on some island or other. He has a restaurant there, he says—or it belongs to his mother-in-law, something like that. He's very proud of it. He showed me a photograph of it—a ghastly looking place under some trees with fairy lights rigged up all round it—to attract the tourists. It's called the Restaurant Sport Terrific. Can you imagine that? How tacky."

"It must mean a lot to him," said Pat.

"Oh yeah, oh yeah . . . Great place. Two Michelin stars, probably."

They moved into the hall. Bruce looked around him. "Who else lives here?" he asked.

"I've got two flatmates."

"Boys or girls?" asked Bruce.

"Girls."

"Nice!" said Bruce. "I love Edinburgh flats full of middle-class girls like you, Pat. Well-brought-up girls, maybe even Watsonians—at a pinch. No offence. Where are they? Are they here tonight?"

"They're both out. They've gone to a movie together."

Bruce winked. "Oh yes? Are they . . . are they an item?"

Pat struggled to control herself. Bruce, after all, was doing her a favour and she should be civil. "No," she said. "They both have boyfriends."

"Pity," said Bruce. "Where are the boyfriends? Have they gone to a movie together as well?"

Pat ignored this. "If you go and sit in the living room," she said. "I'll bring Matthew and Elspeth through."

She led Bruce into the living room, which had been tidied for the occasion. The room served as a dining room too, with a fair-sized table in the bay window at the far end. This had been set for dinner, with near-matching crockery and an assortment of glasses from the eccentrically stocked kitchen.

Bruce moved over to look out of the window. "Good view," he said, and then added, "of nothing."

Pat left him there and made her way back into the kitchen. "He's arrived," she whispered to Matthew and Elspeth.

Matthew made a face. "I suppose we'd better go and talk to him."

Elspeth said, "You used to like him, didn't you?"

"We occasionally meet in the Cumberland Bar," said Matthew. "But I don't really like him."

"Does anybody?" asked Pat.

Matthew turned to her. "You did. You used to go out with him, didn't you?"

Pat looked resentful. "And I used to go out with you," she said.

"Oh really?" said Elspeth.

Matthew frowned. "You knew that," he said to Elspeth.

"We didn't go out for all that long," said Pat. "And it was a long time ago."

"Yes, ages," said Matthew hurriedly. "Let's go and see Bruce."

They made their way into the living room, where Bruce, standing near the window, was paging through a magazine.

"Look at this," he said. "Have you seen this mag?"

"It belongs to one of my flatmates," said Pat. "She gets it, I don't."

"But I bet you read it," said Bruce, "Cover to cover. All the celeb news that's unfit to print. There's this article here about who's got a tattoo and who hasn't. And where. You wouldn't believe it."

"So," said Matthew. "Who's got a tattoo then?"

"The Pope," said Bruce. "For one."

"I don't believe that," said Elspeth. "The Pope would never get a tattoo. He just wouldn't."

"They must have interviewed him," he said. "Maybe they said: Hey, Frank—you got a tattoo?"

The doorbell rang, and Bruce replaced the magazine on a side table. "That's them?" he asked.

"Probably," said Pat. "I'll go and let them in."

Matthew looked sideways at Bruce. "Nervous?" he asked.

Bruce shook his head. "Why should I be nervous, Matt, old chap? This is all in a day's work."

Matthew smiled. "I hope it doesn't misfire. What if she takes against you at first sight?"

Bruce grinned. "Never happened before," he said.

There was the sound of voices in the hall. Then the door, which Pat had closed behind her, was opened. She came in first, followed by Anichka and Dr. MacGregor.

"You know everyone here, don't you, Daddy? But Anichka, you've not met Elspeth and Matthew . . . and Bruce."

Anichka's eyes moved from Matthew to Elspeth and then to Bruce, where her gaze stopped—and was held. "I've always liked meeting new people," she said. "It keeps life interesting."

Pat exchanged a glance with Matthew. "Matthew—come and help me get drinks for everybody."

Matthew stepped forward, but stopped. Dr. MacGregor held up a hand. "Let me help you, Pat. I know your kitchen."

Once in the kitchen, Dr. MacGregor closed the door and looked at his daughter with concern. "Darling, why have you invited that boy?"

"Bruce?"

"Yes, him. You aren't together with him again, are you? I couldn't bear the thought if you were."

Pat shook her head. "No, Daddy, I promise you—I'm not. I'm really not."

"Well, that's a great relief. You remember what I told you about him way back. Remember?"

"That he's a narcissist. You said he was a narcissist."

"Yes, I did. And I told you, didn't I, that people like him are a terrible danger to others. They may not know it, but they are."

Pat looked away. Of course Bruce was a danger to others, and here he was, aimed at the woman whom Dr. MacGregor loved, but who was clearly planning to deprive him of everything.

"Daddy, I promise you: I'm not involved in any way with Bruce. I've invited him here because he's lonely—that's all. I bumped into him and invited him on impulse."

Liar, she thought; but it was too late, far too late, for self-reproach.

56. I'm Going to Try Now

Dr. MacGregor lined up the glasses on the kitchen table while Pat retrieved a couple of bottles of wine from the fridge.

"Now," he asked, "how many are we?"

"Matthew and Elspeth, Bruce, Me," she said. "That's four. And then there's you and . . . Anichka." She stumbled on the name, not for its unfamiliarity to the Scottish tongue but because of a psychological barrier: the names of those we dread may not always be easy to say.

She realised immediately that her father had noticed. He looked up sharply, and their eyes met: his probing, hers guilty. He was holding a glass, and he dropped it.

"Oh, no . . ." He went down on his haunches to pick up the pieces.

"Careful," she said. "You'll cut yourself. I'll get a pan . . ."

But it was too late. He stood up, and sucked quickly at his right hand.

"Oh, Daddy . . ."

"It's nothing." He was, after all, a doctor, although it was decades since he had ministered to a physical injury. "It'll be all right if I stick a plaster on. Have you got one?"

"Of course." She opened a drawer beside the fridge and took out a small box of sticking plasters. "One of these."

He came towards her, and held out his hand. "You know, I was always rather squeamish. I hated the sight of blood, would you believe it? But you never seemed to mind, did you? Even when you were very small you never seemed to bother."

Peeling off a protective strip, she applied the sticking plaster to the cut. "There, that should do it." She paused. "Surely being squeamish must have made medical school a bit of an ordeal for you?"

"I coped. I rather enjoyed dissection, as it happens, but actual cuts were different." He looked at the plaster on his finger. "Thank you, darling. I'm sorry I dropped that glass, it's just that . . . Well, I can tell that you're finding this difficult. You are, aren't you?"

She protested her innocence. "Finding what difficult?"

"Oh come on, darling. I can tell. You find it difficult to accept Anichka."

She bit her lip.

"It's probably better for you to express your feelings," Dr. MacGregor continued. "Bottling up hostility rarely helps."

Pat looked away. "I'm not hostile." The words—the direct opposite of her true feelings—were glibly uttered.

"But you are, you know. I can tell."

She felt torn. She had never been able to hide her feelings from her father; it was hard as a child, and it was impossible as an adult.

Her father took her hand. "You see, darling, once you begin to lie, it becomes terribly easy. Like running downhill."

She struggled to control herself. She could sense that tears were not far away. "I'm concerned about you, Daddy. I want you to be happy, and yet I think that woman . . ."

"Anichka," he corrected her. "Even our enemies have names, you know."

"I'm concerned that Anichka is with you . . . for what she can get. In fact, I'm sure of it. You only have to look at the way she behaves."

He sighed. "You really believe that, don't you?"

She nodded.

"And there's nothing I can say that will make you think differently?"

"You're not going to say it. You're in love, and people in love can't think straight."

He sighed. "Do you know anything about her? I don't think you do."

She had been avoiding his gaze. Now she turned back to

face him. "I know that she looks at everything—and I mean everything—from the point of view of what it costs. She's adding it all up—can't you see? She's working out how much she can get away with once she . . . once she dumps you—which she will, you know."

He looked wounded. "How can you say that?"

"Because it's glaringly obvious. Because I can see it a mile off, even if you can't."

He reached out for her hand. She pulled it away.

"She's Czech," he said.

"Is that some sort of excuse?"

He sighed again. "If you knew anything about it, you might just begin to understand. Where we come from may play a big role in how we look at the world. I know that sounds obvious, but you don't seem to be aware of it, darling, and you might like to give it a moment's thought."

She shook her head; she wanted this conversation to stop.

"No, Pat, you can't just brush it under the carpet," said Dr. MacGregor. "You're going to have to listen." He paused. "I'm not sure how much you know of the history of Eastern Europe—not much, I'm sorry to say. And I hasten to add that's not your fault—you've been brought up in a country that hasn't had anything really nasty happen to it for a good long time. Well, the twentieth century for people in Eastern Europe was a very different matter."

"I don't want a history lesson, Daddy. And they're waiting for drinks . . ."

He stopped her. "No, listen to me for a moment. Anichka's grandparents were both murdered. A pogrom—you know what those are, do you? And then her parents found themselves on the wrong side of the Communists and her father was sent to a labour camp. He died there of TB. Her mother drank herself to death. Anichka had nobody then—nobody, and nothing. Are you surprised that she experiences insecurity?

Are you surprised that she takes an interest in what things are worth? Has it occurred to you that you might do the same if you had nothing yourself?"

Pat closed her eyes.

"So just think about it for a few moments," Dr. MacGregor went on. "Before you dismiss somebody about whom you know virtually nothing—just think about it. She is kind to me and I have been able to give her some of the security she has never had. She looks after me in return. I think that's a perfectly reasonable bargain, don't you think?"

Pat thought: *I have been utterly unfair. I've taken it upon myself to interfere in something that really is none of my business.*

She opened her eyes and moved towards her father. She embraced him. "I'm so sorry," she said. "I've been very thoughtless. I'm going to try now. I really am."

He seemed doubtful. "Are you?"

"Yes, I am. I promise you—I am."

57. The Switching On of Magnets

There was still time, of course. Bruce was primed, but could be disarmed, or whatever it was that one did to a missile one no longer wished to launch. As she returned to the living room, Pat saw that Anichka was deep in conversation with Elspeth, while Bruce and Matthew were standing by the window, with Bruce holding forth volubly to his cornered friend. Matthew caught Pat's eye with one of those looks that plead for social rescue. She would go to his aid, but for the moment she was relieved to see that the situation was clearly controllable. All she would have to do was discreetly to alter the seating plan and then have a quiet word with Bruce, telling him that the whole plan was off.

She crossed the room to join Matthew and Bruce. Bruce was talking about Dublin.

"Great place," he said. "I went over when we last played Ireland. We lost, but it wasn't our fault."

Pat smiled. "Whose was it, then?"

Bruce looked at her with condescension. "Do you know anything about rugby, Pat?"

"I've seen it played."

Bruce laughed. "Oh, in that case you'll know what I mean when I say that the Irish distracted the ref. That's what they always do—they distract the ref so that he doesn't see what's going on."

"But you do?"

"Too true. If they hadn't distracted the ref, we would have scored another couple of tries."

Pat raised an eyebrow. "Oh well."

"But Dublin is a great place to go for a weekend, no matter what happens," Bruce continued. "We went to this pub called the Palace Bar. Near Trinity. Fantastic *craic*."

"Interesting word," said Matthew.

"*Craic*?" said Bruce. "Yes—if you need to ask what it means, it means you're not having it."

Pat caught Matthew's eye again. She lowered her voice. "The plan is off," she said.

"What?" asked Bruce.

Pat leaned forward. "Don't do it," she whispered.

Matthew frowned. "What's changed?" he asked.

Pat looked over her shoulder. "Everything," she said. She looked intently at Bruce. "I just don't want you to exercise your charm. It's off."

Bruce rolled his eyes. "You sure?"

"Yes, I'm very sure. I think I'm wrong about . . ." She lowered her voice still further even though there was no danger of her being overheard: Elspeth and Anichka were at the opposite end of the room, having now been joined by Dr. MacGregor. They seemed immersed in their own conversation and would not be able to pick up what Pat was saying. She completed her sentence. "I'm wrong about *her.*"

Bruce made a gesture of resignation. "Oh well," he said. "Her loss."

Matthew gave him a withering look, but it went unnoticed.

"I'll change the seating arrangements," said Pat.

Bruce held up a hand. "No, don't do that. Let me sit next to her—as per plan. I give you my word I won't switch on the magnets."

"Why do you want to sit next to her?"

"Interest," said Bruce.

"You promise you won't try it on?"

Bruce gave her a broad smile. 'Do I look like the sort of man who would try it on? Is that what you think of me?"

Pat ignored his question. "I think we should start the meal," she said loudly, to the entire room. And then to Matthew, "Will you help me bring stuff through?"

Matthew agreed, and when they were both in the kitchen, Pat said to him, "How can you tolerate it, Matthew? How can you put up with him?"

"He's largely harmless," said Matthew. "He's just being Bruce."

Pat shook her head. "How can you say that? It reminds me of what a prominent politician said of one of his colleagues who had just done something completely inappropriate. He said, 'Fred's just being Fred.' I thought: what a thing to say!"

A few minutes later, seated at the table, with their main course on their plates before them, Pat was able to relax for the first time that evening. She felt immense relief that she had been able to call off her plan—she had been very much weighed down by the subterfuge she had embarked upon, and that weight was now gone. Of course, it meant that she still had to contend with Anichka, but if the Czech woman made him happy, and if she was only the way she was because of several hundred years of European history, then Pat could tolerate her.

The meal began. Pat was seated next to her father, who seemed anxious to move to uncontroversial topics. That suited her too, and when he raised the topic of a gallery exhibition he had recently been to, she responded enthusiastically.

"Cowie," he said. "James Cowie. He was a wonderful draftsman."

Pat agreed. "And that portrait of the four friends in the Scottish National Gallery of Modern Art—I love that picture. I've sometimes thought I could write a book about it."

"Could one write a whole book about one picture?" asked Dr. MacGregor.

"Oh yes. I've got a book about Hopper's *Nighthawks*— you know that painting of the people at the bar of the diner? And then there's a book all about Poussin's picture of the man killed by the snake. That's all it's about—that one picture."

Dr. MacGregor shook his head. "Poussin leaves me cold, I'm afraid. I find him bloodless. I know that plenty of people . . ."

He did not finish, and Pat who had been looking towards the other end of the table, now turned to look at her father. He, in turn, was looking across the table to where Anichka was sitting next to Bruce. The two of them were talking, and Pat noticed that Anichka was leaning sideways in her chair, gazing at Bruce. And then, as Bruce emphasised some point, her hand touched his forearm and remained there. There was no mistaking it; any witness of the scene who failed to diagnose fascination might well be accused of being chronically unobservant.

Pat felt dismay overwhelm her. Bruce had promised to

refrain from flirting, but his resolution was irrelevant now. Flirting was in full sway, and there was no doubt about who was flirting with whom: Anichka had seized the initiative.

Pat saw that her father had noticed this. She glanced away, and then looked at him again. He had lowered his eyes. *He saw*, she thought.

She was about to say something to him, to make light of what was so clearly happening, but he spoke before she did.

"You know, darling, I'm not feeling terribly well. Would you mind if I just slipped out and went home? Would you mind terribly?"

"But Daddy . . ."

He had already risen to his feet. He did not say anything to anybody else; indeed Anichka, busy with Bruce, did not even see him go.

58. A Meeting with Marchmont

The Lord Provost's party in the City Chambers was in full swing when Angus Lordie and Domenica Macdonald met the Duke of Johannesburg. The Duke was wearing a lightweight linen suit, a red neckerchief, and a pair of brown suede brogues. He had reminded Angus of their previous meeting, which was at a whisky nosing conducted by the Duke himself, an authority on the subject and author, under a nom de plume or, as he put it, a *nom de malt,* of several books on the whiskies of Scotland.

Angus had forgotten the occasion but, prompted by the Duke, now remembered it. "We had some very peaty island malts, as I recall," he said. "You used some colourful terms to describe them."

The Duke laughed. "Our whisky-nosing terminology is much less pretentious than our dear colleagues in the wine business," he said. "They're always going on about things being *very agreeable* and *flinty* and so on. They actually don't have all that many terms to use, anyway. Once you've said something tastes of black currant, you've said it all."

"I think you described one of the whiskies as tasting of diesel oil," said Angus. "And another reminded you of the leathery smell of an old Rover car's interior."

"Very probably," said the Duke. "We call a spade a spade in the whisky business." He took a sip of his host's wine, and made a face. Then he leaned forward to whisper a confidence to Angus. "Would you fancy a pukka drink? I mean an actual dram . . . ?"

Angus smiled. "Is there any? You never see whisky on these occasions?"

The Duke patted the pocket of his jacket. "I have a hip flask to hand," he said. "Never go anywhere without it. Be prepared! As Baden Powell used to say to the boys. Purely for emergency use, you understand, but I think this counts as an emergency."

He turned to Domenica. "Mrs. Lordie? Would you care for a dram too?"

Domenica declined. She was not a whisky drinker. "You go ahead," she said to Angus.

The Duke fished a small silver hip-flask out of his pocket, along with two small silver beakers engraved with a coat of arms. He poured a dram into each, replaced the hip-flask, and raised his beaker in toast. "*Slàinte!*" Angus reciprocated.

"This is actually rather a special whisky," said the Duke. "They asked me to write some tasting notes for them. What do you think of it?"

Angus took a sip of the whisky. "Peppery?" he said.

The Duke nodded. "Yes, a good amount of pepper. There's a prickliness, I'd say."

"What is it?" asked Angus.

The Duke drew him aside. Domenica had now drifted off to

make conversation with somebody she had spotted in a knot of people near the door, leaving Angus and the Duke together.

"This," he whispered, "happens to be the oldest casked whisky in Scotland. 1939, would you believe, and they're only now getting ready to bottle it. How about that, Angus— 1939?"

Angus was thinking. "Do you know that poem by Auden? *September 1, 1939*? The one that begins with his sitting in a bar in New York and reflecting on—what did he call it?—'a low dishonest decade'?"

The Duke did. "He disowned it, didn't he? The poem, that is—not the world."

"He did," said Angus. "He thought it was meretricious. He didn't like political posturing."

The Duke made a face. "Who does? People are so keen to wear their heart on their sleeve and . . ." He trailed off, peering into the far corner of the room. Angus followed his gaze.

"That chap over there," whispered the Duke. "His face looks vaguely familiar. You don't know who he is?"

Angus followed the Duke's gaze. A well-groomed man, wearing a light brown tweed jacket, was talking to a small circle of guests. "That's Adam Bruce."

The Duke frowned. "Have I met him? I think I have, but I can't quite place him."

"He's Marchmont."

"Marchmont? Lives in Marchmont?"

Angus shook his head. "No, Marchmont Herald. He's one of the Lord Lyon's men. He used to be Unicorn Pursuivant, but now he's Marchmont. He's pretty knowledgeable on heraldic matters." Angus paused. "In fact, I think I saw Unicorn here as well. Somewhere or other . . ." He looked about the room and then pointed to a far corner of the gathering. "Yes, Unicorn's over there."

The mention of these ancient heráldic offices would have caused no more than slight interest in most circumstances, but the effect on the Duke of Johannesburg was profound. The confident, cheerful demeanour, exemplified in the red neckerchief, became almost immediately furtive, the sanguine complexion drained of colour.

"The Lord Lyon's men . . ." stuttered the Duke.

"They're in plain clothes," observed Angus. "No tabards or anything like that. Obviously not on duty—not looking for any false display of arms or anything like that."

The Duke was silent. Angus noticed that he was looking towards the door, as if calculating the distance between it and himself.

"Are you feeling all right?" asked Angus.

At first, the Duke seemed almost too preoccupied to answer. But then he turned to Angus and said, "Look, you do know, don't you, that I'm not quite the real McCoy? You know that, don't you?"

Angus shrugged. "I'd heard something said in the Scottish Arts Club. Somebody said your claim was a bit dodgy . . ."

"Not a bit dodgy—not recognised by Lyon at all, I'm sorry to say. Morally, yes, but not strictly speaking in, how shall we put it, a legally watertight sense. You know how pedantic some people can be."

Angus laughed. "I wouldn't worry if I were you. The Lord Lyon and his people have got far better things to do than chase after people calling themselves this or that."

"Better things to do?" said the Duke. "Such as?"

"Oh, I don't know," said Angus. "They keep quite busy, I believe."

It was at this moment that Marchmont Herald looked across the room. The Duke stiffened, reaching for Angus's forearm. "Oh no," he muttered. "He's seen me."

Angus looked across the room. At first he had doubted the Duke, but now he saw that Marchmont was indeed looking in his companion's direction—and frowning.

The Duke's grip on Angus's forearm tightened. "Look," he whispered, "I'm going to have to make myself scarce. Would you mind terribly helping me? It'll look far less suspicious if the two of us make for the door—deeply engaged in conversation about something. If I scarper by myself, they'll think that . . . well, they'll think I'm scarpering."

Angus could hardly refuse, and he accompanied the Duke as he began to sidle towards the door. One or two people, recognising the Duke on his way out, tried to engage him in conversation, but were quietly but firmly fobbed off.

"Terribly sorry," muttered the Duke. "Another engagement. How nice to see you."

They reached the door, and Angus turned round.

"Marchmont's following us," he said to the Duke. "What now?"

59. Fear and Jeopardy in Mary King's Close

They stopped immediately outside the door.

"Listen," said Angus. "I can't leave the party just like that. My wife's still in there and I haven't spoken a word to the Lord Provost—he is our host, after all."

The Duke looked anxiously back into the room in which the party was being held.

"You can return," he said. "All I'm asking you to do is to help me get away from Marchmont."

Angus sighed. "All right. I'll help you get a taxi—something like that. Let's go."

They began to make their way along the corridor leading to the stairs. As they did so, Angus looked over his shoulder. Marchmont was still following them, walking fast and with a determined look on his face. Angus nudged the Duke, who looked back too and gave a small cry of alarm. "Oh no," groaned the Duke. "It looks as if he means business."

"Let's run for it," said Angus.

They ran as quickly as they could down the red-carpeted staircase, taking two or three steps at a time, launching themselves downwards with as much dispatch as they dared. As they reached the bottom of the staircase, they saw that their pursuer, eager to match their speed, had tripped on the first of the stairs and taken a tumble. He was now picking himself up, but the delay gave them precious seconds.

"That way," said the Duke, pointing down another corridor. "Come on!"

Angus and the Duke hurried along the darkened corridor. They ran past several closed doors until they reached a turning; the Duke hesitated for a moment before urging Angus to follow him. "Mary King's Close," he said. "We'll throw him off down there."

Angus paused to recover his breath but was encouraged not to linger. "No time," muttered the Duke. "He'll be here in a second—just follow me."

Angus did not argue. The whole situation was so unreal: this cannot be me, he told himself; this cannot be me running away like a delinquent schoolboy; this cannot be me, the portrait painter, the member of the Royal Scottish Academy, the former convenor of the Scottish Arts Club Social Committee, the husband of the anthropologist Domenica Macdonald . . . the list of positions and roles acquired by accretion over the years could have continued, but the absurd contrast was already made.

Yet ridiculous though the situation may be, it was still real enough. There was no doubt but that Marchmont Herald was keen to speak to the Duke—presumably on a matter pertaining to heraldry and, Angus imagined, the broader issue of misdescription. Angus was vaguely aware that the Court of the Lord Lyon had a criminal jurisdiction, and that people who used crests or coats of arms without proper permission could be prosecuted by the Lyon Court's procurator. Angus imagined that fines could be imposed, and perhaps even a sentence of imprisonment in an egregiously bad case, but would anyone bother these days—particularly with somebody like the Duke of Johannesburg who, even if not a real duke in the strictest sense, nonetheless *looked* like one? Who was harmed by this piece of innocent nonsense?

These were his thoughts as they rushed down the steps into Mary King's Close.

"It'll be dark down there," the Duke said. "We'll find somewhere to hole up for a while and then, when the coast is clear, we can nip out again."

The steps negotiated, they began to run along a narrow, descending cobbled alleyway, part of the whole network of streets and dwellings that had been entombed beneath the buildings above it, now the City Chambers, since the seventeen hundreds. These streets had once been part of the bustling centre of the Old Town but had been sealed off for centuries, preserving the houses and shops much as they were when they were last part of the city's living heart.

The faint glimmer of light from above that had enabled them to see their way into the beginning of the close had now faded, and they were surrounded by pitch black. The Duke, though, had a box of matches with him, and he now rolled up the Lord Provost's letter of invitation to form a rough and brief brand. It was by this short-lived light they saw a room open up a few steps away—a room that had once been a ground-floor kitchen or living room for a family in that vanished Edinburgh. At the back of this room they could make out a small area recessed into a wall—an ancient cupboard or storeroom—that the Duke suggested would be a perfect place to hide.

There was just enough room, and there was just enough time to conceal themselves within the cupboard before they heard the sound of approaching footsteps—and the low rumble of voices.

"Two of them," whispered the Duke. "He probably went off to fetch Unicorn."

Angus shivered. "I think they've got hold of a torch," he said under his breath. He had seen a light play across a wall and then disappear into the darkness.

"It's a long time since I hid anywhere," whispered the Duke. "I think I was a teenager."

Angus, also whispering, replied, "Surely it's a bit late to be playing hide-and-seek when one's a teenager?"

"Not hide-and-seek," said the Duke. "Sardines. That's a great game for teenagers. A couple of people go off and hide somewhere in the house and then everybody else creeps around until they find them. Then they join them in their hiding place—getting as close as possible—hence the name—until eventually they're all hiding together and the last person turns up. The last person to find them loses."

Angus remembered. He had played that once when he was sixteen. He had found himself hiding with a girl and had hoped that nobody would discover them. That was so long ago, when everything was so fresh, so unsullied, so innocent—well, not entirely innocent.

60. *I May Be Some Time*

Hiding with the Duke of Johannesburg in Mary King's Close, aware of the presence elsewhere in that dark warren of Adam Bruce, Marchmont Herald, intent on finding them, Angus Lordie's mind naturally turned to the subject of fear. When had he last felt frightened? It was a question that he could not remember ever asking himself, which meant that it contained, in its very posing, a pointer to the absence of fear in his life. He had felt anxiety, of course, but not actual fear—raw, physical fear; he had felt anxiety over Cyril, his dog, whose canine life, it seemed, was led at an entirely different level and to a mood music considerably more ominous than that which accompanied his own life. Dogs faced constant challenges from other, bigger dogs—those burly mesomorphic breeds—Rottweilers, whose dire press precedes them; the Neapolitan Mastiff, the keeping of which, in Romania at least, requires a certificate of psychological fitness to be obtained by the owner; or the Maryhill Terrier, a short-legged Glaswegian breed, whose style of fighting with other dogs involves head-butting, a rare phenomenon in the canine world. All of that was faced by Cyril, but not by Angus, whose life had been largely without any saliences marked out by fear.

And yet here he was, at precisely the stage of life in which little should disturb equanimity, experiencing real dread. Of course, he knew that even if Marchmont Herald found them, there was little he could do. This was the twenty-first century. Outside, in the street, cars moved in the light rain that had now set in, their tyres hissing over the cobblestones; streetlights blazed; rationality prevailed (to an extent, of course—there were exceptions); Scotland was not a dark place. But down below, in their world beneath a world, it felt quite different; only a short distance, a breath, a sigh, lay between them and the seventeenth century; only a touch away were the very walls they felt, those people who had plagues and witchcraft and all the rest to contend with.

There was no real reason for the Duke to be so afraid. The Lord Lyon and his staff would not be unreasonable—they could remonstrate with the Duke—warn him, perhaps, or write his name down in some notebook, but was there anything more to be feared? Surely not. And yet the ancient terror of the pursued at the mercy of the pursuer could not be ignored. Marchmont had the torch; they had only the darkness.

The Maryhill Terrier

He strained to hear footsteps, but there was nothing.

"I think they might have given up," whispered the Duke. "I can't hear a thing—can you?"

Angus listened again. "Not a sound," he whispered back.

"But they might just be standing still," said the Duke. "They might be waiting for us to show our hand. That's an old trick—I've seen it time and time again."

Angus wondered what lay behind that remark. Could the Duke have been pursued in the darkness before? It was unlikely, and yet he claimed to have seen it time and time again. Perhaps he had been in intelligence work—the most unlikely people have turned out to have been spies in the past and the Duke was, in fact, a Maclean—and there had been plenty of Maclean spies over the years: Fitzroy Maclean had been a very brave and distinguished agent and then there was . . . well, working for the other side in the Cold War, Donald Maclean, one of the Cambridge spies who had defected to Moscow from the Foreign Office. Of course the Foreign Office had been full of spies at the time and so perhaps one should be understanding; perhaps being a spy for the other side was part of the career path, the *cursus honorum* . . . The Americans had been so angry when Philby and Maclean had revealed their hands, but then the Americans were a bit hazy on the concept of a gentleman and did not appreciate why nobody would have suspected a gentleman like Philby of being such a consummate liar . . . Hah! thought Angus—how times had changed: now *everyone* lied, it seemed . . .

The Duke interrupted these thoughts. "I think they may have gone," he said, his voice slightly louder than before. "In fact, I'm going to stretch my legs a bit."

Angus was more cautious. "They might still be lurking, you know."

"I doubt it," said the Duke, standing up and brushing down his suit. "Dusty place, this, don't you think?"

Angus, who had been crouching, now stood up, feeling a momentary dizziness as he did so. "That's a relief," he said.

The Duke laughed, and lit a match. Angus half expected to see Marchmont standing in front of them, triumphant at the success of his ruse, but there was nobody. "You should get back to the party," said the Duke. "I'm just going to have a quick stroll."

"Are you sure?" asked Angus.

By the light of the fading match, he saw his companion nod. "Yes," said the Duke. "I'm just going outside. I may be some time."

Using a handful of matches given to him by the Duke, lighting the new from the old as they died, Angus made his way up and out of Mary King's Close. Soon he was back at the Lord Provost's party, where he found Domenica wondering where he had been.

"It's a bit complicated," he explained. "And a bit unlikely."

"This whole city is unlikely at times," said Domenica. She looked about her. "Where's the Duke?"

Angus sighed. "I worry about him, you know. He appears to be on the run from the Lord Lyon's people."

Domenica gave Angus a sceptical look, but said nothing.

"He said that he was going for a stroll," said Angus. "Outside. He said that he was just going outside and may be some time."

Domenica frowned. "Did he now?" Her frown deepened. "There's something familiar about those words, you know."

Angus thought. "Captain Oates?"

"Yes," said Domenica. "And look what happened to him."

Angus laughed. "But that's ridiculous," he said.

Domenica made a gesture that implied that one should not too readily assume the unlikelihood of the ridiculous—that sort of gesture: eloquent, expressive, and ultimately persuasive.

And it was then that the Duke returned. He seemed jaunty, and immediately crossed the room to join Angus and Domenica.

"Bumped into Marchmont outside," he said. "No problem. He made me sign a bit of paper about not claiming to be the Duke of Johannesburg. That's all he wanted."

"And you signed?" asked Angus.

"Of course," said the Duke airily. "But he didn't see me cross the fingers of my other hand. Hah! Old trick—I've seen it time and time again. Always works."

Domenica made another gesture that might have meant anything, or nothing; Angus was not quite sure.

The Duke looked about him. "I must say that the Lord Provost gives rather a good party," he said. "Taking all things into consideration."

61. *Friends and Others*

The acquisition of his kilt had brought Bertie a promise from his grandmother that the following Saturday they would visit his friend, Ranald Braveheart MacPherson, in Church Hill. Ranald was Bertie's particular friend; in fact, on one view of the matter, he was Bertie's only friend. There were, of course, plenty of members of his class at school who claimed his friendship, but for one reason or another few of those were ideal. This was the case however much they were encouraged by his mother, Irene, who regarded it as her responsibility to choose suitable friends for her son.

"Mummy trusts you to make the right choice when it comes to friends," Irene had said. "But all of us—myself included—can do with a bit of guidance in some of these important life decisions, Bertie."

Bertie listened, but said nothing. He had learned that it was often best to say nothing when his mother spoke: should he protest, as he very much wanted to do, he knew this would simply provoke his mother into longer and longer explanations of what she really meant and of how he would, if he thought about it, come round to her way of thinking.

Irene particularly favoured Olive, mainly on the grounds that she was a girl and would therefore provide the feminine influence Bertie so clearly needed. The fact that Bertie appeared to detest Olive was of no real relevance; children of that age were often confused as to their real feelings, and persistence could always correct a fundamentally misguided antipathy. Bertie professed to find Olive bossy, but that was simply because his innate male desire to dominate was being thwarted by Olive's strength of character. That was something that was fundamental to relations between the sexes and it was encouraging, thought Irene, to see the extent to which male dominance was being curbed by quite proper, indeed grossly overdue, female assertiveness. Men had to be taught their place, and it was undoubtedly best to start that process of education in the nursery . . . as it used to be called; Irene rejected the term, of course, as it was an entirely bourgeois construct. Who had nurseries these days? Certainly there was a room in the Pollock flat given over to the two boys, Bertie and his brother, Ulysses, but the room was never called a *nursery*— Heaven forfend (not that Heaven existed, it too being an archetypical bourgeois construct). The room in question was referred to by Irene as the Growth and Development Room, a name that expressed exactly what the point of the room was without any overtones of long-abandoned middle-class notions of the separation of children from the adult sphere.

In spite of the backing she received from Irene, Olive's role in Bertie's life was minimal. He was a polite boy and replied to remarks that Olive addressed to him when the only alternative would have been a rude ignoring of her, but for the most part he simply pretended not to hear what Olive said to him. This worked—to an extent—but occasionally provoked Olive into shouting loudly into his ear. "I think your hearing is not what it might be, Bertie," Olive yelled. "Wax, you know. Your ears are probably full of it. Shall I have a look for you?"

Such incidents understandably embarrassed Bertie, especially when at the school craft display Olive entered a small yellow-brown candle she had made under the heading: "Fully functioning eco candle made entirely out of wax retrieved from Bertie Pollock's ears. 100% organic."

This candle was removed by one of the teachers, but not before it had been seen—and admired—by half the school and Bertie had received several requests to save any further wax from his ears for other prospective candle-makers.

That was Olive. Then there was her lieutenant, Pansy, who, although less forceful than Olive, nonetheless provided her friend with additional firepower. Pansy tended to echo everything that Olive said, adding a certain edge by raising her voice at what she felt were appropriate points. Like Olive, she was quick to spot slights, which would be immediately reported to Olive for further action.

As for the boys in the class, these provided scant opportunities for friendship. Tofu was the boy with whom Bertie had most dealings, but this was at Tofu's insistence rather than Bertie's. Tofu's main drawback as a friend was his tendency to spit at anybody, including those whom he regarded as friends or allies, when they said anything with which he disagreed. He also showed incipient criminal tendencies, running a regular protection racket to which the other children were invited to subscribe—"in order to avoid unnecessary difficulties" as he put it. His numbers racket, which he organised at the end of each week, was also more compulsory than voluntary, and was, on most occasions, won by Tofu himself, who had a seemingly uncanny ability to pick the number that he said had been reached by blind selection.

"It's just the way things are," Tofu said. "Some people are luckier than others. I can't help that, can I?"

Then there was Ranald Braveheart MacPherson, who went to a different school, but whom Bertie had met in the Cub Scouts. Ranald was physically smaller than Bertie—they were roughly the same height, but Ranald weighed far less, mainly because of his spindly legs. He was, however, a loyal friend to Bertie and often telephoned him in the early evening for no particular reason other than to check up that Bertie was all right.

Irene discouraged Bertie's friendship with Ranald on the grounds that Ranald's father had conservative leanings and was possibly even a bourgeois nationalist.

"I cannot see myself going to that house," said Irene to Stuart one evening. "I simply cannot bring myself to do anything that might encourage them."

"I'm sure they're okay," replied Stuart. "I met him once and he seemed fine to me."

Irene looked at him with scorn. "Fine—if you ignore his *Weltanschauung*."

"Oh, I don't know . . ."

"Well, I do, Stuart, and I'm not having Bertie going to that house. You can imagine what he might pick up."

"A report of the Adam Smith Institute?" said Stuart.

Irene's eyes narrowed. "It's not something about which one should make flippant remarks, Stuart. We're talking about Bertie's upbringing here."

Stuart had sighed, but said nothing further. It was not for him to defend Ranald Braveheart MacPherson's father. It was not for him to question Irene's views of where Bertie should go or should not go. It was not for him to . . . He stopped. If there were so many things it was not for him to do, then what exactly was his role?

62. At the Scotch Malt Whisky Society

"Of course I'd be very happy to see you," said the Duke of Johannesburg to Matthew over the telephone. "I'm happy to see anybody, as it happens." He paused. "Tomorrow? I shall be in the Scotch Malt Whisky Society rooms down in Leith. The Vaults. You know them, I imagine."

Matthew did, and at lunchtime the following day he found himself in the eighteenth-century claret vaults now occupied by the Scotch Malt Whisky Society. The Duke was already there, seated in a red leather armchair, a copy of *The Scotsman* newspaper open on the table in front of him, a small glass of whisky at his side.

"My dear fellow!" said the Duke. "I do hope you don't want your money back for the house or anything like that."

Matthew laughed. "Not at all," he assured him. "We're delighted with it. There's so much room—more room than we had imagined."

He had not meant it, but it was an indirect way of referring to the discovery of the concealed room. He wondered whether the Duke would take the reference, but there was nothing in his demeanour to suggest this. *He doesn't know*, thought Matthew.

The Duke rose to get Matthew a whisky. "Our own stuff," he said. "You can't get this in any old pub or wine merchant. This is just for members—single-cask whisky. There's no mention of the distillery, just the numbers of the cask and the tasting notes. But you could join, you know—anybody can. You get this place and Queen Street and a place down in the City of London—not that I ever go there myself—but highly convenient for those who do." He smiled. "I like the idea of London, Matthew, but the best prospect for a Londoner is undoubtedly the road to Edinburgh. I've always felt that."

"The opposite of what Dr. Johnson said," remarked Matthew.

"Not everybody likes this country," said the Duke. "There's no accounting for taste. But *chacun à son goût*. You know, when I was a boy I thought that meant *everyone gets gout sooner or later*. Such a misconception, although gout, I gather, is on the increase. More and more people are getting it because of unhealthy lifestyles."

"I've heard that," said Matthew. "I have an uncle who has it. He did nothing to deserve it."

"Uric acid is not a matter of deserve," said the Duke. "But people still laugh at gout. They think it a vaguely comic condition—which it isn't. Mind you, I did hear of the existence of the UK Gout Society and I must admit I allowed myself a mental picture of the Gout Society's annual dance—it wouldn't be much fun, I thought."

They sat down and the Duke raised his glass, "*Slàinte!*"

"*Slàinte*," replied Matthew.

"So," said the Duke. "You said on the blower that you wanted to speak to me about a delicate subject. I've been racking my brains to think of what delicate subjects are left, now that we can talk about everything so openly. We've abolished delicacy, I would have thought."

Matthew went straight to the subject. "Did you know that the house in Nine Mile Burn has a concealed room?"

The Duke smiled. "Of course. Did the sale particulars not mention it?"

Matthew was deflated. "No . . . No, they didn't."

"Well, that's my fault," said the Duke. "I meant to put in something about it, but obviously didn't. I never spoke about it, you know."

"Why not?"

"Because it's a bit tactless to speak about things that you have that other people don't have," said the Duke. "You have no idea how envious people can be. People don't like others who have more than they have—of anything. I get quite a bit of that, you know, as a duke." He looked down at the floor, almost apologetically. "Even if, as you know, I'm not quite the real thing. I had a run-in with the Lord Lyon's men the other day. A bit of a close shave, if the truth be told, but there we are."

"I see," said Matthew. "So you closed off that room?"

"Yes," said the Duke. "I built a bookcase in front of it. Or rather, I had a joiner do it. There was a very good man in Peebles who could make anything; dead these days, of course, as most people who can make anything are. But there we are. He made a very good job of it."

Matthew took a deep breath. "I found some paintings in it," he blurted out. "Three rather good ones. One very good, in fact."

"Oh those," said the Duke. "I left some stuff in there because I couldn't find anywhere for it and couldn't be bothered. They aren't any good, by the way—just some rubbish that my grandfather picked up. He was interested in the arts. He was a member of the Glasgow Arts Club for a long time. He knew Bunty Cadell and Peploe and some of the others. He had a good eye, but he also had a lot of stuff of no real interest."

Matthew could barely believe what he was hearing. "But these paintings are wonderful," he protested. "There's a Vuillard."

"Edouard Vuillard?" asked the Duke. "The Post-Impressionist?"

"Yes," said Matthew.

"Oh," said the Duke. "My mistake then." He paused to take a sip of whisky. "What are you going to do with them? Sell them?"

Matthew's heart stopped. "They're not mine to sell."

"Of course they're yours," said the Duke. "They're not mine. You bought the house and the contents. They're yours."

"I can't," said Matthew.

The Duke smiled. "I knew it! I knew you'd be the sort to

appreciate that not everything should be reduced to commerce. Good for you! So you're going to keep them and enjoy them?"

Matthew hesitated. It was a moment of profound significance. The Duke was right: art should be above the marketplace. Art was about beauty and about being possessed, rather than possessing. "I thought I might share them with you," he said. "You take . . . you take the Vuillard, and the Fergusson, and I'll take the Cowie. Then we'll both be able to enjoy them on our walls."

He had offered the Duke the two most valuable paintings, leaving the least valuable for himself.

"Well, that's frightfully generous," said the Duke. "But you take the Vuillard and the Fergusson. I'll take the Cowie. How about that?"

"No, you take the Vuillard and the Cowie," said Matthew. "I'll take the Fergusson."

"Fine," said the Duke. "Except you keep the Vuillard. I'll take the Fergusson and the Cowie."

"All right," said Matthew. "I love the Vuillard. I love it. I'll put it in my study. I'm very happy."

"My dear chap," said the Duke. "That's what happens when one begins to appreciate things for what they are, rather than for what they cost. One feels happiness." He looked thoughtful. "You know, I was wondering about this recent difficulty I've had with the Lord Lyon's people. I was wondering whether I should stop being the Duke of Johannesburg and become, instead, the ex-Duke of Johannesburg."

Matthew pondered this. Demotion to ex-duke was inappropriate if one were not a genuine duke to begin with; "*soi-disant* duke" or "alleged duke" might be better. He did not say this, though. Instead, he said, "That sounds very distinguished. It sounds rather like ex–King Constantine of Greece. A pretty grand moniker."

"Or ex–King Zog of Albania," the Duke mused. "Do you know that when Zog travelled from the United Kingdom to Egypt in 1946 he took two thousand pieces of luggage? There were questions asked in the House of Commons about it."

"Imagine checking in at an airport with that," said Matthew. "When they asked how many pieces to check in, you'd have to say 'Two thousand.'"

"Zog was a bit of an enigma," said the Duke. "My grandfather met him, you know. He had his detractors who were somewhat harsh on him. They said he never really learned Albanian grammar and he only read two books in his lifetime, and both of them were about Napoleon. Probably not true. He had a difficult task trying to rule that place. Mind you, it probably is true what they said about the tutor Zog had as a boy; apparently the tutor was illiterate and a consummate schemer. Such a teacher would be bound to be suspended in Scotland today, don't you think? We're so censorious."

Matthew laughed. It was such a wonderful thing to say. "Please don't stop being a duke," he said. It was a heartfelt request; entirely meant, entirely intended.

"Fine," said the Duke. "Another dram?"

63. *In Valvona & Crolla*

Nicola had no such compunctions about taking Bertie to Ranald Braveheart MacPherson's house. Indeed it was when she learned that Irene looked on Ranald's family with disfavour that she made the firm decision to take him there.

"Mummy doesn't like me going to Ranald's house," Bertie said. "She gets cross if I ask her if I can go there. She says I should go to Olive's house instead, but I hate going there because Olive makes me play Doctors and Nurses—and I always have to be the nurse."

Nicola listened sympathetically. "That's unfortunate, Bertie," she said. "You do know, though, that male nurses are often very kind; they help people a lot. You know that, don't you?"

"Oh, I know that," Bertie assured her. "But I don't want to play Doctors and Nurses anyway. I'd much prefer to play Cowboys and Native Americans."

Nicola raised an eyebrow. "Cowboys and Native Americans? That sounds interesting, Bertie. Who gave it that name, I wonder?"

"Mummy calls it that," said Bertie. "She also made different rules. The cowboys are meant to help the Native Americans establish community centres. It's a bit boring, but it's better than Doctors and Nurses."

"I see," said Nicola, smiling grimly. "I think, though, that you should go to Ranald's house, Bertie. I'd be very happy to take you next Saturday. We can go there in the afternoon after we've been to a pizza restaurant I've discovered on Rose Street."

Bertie's eyes widened. "A pizza restaurant?"

"Yes," said Nicola. "We can go and have a pizza—lots of toppings—and then go on to Ranald's house mid- to late-afternoon. You can wear your kilt if you like. You say that Ranald's got a kilt—the two of you could both wear them." She paused. "Would you like that, Bertie?"

Bertie's delight was very apparent—even without his saying a word. Pizzas were normally strictly forbidden by Irene, but since Nicola had arrived they had been included in the family diet at least twice a week. The thought of going to a restaurant dedicated to pizza was almost too delicious to bear—especially if he would be wearing his kilt for the outing.

When Saturday came, Bertie was scarcely able to contain himself. He was not sure that he would be able to survive until one o'clock when they were due to set off for the pizza restaurant, but a suddenly announced expedition to Valvona & Crolla with his grandmother and Ulysses in his pushchair would at least pass the time before they set off. Ulysses, of course, would not be going with them to the restaurant, but would be staying at home with Stuart.

"There's no point giving him pizza anyway," remarked Bertie. "He'd just sick it up. He always does." He paused. "And the other people in the restaurant wouldn't like to eat their meal with all those rude noises he makes. It wouldn't be fair on them, Granny—it really wouldn't."

"Yes, it probably will be best for him to stay at home, Bertie," said Nicola. "But the poor little mite can come with us to the delicatessen—he always loves that."

They left for Valvona & Crolla at ten o'clock, walking along London Street and then making their way up Broughton Street. As they walked up the hill, Ulysses pointed at the shop fronts excitedly, giving rise to comment from his brother.

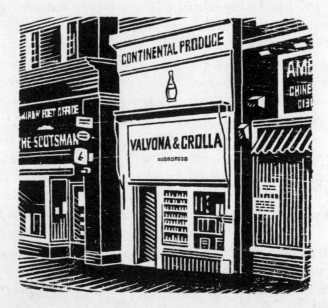

"Ulysses always does that in Broughton Street," observed Bertie. "Do you think he's gay, Granny?" Broughton Street was at the heart of the gay area of Edinburgh, and several cheerful-looking cafés and bars displayed the rainbow flag in their windows.

Nicola smiled. "I have no idea, Bertie. I think you should just wait and see. It will be many years before Ulysses knows what he wants in life."

"I just want him to be happy," said Bertie.

Nicola nodded gravely. "That's quite right, Bertie. Most people want other people to be happy, I think. Very few people actually want to make others unhappy, I suspect."

"Maybe they don't think about it," said Bertie. "Maybe they don't realise how the things they say and do can make other people feel unhappy."

"Maybe they don't," said Nicola. "I think you're right, Bertie."

In Valvona & Crolla they bought the staples: extra virgin olive oil, sun-dried tomatoes, star anise, Himalayan flower salt, and artisan seaweed flakes. Bertie knew where all of these were shelved, and after he had collected them, he pointed longingly to the generous display of *panforte di Siena*. The characteristic octagonal boxes, arranged in their various sizes, bore pictures of their factory of origin printed in the colours of Italian majolica; on the sides of the boxes, certificates of purity were displayed along with lists of contents.

"Do you like *panforte*?" asked Nicola.

Bertie nodded. He was allowed it only very occasionally, and even then in small, carefully rationed pieces.

"In that case, choose one or two big ones," said Nicola. "In fact, how about three, Bertie?"

On the way back, Bertie nursed the boxes of *panforte*, all neatly wrapped, against his chest. His heart had rarely been so full: *three* boxes of *panforte di Siena* to be consumed, Nicola told him, at his discretion. "Not all at once, Bertie," she said. "But certainly one a day—if you feel so inclined. But remember to leave room for pizza."

Back at the flat, they left Ulysses in the charge of Stuart. Bertie, now wearing his kilt, the new sporran given to him by Angus, and a dark green jersey that Nicola had knitted for him in Portugal, led the way to the bus stop where the 23 bus would take them into town. There they would interrupt their journey at a pizza restaurant on Rose Street before re-boarding the bus to Church Hill.

The restaurant was busy but they had no difficulty getting a table. Bertie was shown the menu and ordered a large pizza with seven toppings. Nicola chose a smaller one, but compensated for this with her order of a large gin and tonic.

Bertie looked at his grandmother across the table. She smiled back at him, raising her glass in toast. "Here's mud in your eye, Bertie," she said. "Happy landings, my darling."

Bertie looked at her fondly. In his short life, he had never been so happy, and he felt now that he should tell her that. But what words could he use to convey what he felt; the sense of freedom that seemed to have come over him, the sense that somehow the boundaries of his world, previously so constrained, now embraced possibilities of which previously he had only dreamed? Three words came to the fore—three words that were not so much the product of the mind, but of the soul. "Please stay forever," he muttered.

She heard him, and her heart gave a leap. The young believe that forever is possible; the old know otherwise.

64. At St. Fillan's

"Did Fersie MacPherson ever come to Edinburgh?" asked Bertie as he and Nicola resumed their journey to Church Hill.

Nicola thought for a moment. "Yes, I believe he did," she said. "He came one summer when he was about eighteen, I think. He had been at the Pitlochry Highland Games and decided to come down for a quick visit."

"And did they like him here?" asked Bertie.

Nicola nodded. "They liked him very much. He was a big success in Edinburgh."

"Did they know how brave he was?"

"Oh yes, they knew. His visit was a bit like the visit that Robert Burns paid to Edinburgh. You know that Robert Burns came to Edinburgh, Bertie?"

"Yes, I know that. He read his poems to all the Edinburgh people and they thought they were very good. They liked him, I think."

Nicola smiled. "Well, it was much the same with Fersie MacPherson."

Bertie looked out of the window. "Did they ask him to go and biff some of the people down in England?" he asked.

Nicola made an effort to control herself. "Not exactly, Bertie. In fact, they asked him to go and biff some people over in Glasgow."

"And did he?"

Nicola closed her eyes. She liked Fersie MacPherson and was rather glad she had invented him.

"No, Fersie MacPherson didn't like that sort of thing," she said. "He liked the people in Glasgow, as long as they didn't make too much noise. He found Edinburgh a tiny bit on the stuck-up side—just a tiny bit, hardly noticeable, but there we are. He thought that everybody was doing their best and the Edinburgh people couldn't really help it if they were a bit that way, because that was the way they had been brought up." She paused. "But let's not talk too much about Fersie MacPherson. Would you like to go to some Highland Games, Bertie?"

Bertie said that he would, and they spent the remainder of the journey talking about which of the trials of strength he would prefer. Then it was time to alight from the bus and walk the short distance to the nineteenth-century stone villa, *St. Fillan's*, in which Bertie's friend, Ranald Braveheart MacPherson, lived with his father, who opened the door to them when they arrived, and his mother, who appeared shortly thereafter with a tray of lemonade, scones and Tunnock's Tea Cakes.

The adults retired to the drawing room while Bertie and Ranald went out into the garden. Ranald, forewarned that Bertie would be wearing his new kilt, had his kilt on as well.

"Shall we play Highlanders?" Ranald asked.

Bertie frowned. "I'd like to," he said. "But I've never played it before."

"It's quite easy," said Ranald. "The lemonade can be pretend whisky. You drink the lemonade and then you start singing."

"Is that all?" asked Bertie.

Ranald looked thoughtful. "You can do a bit of fighting if you like."

"Is that all?" repeated Bertie.

Ranald scratched his head. "We could apply for a grant," he said. "My Dad said that grants come into it. He said something about grants, but I don't know what they are."

"I'm not sure if I want to play," said Bertie. "Couldn't we build a gang hut instead?"

Ranald looked doubtful. "We could play Jacobites," he said. "You can be Bonnie Prince Charlie, Bertie. You can go and hide and I'll come looking for you. I'll be a Campbell, if you like. I'll even be the Duke of Argyll. I'll come and catch you."

Bertie agreed, but insisted that Ranald Braveheart MacPherson should close his eyes while he went to hide behind a California lilac bush in the far corner of the garden. He heard Ranald counting to one hundred, and then running across the lawn directly to his hiding place.

"You must have looked, Ranald," said Bertie. "You cheated."

Ranald looked down at the ground. "I'm meant to be a Campbell, Bertie."

From the window of the *St. Fillan's* drawing room, George Balerno MacPherson watched the two boys playing in the garden. "They get on very well," he observed. "Ranald and Bertie look like two peas in a pod, out there in their kilts, playing whatever it is they're playing."

"It looks like fun," said Nicola. "And how nice for Bertie to have the chance to play some real, rough-and-tumble games. You know what his mother was trying to persuade him to play a few months ago? You'll never believe it."

Sensing an identity of attitude towards Irene, George Balerno MacPherson raised an eyebrow. "She's a most unusual woman, I think."

"Thank heavens," said Nicola. "I would hate her to be the norm."

Ranald's father smiled. "And the game?"

"Scottish Enlightenment," said Nicola. "Bertie told me. She organised a game of Scottish Enlightenment in Scotland Street. Apparently the children sat around on chairs and were meant to pretend to be Enlightenment figures. Bertie had to be David Hume. Really, I ask you . . ."

"One despairs," said Ranald's mother.

"Indeed," said George Balerno MacPherson. He looked at his watch. "Sun's over the yardarm, I believe. Would you care for a G&T? Or even a martini?"

Nicola clapped her hands together. "A martini would be divine," she said.

"George makes killer martinis," said Ranald's mother.

"It's an offshoot of the Scottish Enlightenment," said George.

Nicola laughed. She liked these MacPhersons. She liked their assessment of Irene. She liked the freedom that Ranald was given. She liked the absence of holier-than-thou piety and attendant disapproval. These were her sort of people.

"Here's tae us," said George as he raised his martini glass a few minutes later. "Wha's like us?"

"Damn few," said his wife.

"And they're a' deid," finished Nicola.

Ranald's mother looked at Nicola. "The thing about that toast, you know, is that George actually believes it."

And it was then, just as Nicola took her first sip of martini, a taste so redolent of past happiness, that her mobile telephone rang. Apologetically she answered it.

It was Stuart. "She's back," he said.

65. A Nice Surprise for Bruce

Bruce felt pleased with himself. This was not an uncommon situation; Bruce had felt pleased with himself since early boyhood, probably from the very first time he was conscious of the fact that somebody had passed an admiring remark about his appearance. The creation of personality is a process of accretion: small things, minor events, the most subtle of human currents, lay down the solum on which the personality is nourished; in Bruce's case, it had been the compliments passed by his mother's friends, by people in the street—by just about everybody, in fact—that had made him aware that he had the power to charm—just by being. That was a powerful discovery, dimly glimpsed as it might have been by the immature mind, and it set the stage for the development of narcissism. So there was no incident beside a pool when, watched by some shy Perthshire Echo, he peered down into the pool at his own reflection and fell in love; rather there were numerous moments in the High Street in Crieff when holding his mother's hand, the young Bruce became aware that some passing woman was crouching down to gaze at him and mutter, "How bonnie!" Believing that such compliments were his due, he came to expect them, and if heads failed to turn, then there was something wrong with the heads in question.

Now, opening the shutters of his flat in Abercromby Place, he reflected with some satisfaction on his behaviour the previous evening. Pat's dinner party had, in his view, been a success, even if the whole purpose behind it had been thwarted by a sudden change of plan. Bruce, primed to tempt Anichka to reveal herself to Dr. MacGregor as the gold digger that Pat suspected she was, had, in military terms, been stood down.

That had been mildly irritating, but what pleased him

was that he had responded in such a self-effacing way. He had found Anichka attractive—even if she was well into her thirties—and there had been moments when he had been tempted to ignore Pat's request to call the whole thing off. But he had not done that, and had not even given Anichka his telephone number. That was an achievement on his part, and he felt justly pleased with himself for it. Pat should be grateful to him; Pat owed him now, as he might point out to her at some point. She, after all, was not so bad, and if old fires could be stoked up occasionally—just for those occasions when the dance card, so to speak, was not particularly full, then there was no harm in that. As long as she didn't cling . . . That was the problem with women, Bruce thought—they clung. Or was it clang? No, clung. Sometimes they failed to realise it, but they were clinging, slipping their emotional hooks into some poor man who was just trying to get by without being unduly clung to. Give them an inch, thought Bruce, and they take a mile.

Standing at his window, he contemplated the day ahead. It was a Saturday and he had no plans beyond a vague arrangement to meet the boys at the Cumberland Bar early that evening. That could lead to something—there was always a party that somebody knew about, and that could go in all sorts of interesting directions. Bruce had never felt unwelcome at any party—even those to which he was not actually invited in the full sense of the word invited: invitations were for . . . well, for those who *needed* them, whose looks did not mean they were always welcome—it was a subtle distinction.

He glanced at his watch. He had slept in and it was almost ten. He would go out for breakfast, he decided—that place round the corner, Big Lou's or whatever she was calling it now, had started serving croissants—about time, he thought— and he could have one there with a cup of coffee and a flick through the latest issue of *GQ*. He had bought it yesterday and had not yet had the time to read it; it was a great mag, that, Bruce said to himself: all those gadgets, and fashion, and cars. Perfect.

He let himself out of the flat and crossed the street. A woman was walking her dog, heading for the Queen Street Gardens, and Bruce noticed her admiring glance. He nodded a greeting, and she blushed. Poor woman, he thought. If only I had time I could do so much for her confidence and sense of well-being . . . but there was never enough time. One could not look after the whole world.

As he passed the top of Dundas Street he paused at the Open Eye Gallery, where a John Bellany exhibition had opened that week. Bruce liked Bellany—he liked the yellows and the reds. He liked the seagulls and the boats and the occasional puffin. He liked the elongated faces with their wide eyes. There was a lot to look at in a John Bellany painting, thought Bruce.

He was gazing at one of the paintings through the window when he became aware that somebody was standing behind him. It was the reflection in the gallery window that made him aware of this—the reflection of a woman. He turned round.

Anichka was smiling at him.

He opened his mouth, but the words he needed—if any— did not emerge.

Her smile became coy, almost reproachful. "You did say to look you up."

He drew in his breath. What exactly had he said?

His voice sounded weak. "Did I?"

"Yes. You said that we should meet up some time."

It was possible; it was just possible. But of course one said that sort of thing to people all the time and did not mean it. The problem was that she was foreign and did not understand that often people did not mean what they said. The last thing that "We must have lunch sometime" meant was that we should have lunch.

"Could we have a cup of coffee?" she asked. "I saw a place just round the corner."

Bruce hesitated.

"Come on," she said. "I'll buy you a cup."

There was something commanding in her manner—something that made him feel that resistance if not futile, would at least be difficult.

"I was just on my way to your place," said Anichka. "It's back there, isn't it?" She pointed in the direction of Bruce's flat.

"How did you know?"

"I asked Pat," she said.

Bruce bit his lip. "Oh."

"Will you show it to me afterwards? After we've had coffee?"

"I was going to go . . ."

She cut him short.

"Thanks," she said. "I'm very interested in people's flats."

They began the descent of Dundas Street towards Big Lou's.

"You know, I was with somebody at dinner last night," said Anichka.

"Yes," said Bruce, not without relief. "That's great."

"Not so great now," said Anichka. "He's finished with me."

66. *You Have a Good, Hollow Back*

Bruce felt trapped. This meeting with Anichka was not what he had had in mind the previous evening. He had spoken to her at the dinner table, but he had certainly not gone out of his way to charm her, as had been the original plan. As he was more or less propelled towards Big Lou's coffee bar he wondered whether he had said anything that might be misconstrued as encouragement. He did not think he had; in fact he thought that he had at times been quite cool towards her. How could she possibly have assumed that he had any greater interest in her than one dinner guest normally has for another next to whom he finds himself seated. Politeness was as much as he had shown; and that was something quite different from romantic interest.

"I do not know this part of town," Anichka said. "It is very pleasant, I think."

"It's great," said Bruce. "I like it here."

"I wouldn't mind living here too," said Anichka. "It is more convenient than my current flat."

"It's more expensive," Bruce said quickly.

"Unless you share," said Anichka. "I love sharing. Don't you?"

"No," said Bruce.

Anichka laughed. "You should try it, Mr. Bruce."

Bruce winced. "Please don't call me that," he said. "Mr. Bruce."

She looked at him askance. "What's wrong with your own name?"

"It's my first name," said Bruce. "We don't add mister to first names. We just don't."

"Is it rude?" asked Anichka.

"No, not rude. Just . . . Well, we don't do it."

Anichka flounced. "You Scotchmen are very . . . how do you say it? Inhibited. You do not like to bare your souls. You should, you know. Having all that passion wound up inside is not good for you. It is like a pressure cooker. Then suddenly, bang—and you start shouting. Scotchmen need to undo their buttons."

"And don't call us Scotchmen," said Bruce. "The word is Scotsmen."

"I like that word very much," said Anichka. "My funny Scotsman. Like that song about funny valentines. You are my funny Scotsman! That sounds good, doesn't it?"

Bruce said nothing. They had reached the steps to Big Lou's coffee bar. He led the way, with Anichka behind him. As he descended, he felt a hand on the small of his back.

"You have a good, hollow back," said Anichka. "It is very firm. Strong. I think that Scotsmen have very firm backs. It is nice for a Czech lady to feel a Scotsman's back. It makes her think of how lucky she is."

Bruce narrowly avoided tripping. He felt himself blushing.

"I can see that you are blushing," whispered Anichka. "That is a good sign, you know. If a man blushes, then that shows he has a good blood supply. It is very important to have a good blood supply."

They entered the coffee bar. Bruce noticed that Big Lou was not there. He had seen her new assistant once or twice, and had exchanged a few words with her. What was she called? Hettie, he remembered. And he remembered that she came from somewhere up where Lou came from. Montrose or somewhere like that. Arbroath. Somewhere up there.

He nodded to Hettie and then turned to Anichka. "If you sit down over there I'll get you something. What sort of coffee?"

"Strong coffee," said Anichka. "Big strong coffee to drink with a big strong Scotsman."

Bruce placed the order and returned to the table. He was trying to order his thoughts: he would have to make it very clear.

He sat down. "I think you ought to know something, Anichka," he began.

She stared at him. "You think I should know something?"

"Yes, there's something I need to tell you."

She looked at him through eyes that had suddenly become frightened. "You want to tell me that you . . . that you don't like women. That's it, isn't it?"

Bruce's mouth opened. "I . . . Well, no, I do like women."

She looked flustered. "You mean you like women as well as men? Is that what you're trying to tell me?"

"No," said Bruce. "I like women. I like women a lot."

"As friends?" said Anichka. "Is that how you like them?"

Bruce felt himself becoming increasingly impatient. Conversation with this woman, he thought, is like wading in treacle.

"No," he said. "I like women as friends, but also as lovers. I do not like men in that way."

Anichka's expression lightened. "You mean you're not . . ."

"No, I'm not," said Bruce. "I have nothing against people who are, but I'm not."

"What a relief," said Anichka. "I suddenly thought that there was no chance for me if you were more inclined to like men. But now I know you like me, it's easier. Now I know what you meant when you told me last night. You did not mean that you just wanted me as a friend."

"Told you what?" snapped Bruce.

"Told me that you'd like to see me again. Now I know that you wanted an affair, not just a friendship. That is much better from my point of view. That is what I want, you see. I am a very physical woman. I am very interested in physical conversation. And now that I'm free . . ."

"Well, I'm not free," said Bruce. "I have somebody else."

"But you were by yourself at the dinner. Pat said to me that you were single. She said that."

Bruce felt desperate. "I'm not," he said. "I'm just not."

"I think you really are," said Anichka. "I think you are a free spirit. I think that even if you have some small entanglement at present, it is not an entanglement of the soul."

Bruce looked about him in despair. He saw Hettie standing behind the counter. She was looking at him. On impulse he stood up and made his way over to her.

"You're Hettie, aren't you?" he said, his voice lowered.

Hettie flushed. A good blood supply, thought Bruce. "Yes," she said.

"I've admired you for some time," said Bruce. "Would you give me a kiss?"

"Ah, jings!" said Hettie. "What an invitation! But of course I will. Here."

She planted a kiss on his mouth.

"One more," said Bruce.

He glanced over his shoulder at Anichka. She was watching him, wide-eyed. *I had to do it,* he thought.

Hettie was whispering to him. "I get off at five," she said. "Lou comes back then."

"Five?" asked Bruce vaguely.

"Yes," said Hettie. "See you then."

67. *A Father Forgives*

Pat walked up the path to her father's front door, past the lavender bushes that always made the scent of lavender so evocative for her of home and the warm feeling of security that home entailed. Now, though, the lavender only seemed to accentuate her feelings of guilt. She had hardly slept that night of her dinner party, rehearsing over and over the folly of her ridiculous plan. She had tried to call it off—in fact she had done everything she could to call it off—but it seemed to have worked anyway. And the result had been her father's departure from the party and without Anichka.

She had not telephoned in advance as she was not sure what

she would say. She would see him instead, and try to explain, if she had the courage to do so—which she rather doubted.

She had her own key and let herself in.

"Daddy?"

The house was in silence, and for a few moments she panicked. She imagined finding him on the floor, unmoving. She imagined finding a note.

"Daddy?" her voice had an edge of dread in it.

He answered from the kitchen. "In here."

Relief flooded over her as she opened the kitchen door and saw him standing at the work table. He had a bag of flour in his hand and had been measuring a quantity of it into the pan of a set of scales.

"What are you doing, Daddy?"

"Making bread," he said.

His voice sounded quite normal, and she breathed again.

"I didn't know you made bread. You didn't tell me."

He turned to her. Were his eyes red? She took a step closer to him.

"I bought a book," he said. "A book of bread recipes. I made a Neapolitan loaf the other day. I've still got some of it." He paused, and put down the bag of flour. "No, we don't have to talk about bread . . ."

His voice faltered, and she rushed to him, flinging her arms around him. For a while they said nothing; he patted her back, and she joined her hands and hugged him hard.

"Don't knock all the wind out of me," he mumbled. "Breathing is important to me, you know."

She wanted to laugh, but it was tears that came instead.

"There, there, my darling." He patted her back again. "My darling, you mustn't cry. There's no need to cry—none at all."

"I'm so sorry, Daddy. I'm so, so sorry."

"Sorry for what? You've got no reason to be sorry. It was nothing to do with you."

"But . . ."

He drew back, and looked into her eyes. He brushed at her cheek, gently, at a tear.

"I've been foolish," he said. "No. Listen to me. Listen. I've been foolish in the way that all of us—or most of us—are foolish at one time or other. I closed my eyes to something that must have been so obvious to everybody else. I don't know how I could do it."

"Oh, Daddy, you were just being kind . . . You've always been kind."

He shook his head. "You're the one who's being kind. No, I was stupid. My head was turned because a woman who was much younger gave me some attention. I was flattered, I suppose. And I behaved like a teenage boy. I had no judgement at all. All the time I'm telling other people, my patients, how to lead their lives, yet I end up doing something really stupid, making the mistake a sixteen-year-old boy would make."

"Oh, Daddy . . ."

He looked at her lovingly. "And of course you could see it all along. Of course you saw it, didn't you?"

Pat lowered her head. She was ashamed to meet his eyes. "I suppose I thought that she didn't really love you . . . not for yourself, if you see what I mean."

"I see perfectly," he said. "I'm like a man who has a new set of spectacles. Everything is very clear since I put them on."

"I thought that she might be . . ."

"Of course you did—and you were right."

She plucked up her courage. She had to confess; she simply had to tell him.

"I rather hoped that Bruce might . . ."

He smiled. "I knew that."

"Knew what?"

"I knew what you were up to."

She stared at him. She was mute.

"When you brought that young man into things," he continued, I worked out what you were up to. It was pretty obvious, you know."

"You must have been furious." Her voice was weak.

"Not at all. The opposite, in fact. I had suspected it, I'm afraid, but somehow I couldn't bring myself to the final admission that Anichka was using me. It's not an easy realisation, you know, and we tend to put it off until there really is no other conclusion we can reasonably reach."

"So you're not cross with me?"

"No, my darling, how could I be cross with you? All that you did was try to save me, and I suspect that is just what you've done."

"I see."

"Yes." He took her hand. There was flour on his fingers and she looked down and saw it now on her skin—a thin dusting of flour.

"Infatuation is an extraordinary thing, isn't it? You have no real control of yourself. You see, but you don't see; you embrace denial. *Amor furor brevis est.* Love is a short madness—from which we recover, if we are lucky."

"Not all love is like that."

"No, of course not, but some is."

He smiled at her again. "Do you want to help me make bread?"

She threw her arms around him again, kissing him on his cheek. He had not shaved.

"You must go and shave. Then we can make bread."

"Why do daughters push their fathers around so much?"

She gave him the answer without hesitation. "Because they love them. In spite of any of the silly things they do, they love them."

"And fathers love them back?"

"Yes."

He pointed to the recipe book. "A big Puglian loaf? Or a French country recipe?"

She hesitated a moment, and then replied, "Puglian."

"Then that shall be it." He rubbed his hands. "And afterwards? A walk in the Botanics?"

She looked out of the window. "Perfect," she said. "But go and shave now. Go on."

"Mrs. Thatcher," he said.

She looked at him blankly, and he realised that she was too young to remember—and not old enough to know.

68. *The Caledonian Antisyzygy*

"I'd like to make one thing clear," said Irene. "I do not want any sympathy."

She was addressing Stuart and Nicola in the kitchen. The three of them were seated at the scrubbed pine table, finishing the meal that Nicola had prepared—the remnants of a large pot of risotto she had made the previous day. When she had made the risotto, little had Nicola imagined that she would be serving it the following day to Irene, newly returned from almost six weeks in the Persian Gulf—a five-day holiday that had gone spectacularly wrong: losing one's luggage on holiday is one thing—being mistaken for the new wife of a Bedouin sheikh and being immured in a desert harem is quite another.

Nicola frowned and wondered why Irene should not want sympathy; if she had herself been detained in the desert, whether or not in a harem, she would be looking for every available scrap of sympathy, she thought, and for as long as possible. Some people could draw on sympathy for years after the event, as Aunt Ada Doom did in *Cold Comfort Farm*—she had seen something nasty in the woodshed years ago and still needed sympathy . . .

Irene continued. "The Foreign Office counsellor went on and on about Stockholm Syndrome and PTSD and so on. I told them that I had had a very enjoyable spell in the harem and had succeeded in introducing the women to a number of new ideas. I was treated with the utmost courtesy."

Nicola's eyes widened. "And the sheikh . . ."

"I very rarely saw him," she said. "In fact, I think he was unaware of my presence. He had nothing to do with my being there—that was an administrative slip by his harem manager. He was the one who made the original mistake, but he was one of those typical men who can't admit to being wrong. All the women were shouting at him in Arabic to the effect that I was not meant to be there, but he would have none of it. He said that he had signed for me and that was that."

Stuart sighed. "It's difficult to believe that this sort of thing still happens."

"Oh, it does," said Nicola. "I read a book a few months ago on Barbary piracy—you know, the corsairs. They captured numerous people—snatched them from villages on the coast in the South of England. They even went up the Thames to take people into slavery. Whole villages in Italy and Spain were led off into captivity."

"And yet they gave us mathematics," mused Stuart.

"Mind you," Nicola went on. "Barbary pirates flourished in the eighteenth century. It didn't really go on into the nineteenth, let alone the twentieth."

"I did not consider myself a slave," said Irene sharply. "I considered myself a guest."

"A sort of guest-concubine," suggested Nicola. "Rather like a *Gastarbeiter*."

Irene shot her a glance. "Hardly the same thing," she said.

"And I was never a concubine. Nothing of that nature took place."

"Well, we're so pleased to have you back," said Stuart. "All of us." He looked at his mother, who was staring fixedly at the floor.

"Of course," said Nicola. "It's a great relief."

"I must thank you for looking after the boys in my absence," said Irene. "It was very good of you to come all the way from Portugal." She paused, and then turned to Stuart. "Have you checked tomorrow's flights?"

He paled. "Tomorrow's flights?"

"Yes, for your mother. To go home."

Stuart muttered something indistinct.

"Well, Stuart?" pressed Irene. "You can book online these days. It's terribly simple."

Nicola rose to her feet. She was trying hard; nobody noticed her clenched fists and whitened knuckles. For a moment—a glorious, irrational moment—she imagined herself lunging at Irene. She saw herself grabbing her hair—that ridiculous hairstyle of hers—and pulling hard, so hard that at least some hair would come out at the roots. She imagined scratching her—digging her nails in so that Irene shrieked in her . . . in her dreadful, politically correct way. A politically correct shriek? What on earth would that sound like?

She hesitated. It would be easy, oh so easy, to succumb to the temptation. It would be easy to take the three steps that separated them and do exactly this. Irene so richly deserved it. She had had it coming to her for years and years and nobody had done what so many must have dearly wished to do. But the moment passed. This was Edinburgh. These things did not happen in Edinburgh, no matter how far the famed Caledonian antisyzygy made for a divide in the soul, a divide between respectability and the dark domain of violence.

She left the room, muttering something about having to make a start on her packing. Bertie and Ulysses had been put to bed, but as she went past Bertie's door she heard a noise, a small sound, a whimper perhaps. She pushed at his door; the night-light was on in his room, and she could make out the small figure of her grandson lying under the space-rocket duvet cover, his head on the pillow on which further space rockets passed by shooting stars and ringed planets. And she heard that he was crying.

She crept in and crouched down at the head of his bed.

"Dear Bertie," she said. "You mustn't cry."

But perhaps you should, she thought; perhaps that's precisely what you should do; perhaps you need to cry.

She wondered what she could say. The poor little boy had glimpsed freedom and a life untrammelled by all the things that had enclosed his world—the yoga, the psychotherapy, the Italian *conversazione*. Now all of that would return, and freedom, that blessed state of being able to be a little boy, would recede from his grasp.

"Would you like me to tell you a Fersie MacPherson story?" she whispered. "It will help you to get to sleep and might cheer you up a bit."

He moved his head against the pillow—an attempt, in his misery, at a nod.

She reached out to touch his cheek, damp with his tears.

"Fersie MacPherson, the Scottish person, lived in Lochaber, as well you know. Sometimes he went out to stay with his uncle on South Uist when he was a small boy—a very strong small boy, remember—and he used to walk down to the machair—you know what that is, don't you: the strip of sand and grass and shells between the water and the land—and he would pick up shells and listen to them and hear the sea in them . . . And he would think of the things that made him sad and realise that they would not last forever and that if he was unhappy now he was bound to be happy tomorrow, if he waited patiently enough . . ."

69. *In Drummond Place Gardens*

"I'm going out for a walk," called Nicola from the hallway. She could not bring herself to enter the kitchen, where Stuart and Irene were. She was no coward, but she could not; not in her heart-sore state.

"All right," called Irene. "Enjoy yourself."

Nicola pursed her lips. How dare she! *Enjoy yourself!* For a moment she struggled with a strong impulse to turn round, storm back into the kitchen, and scream at Irene at the top of her lungs, like a Musselburgh fishwife. But she controlled herself and merely seethed for a minute or so. Then she thought: how unjust we are to fishwives. Presumably they were no more vocal than any other class of the community, and anyway it was an ancient form of words now. There were no fishwives left as far as she knew, which meant that a new expression needed to be developed, taking into account modern occurrences of shrill conduct. Who screamed in an unseemly way? She smiled as she thought of her candidates.

She made her way downstairs and out onto Scotland Street. She would miss Edinburgh once she went back to Portugal. She would miss the stoniness of the buildings, the attenuated light, the rapidly changing skies. She would even miss the weather, the sudden squalls, the fleeting, weak sunshine, the way the light came at you at an angle, brushed against you, rather than fell heavily on you, as it did in Portugal. Scotland, she thought, has so much wrong with it, but it is my place, the place that will always be home to me, no matter how beguiling

Portugal might become: coloured tiles, vineyards, arresting smiles, white dust were all very well but I, she thought, am a woman of our latitudes rather than theirs.

She walked up the street. The Drummond Place Gardens were bathed in evening sunshine, and she had a key in her pocket. She would go there, she decided, and calm down. There was nothing like greenery to reduce anger, she felt. Green was the most calming of colours; red the most enraging.

In the gardens she began to walk along the path that ran round the circumference. There was nobody else there and she was able to mutter under her breath without risking being overheard. *Irene*, she murmured. *That woman. Unbelievable. Incredible. Ghastly.*

She stopped. Domenica Macdonald was approaching her on the path.

"Well, good evening, Nicola," said Domenica. "What a gorgeous sky. Just look at it. One might almost imagine angels flying across it. Or Time's chariot—as in Poussin." She paused. "Are you all right?"

Nicola sighed. "No. I'm not, actually."

"I'm very sorry to hear that," said Domenica. "Can I do anything?"

Nicola looked at her. She liked Domenica, and she felt she could talk to her.

"My daughter-in-law has returned," she said. "She's been released."

She watched for Domenica's reaction—and she was pleased with what she saw. Domenica's face fell.

"What interesting news," said Domenica, in the tone of a general hearing of the rout of his army.

Nicola managed a rueful smile. "I suppose she had to return."

Domenica was silent.

"I'm not happy about it," Nicola continued.

"And Bertie?" asked Domenica. "Is he pleased?"

Nicola shook her head. "The poor little boy. He's putting a good face on it, but frankly I think he would have preferred her to prolong her absence. In other words, no."

"And the younger one?" asked Domenica. "Little Ulysses?"

Nicola shrugged. "Hard to tell. He was copiously sick the moment he saw her. All over her dress. He hadn't been sick for some time—but her return seemed to bring it on."

Domenica made a gesture of acceptance. "Well, what about you?"

"She suggested that I leave more or less immediately. I suppose I have no alternative."

Domenica raised an eyebrow. "Really? She can't tell you where you go. You can stay if you wish—not in her house, of course, but somewhere else." She paused. "I have a friend who's looking for a house sitter. She's going to Sri Lanka for three months and is keen to have somebody look after her house. And her cat. Are you pro-cat?"

"Unconditionally," said Nicola. "If the dogs took over, I'd go to the wall for the cats."

"She has a flat in Moray Place. You know it?"

"Very central," said Nicola.

"She's next door to the Association of Scottish Nudists," Domenica continued. "But she gets on very well with them, she tells me. Apparently they've been having internal issues recently—some sort of power grab by Glasgow—defeated by some deft footwork on Edinburgh's part. They held a party to celebrate apparently—in the Moray Place Gardens, but it was the usual cold Edinburgh evening and several of them were carted off to the Infirmary suffering from frostbite. And exposure too, I imagine."

Nicola laughed. It was the first time she had laughed since she had heard the news of Irene's return.

"I might be interested," she said. "I could stay there and see what I could do to help Bertie."

"You know what the best thing would be," said Domenica. She spoke slowly, choosing her words very carefully. "Sorry to say this, but I think it's the only chance. The best thing might be for Stuart to perhaps . . ."

"Leave her?" asked Nicola.

"Well . . ."

"Oh, I've thought of that," said Nicola. "And when I did, I felt guilty just to think of it. But you're right, you know—she's not going to change."

Emboldened, Domenica said, "We could perhaps introduce him to somebody. We could find somebody who appreciated him. Who would let him be who he wants to be without constantly lecturing him about his failings."

"Somebody who would love him," said Nicola.

"Yes. Somebody who would love him."

"But what about Bertie?" asked Nicola. "Wouldn't she try to keep hold of him?"

"I assume Bertie would divide his time. He'd be half-free, which is better than being completely unfree."

They continued on their walk together.

"The more I think of spending a few months in your friend's flat," said Nicola, "the more desirable a prospect I find it."

"We could phone her straightaway," said Domenica. "We could go round to meet her right now. Why not?"

"Why not indeed?" said Nicola.

70. *In the Cumberland Bar*

"Do people have parties anymore?" asked Matthew.

He was sitting in the Cumberland Bar with Angus Lordie and his dog, Cyril. Matthew and Angus were on bent-cane chairs round a small table, while Cyril lay contentedly under the table, one of his paws resting on his master's foot in a gesture that, although entirely accidental, had a proprietary look to it. A few inches away from his head lay the small dish in which Cyril was served his ration of beer—no more than a few slurps really, but for Cyril the great treat of his life. He liked beer not for its intoxicating effect—and Cyril had only once been drunk, when he had been inadvertently served an excessive amount—but for the smell of hops. Rather like catmint, for which cats would readily commit murder, some dogs find it difficult to resist the smell of hops. Had they the vocabulary, dogs might say: hops was one of the smells of canine heaven—a place of corners yet to be investigated by any other dog; of fields of unflushed birds; of ancient cherished bones; the smell of loyalty and a warm fireside.

"Parties?" said Angus. "I suppose they do."

"It's just that there seem to be so few these days," Matthew continued. "In the old days . . ."

"Ah," said Angus, "the old days! How often do we say 'the old days'?"

Matthew was undeterred. "In the old days, in Edinburgh, there were parties galore on Friday night. You heard them. If you walked along the street in a place like Marchmont, you heard the parties going on. And then people who were a bit more—how shall I put it—'evolved' perhaps—they had dinner parties. People went round for dinner at other people's flats." He took a sip of his beer. "They just did."

"Perhaps they still do," said Angus. "It might just be that we're not invited quite as much. Or not at all, maybe. Invitations decline, you know—not that that should affect people like you, Matthew. How old are you? Thirty? If that." He paused. "Of course, in your case it may have something to do with your having triplets. I think it probably makes a difference if you have triplets. People must hesitate to invite those who have triplets. They must say to themselves: they won't be able to come to anything—now they have triplets."

This conversation, conducted early on a Friday evening, seemed destined to take a melancholy turn, and would have done so, perhaps, had it not been for the arrival of Brian Taylor, a journalist and old friend of Angus's. Joining them at their table, Brian looked at Angus and said, "Don't ask me."

Angus demurred. "Of course not." But then said, "Don't ask you what?"

"To analyse the situation."

This brought a laugh from Matthew. "I understand. It must get a bit much."

Angus smiled. "I was just about to ask you: What do you think of the old days?"

Brian smiled. "Oh, I think they were terrific. We had such fun in the old days. Didn't you? When somebody says 'the old days' I think of St. Andrews. I suspect a lot of people do."

"We each carry our particular old days within us," observed Angus. "Even Cyril down there. He had quite a time—before he went to the vet. Remember those days, Cyril?"

Cyril looked up and flashed a grin. His gold tooth, inserted all those years ago by an obliging dentist who happened to be at a particularly raucous party in the Scottish Arts Club, momentarily caught the light.

"I have yet to find anybody," said Matthew, "who disliked being at St. Andrews."

"They might have existed," said Brian. "But I didn't meet them."

Angus nodded. "Art College dances," he said, looking into his beer. "They were legendary. Parties that went on until . . . however long was deemed necessary. Exhibitions that got people talking. The sense of the world's possibilities."

"Yes, it was full of possibilities," said Brian. "It still is."

"Bliss it was in that dawn to be alive," muttered Matthew.

"I went to Dublin once," said Angus. "Back in the old days . . ."

Brian smiled. "Ten years ago?"

"About that," said Angus. "I went to a splendid bar— you know, one of those marvellous Dublin bars, complete with brewers' mirrors and snugs and a barman with a white apron. Everything. This was called the Palace Bar—it was near Trinity. It had strong literary associations—they all went there, including Brian O'Nolan—or Flann O'Brien as he called himself. Or Myles na gCopaleen. The funniest writer there ever was. His picture was on the wall."

"And?" asked Matthew.

"Well, we went there," Angus went on. "It was just me and

a friend from Glasgow. We both had a painting in a show of contemporary Scottish art—or it was contemporary then— somehow I feel that nobody would regard me as contemporary today."

"But you are contemporary, Angus," said Brian, loyally. "It's just that some people these days are a bit more contemporary than you. That's all it is."

"You're very kind," said Angus. "As always. But anyway, we had this wonderful conversation with somebody who worked for the *Irish Times*. It's their bar, you see—their office isn't far away. And he said: 'There's a party on at such and such a place. Would you care to come?' He then said, 'All the fellows will be there. Racing correspondent. Economics editor. Literary editor. All of them, so they will.' Those were his exact words. The Irish like to add things like 'so they will' to what they say."

"And this party?" pressed Matthew.

"Well, we said that we thought it would be a great idea. So we piled into a taxi and the *Irish Times* chap gave the driver the address. But the driver said, 'But isn't it a bit early to be going along to a party like that? Sure, wouldn't you be better to be going to another party first?' So the *Irish Times* chap said to him, 'You wouldn't happen to know of a better party, would you?' And the driver said, 'As it happens, I do. Should I be taking you fellows along there first?'"

Matthew was intrigued. "So you went?"

"Of course we did," said Angus. "Those were the old days. You did that sort of thing." He paused. "How about a party in Scotland Street? Right now? We'll get a few people along."

Matthew looked doubtful. "You're married now, Angus. What about Domenica? Wives don't like parties being sprung on them."

"But we'll invite her too," said Angus. "Why should the Irish have all the fun?"

71. Friendship, Camouflage, Love

But while Angus and his two friends sat in the Cumberland Bar and talked of the past, of the talent of the Irish for parties, and of other matters that are an antidote to the pressing concerns of the day, Domenica Macdonald, anthropologist and observer of the ways of Edinburgh and the world, author of that seminal paper "On the Home Life of Contemporary Pirates in a Malaccan Coastal Community," was drinking China tea in Scotland Street with her old friend, Dilly Emslie, and discussing conceptual art and the return of Irene Pollock from her ill-starred trip to the Persian Gulf.

"Angus, as you may know," said Domenica, "has little time for it. He gets very steamed up when he reads assessments of Duchamp as one of the greatest figures of twentieth-century art. He says by the same token Mr. Shanks of Barrhead should be considered Scotland's Leonardo."

"Hah!" said Dilly.

"But on the subject of artists," Domenica continued, "I've been reading the most extraordinary book on a most unlikely theme."

"The best sort of book," said Dilly, "is the one we do not expect. There's a wonderful sense of discovery when we come across something we wouldn't otherwise have read."

"Well," continued Domenica, "I picked up a book on camouflage. You know that camouflage artists are called camoufleurs? A lovely word. So poetic—romantic indeed. *To my dearest camoufleur . . .*"

"Not very masculine, of course," observed Dilly. "One would imagine a camoufleur to be an aesthete. Rather *Burlington Magazine*, rather Bloomsbury."

Domenica nodded. "Perhaps. But these camoufleurs were terribly important in the Second World War, apparently. In fact, the book suggests that they won the battle of El Alamein.

So the aesthetes, rather than Montgomery, deserve the credit. They created a whole bogus army, you see—made of hessian and stuffed dummies and the like. The opposition—as we used to call the Germans—were completely taken in. They thought the attack would come from the south rather than the north."

"People often make that mistake," said Dilly. "The south is the sort of place from which attacks might well be expected to come, I would have thought."

"Hah!" said Domenica, and laughed. "Dorothy Parker."

"More Barbara Pym," said Dilly.

"Barbara Pym is in a direct line of apostolic succession to Jane Austen," said Domenica. "But back to camouflage. Apparently these artists all joined up and darted about the Western Desert hoodwinking the other side . . . rather like the Greeks, I suppose. They made a big thing of hoodwinking the Germans, until recently, of course. The Germans suddenly turned round and told the poor Greeks that the game was up. Oh dear."

Domenica poured more tea. "I can just imagine the mythical parallel. There are all the Greek gods on Mount Olympus, or wherever they liked to cavort—cavorting away and having a great time on borrowed funds from those northern gods— Thor, Odin and so on—who of course inhabit northern forests and mountains. Anyway, the Greek gods have a great time and then Thor and Freya and so on get all sniffy and tell them that they have to cut the whole thing out and move down the mountain and get a job, or whatever. A terrible row ensues, with thunderbolts being hurled." She paused. "Myths are so relevant, so timeless, don't you think?

"Anyway, back to camouflage. I told Angus about this book and how the artists had done wonders and he said that one of his lecturers at the Art College had been involved in it as a young man. And then he came up with a rather amusing story—just invented on the spot, as often happens with Angus. He said that he imagined some unit on active service being told that they were to get a camouflage officer to supervise the camouflaging of their equipment. And they wait and they wait and the camouflage officer never turns up. They get in touch with HQ and say, 'Where's this camouflage officer you promised to send us?' and HQ sends a signal back saying, 'Sent him a long time ago.' To which they reply, 'No, you didn't.' And they're all very puzzled, when suddenly this major pops up and says, 'I've been here all along. Didn't you see me?' "

They both laughed.

Then Domenica said, "Speaking of popping up, do you know that Irene Pollock is back?"

"Oh no," said Dilly. "Somehow we all hoped she would . . . would find herself elsewhere."

"Well, she came back," said Domenica. "I saw her on the stairway with that younger son of hers, little Ulysses. He was red in the face from screaming. He seemed less than delighted to have her back."

"And Bertie?" asked Dilly.

"He told me his mother was home. He was very loyal. He said that he was glad, but I can't imagine that this was the case. Poor little boy. He deserves so much better. The grandmother has been here, you know—Stuart's mother. She's such fun. She's brought colour and laughter back into their lives. There was a danger of her going back to Portugal, which has bags of colour and laughter and we need it so much in Scotland. Fortunately, she's decided to stay."

"Things will get better for them," said Dilly. "I just feel that. That woman can't get away with it forever."

"Not if there's any justice," said Domenica.

"Do you think there is? Do you think there is justice?"

"Yes," said Domenica. "There is. And it asserts itself sooner or later. It's there, deep in the wiring . . . of everything. It's there."

They were interrupted by the sound of a key in the front door.

"Only me," shouted Angus. "And a couple of the boys."

Domenica took it in good stead. While Angus poured a glass of wine for everybody, she and Dilly put on a large pan of tagliatelle and prepared a sauce of parmesan, chopped salami, onions, and pitted black olives.

"It's very good of you," said Matthew.

"An impromptu party is always fun," said Domenica. "Now tell me, Matthew, how are the triplets? And Elspeth?"

"They're very well," said Matthew. "They're up in Comrie this weekend—with Elspeth's parents. They love the boys. They keep saying that their happiness is multiplied by three."

"Which it must be," said Domenica. "Yours too."

Matthew hesitated. "Yes, I think so."

Domenica looked at him intently. "It's important to know when you're happy," she said.

"Yes," he said, more enthusiastically this time. "I know that."

The pasta did not take long to cook. Then they sat down at the kitchen table—five friends, in friendship.

"You know," said Matthew, "when we have these little parties in your house, Domenica, Angus has always given us a poem. Do you think you could prevail on him this evening?"

"I think I could," said Domenica. "We've made you tagliatelle. We've made you sauce. Now you can at least reciprocate with a poem, Angus."

He was hesitant, but there were things that he wanted to say. Looking out of the window at that moment, with the late evening sky still light, an attenuated blue, and so high and distant and so empty, he thought about how he loved this

place, these friends, this city, this country; and the words came
to him, easily, and from a place that he thought was probably
his heart, and they said something that he had wanted to
say for some time but had refrained from doing so until the
moment was right, which it now was. And this is what he
said:

When I was a boy, not yesterday of course,
When life, I thought, was a whole lot
More certain than it is today,
I made a list of those I thought
Liked me as much as I liked them—
For at that age we're loved
By just about everybody
Whom we care to love; how different
It is in later years, when affection
Has no guarantee of reciprocation,
When we may spend so very long
Yearning for one who cannot
Love us back, or cares not to,
Or who lives somewhere else
And has forgotten our address
And the way we looked or spoke.

The remarkable thing about love
Is that it is freely available,
Is as plentiful as oxygen,
Is as joyous as a burn in spate,
And need never run out.
And yet, for all its plenitude,
We ration it so strictly and forget
Its curative properties, its subtle
Ability to make the soul-injured

Whole again, to make the lonely
Somehow assured that their solitude
Will not last forever; its promise
That if we open our heart
It is joy and resolution
That will march in triumphant
Through the gates we create.

When I look at Scotland,
At this country that possesses me,
I wonder what work love
Has still to do; and find the answer
Closer at hand than I thought—
In the images of contempt and disdain,
That are still there, as stubborn
As human imperfections can be;
In the coldness of heart
That sees nothing wrong
In indifference to want, in dislike
Of those who are different,
In the cutting, dismissive
Turn of phrase, in the sneer.

Love is not there, in all those places,
But it will be; love cannot solve
Every human problem, but it makes
A start on a solution; love
Is the only compass-point
We need to learn; we need not
Be clever to know it, nor endowed
With unusual vision, love
Comes free, at least in those forms
Worth having, lasts as long

As anything human may last.
May Scotland, when it looks
Into its heart tomorrow
If not today, see the fingerprints
Of love, its signature, its presence,
Its promise of healing.

VISIT THE WONDERFUL WORLD OF

Alexander McCall Smith

© Chris Watt

- **AlexanderMcCallSmith.com**
  Join the official Alexander McCall Smith Fan Club to
  receive email updates on author events and book releases.
  Click on "Newsletter" on the home page to sign up!

- **facebook.com/AlexanderMcCallSmith**

- **twitter.com/mccallsmith**

Available wherever books and e-books are sold

THE 44 SCOTLAND STREET SERIES

**"Will make you feel as though you live in Edinburgh....
Long live the folks on Scotland Street."**
—*The Times-Picayune* (New Orleans)

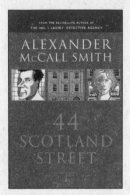

44 SCOTLAND STREET

All of Alexander McCall Smith's trademark warmth and wit come into play in this novel chronicling the lives of the residents of a converted Georgian town house in Edinburgh. Complete with colorful characters, love triangles, and even a mysterious art caper, this is an unforgettable portrait of Edinburgh society.

Volume 1

ESPRESSO TALES

The eccentric residents of 44 Scotland Street are back. From the talented six-year-old Bertie, who is forced to arrive in pink overalls for his first day of class, to the self-absorbed Bruce, who contemplates a change of career in between admiring glances in the mirror, there is much in store as fall settles on Edinburgh.

Volume 2

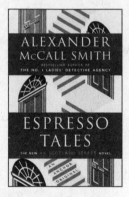

LOVE OVER SCOTLAND

From conducting perilous anthropological studies of pirate households to being inadvertently left behind on a school trip to Paris, the wonderful misadventures of the residents of 44 Scotland Street will charm and delight.

Volume 3

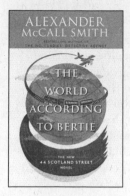

THE WORLD ACCORDING TO BERTIE

Pat is forced to deal with the reappearance of Bruce, which has her heart skipping—and not in the most pleasant way. Angus Lordie's dog, Cyril, has been taken away by the authorities, accused of being a serial biter, and Bertie, the beleaguered Italian-speaking prodigy and saxophonist, now has a little brother, Ulysses, who he hopes will distract his mother, Irene.

Volume 4

THE UNBEARABLE LIGHTNESS OF SCONES

The Unbearable Lightness of Scones finds Bertie still troubled by his rather overbearing mother, Irene, but seeking his escape in the cub scouts. Matthew is rising to the challenge of married life, while Domenica epitomizes the loneliness of the long-distance intellectual, and Cyril succumbs to the kind of romantic temptation that no dog can resist, creating a small problem, or rather six of them, for his friend and owner, Angus Lordie.

Volume 5

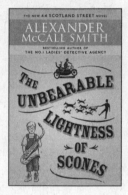

THE IMPORTANCE OF BEING SEVEN

Bertie is—finally!—about to turn seven. But one afternoon he mislays his meddling mother, Irene, and learns a valuable lesson. Angus and Domenica contemplate whether to give in to romance on holiday in Italy, and even usually down-to-earth Big Lou is overheard discussing cosmetic surgery.

Volume 6

BERTIE PLAYS THE BLUES

New parents Matthew and Elspeth must muddle through the difficulties of raising their triplets. Angus and Domenica are newly engaged, and now they must negotiate the complex merger of two households. And in Bertie's family, his father, Stuart, starts to stand up to overbearing mother, Irene—while Bertie has been thinking that he might want to start over with a new family and so puts himself up for adoption on eBay.

Volume 7

SUNSHINE ON SCOTLAND STREET

Scotland Street witnesses the wedding of the century when Angus Lordie and Domenica finally tie the knot. With the assistance of Matthew's new Dane, he is able to fully recover from the trauma of being best man. Meanwhile Cyril eludes his dogsitter, narcissistic Bruce meets his match in the form of a sinister doppelganger, and the unfortunate Bertie yearns for freedom after being set up for fresh embarrassment at school by his mother

Volume 8

BERTIE'S GUIDE TO LIFE AND MOTHERS

Newlywed painter Angus Lordie might be getting into trouble with Animal Welfare when he lets his dog Cyril drink lager at the local bar. And Bertie, on the cusp of his seventh birthday party, dreams about his eighteenth, a time when he will be able to avoid the looming threat of a gender-neutral doll from his domineering mother Irene. Matthew and Elspeth struggle to care for their triplets, contending with Danish au pairs and dubious dukes to boot.

Volume 9

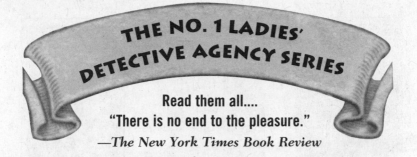

THE NO. 1 LADIES' DETECTIVE AGENCY SERIES

Read them all....
"There is no end to the pleasure."
—*The New York Times Book Review*

**The No. 1 Ladies'
Detective Agency
—Volume 1**

**Tears of the
Giraffe**—Volume 2

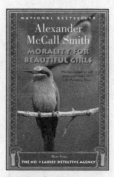

**Morality for Beautiful
Girls**—Volume 3

**The Kalahari Typing
School for Men
—Volume 4**

**The Full Cupboard
of Life**—Volume 5

**In the Company of Cheerful
Ladies**—Volume 6

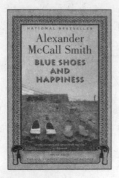

**Blue Shoes and
Happiness**—Volume 7

**The Good Husband of
Zebra Drive**—Volume 8

**The Miracle at Speedy
Motors**—Volume 9

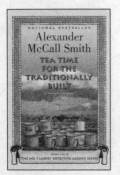

**Tea Time for the
Traditionally Built
**—Volume 10

**The Double Comfort
Safari Club**—Volume 11

**The Saturday Big Tent
Wedding Party**—Volume 12

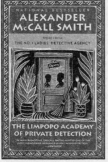

**The Limpopo Academy
of Private Detection
**—Volume 13

**The Minor Adjustment
Beauty Salon**—Volume 14

**The Handsome Man's
De Luxe Café**—Volume 15

**The Woman Who Walked in
Sunshine**—Volume 16

FOR YOUNG READERS, INTRODUCING PRECIOUS AS A YOUNG GIRL

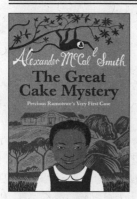

THE GREAT CAKE MYSTERY

In her first case as a young girl, Precious sets out to find the real thief of a piece of cake. Along the way she learns that your first guess isn't always right. She also learns how to be a detective.

Volume 1

THE MYSTERY OF MEERKAT HILL

Precious has a new mystery to solve! When her friend's family's most valuable cow vanishes, Precious must devise a plan to find the missing animal! But she needs the help of another to solve the case. Will she succeed and what obstacles will she face on her path?

Volume 2

THE MYSTERY OF THE MISSING LION

Precious gets a very special treat: a trip to visit her aunty Bee at a safari camp. On her first day there, a new lion arrives. But this is no average lion: Teddy is an actor-lion who came with a film crew. When Teddy escapes, Precious and her resourceful new friend Khumo decide to use their detective skills to help track down the lion and find out where he has gone.

Volume 3

Illustration © Iain McIntosh

THE ISABEL DALHOUSIE NOVELS

"The literary equivalent of herbal tea and a cozy fire....
McCall Smith's Scotland [is] well worth future visits."
—*The New York Times*

The Sunday Philosophy Club—Volume 1

Friends, Lovers, Chocolate—Volume 2

The Right Attitude to Rain—Volume 3

The Careful Use of Compliments—Volume 4

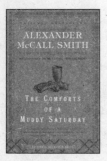

The Comforts of a Muddy Saturday—Volume 5

The Lost Art of Gratitude—Volume 6

The Charming Quirks of Others—Volume 7

The Forgotten Affairs of Youth—Volume 8

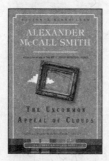

The Uncommon Appeal of Clouds—Volume 9

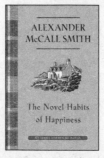

The Novel Habits of Happiness—Volume 10